How to Build a Heart

How to Build a Heart

Maria Padian

ALGONQUIN 2020

Published by Algonquin Young Readers
an imprint of Algonquin Books of Chapel Hill
Post Office Box 2225
Chapel Hill, North Carolina 27515-2225

a division of Workman Publishing
225 Varick Street
New York, New York 10014

Library of Congress Cataloging-in-Publication Data
Names: Padian, Maria, author.
Title: How to build a heart / Maria Padian.
Description: Chapel Hill, North Carolina : Algonquin, 2020. |
Summary: Izzy Crawford's family has been selected for a new home by
Habitat for Humanity, near where the very attractive Sam lives,
but just when her neighbor and best friend needs her most.
Identifiers: LCCN 2019007625 | ISBN 9781616208493 (hardcover : alk. paper)
Subjects: | CYAC: Home—Fiction. | Single-parent families—Fiction. |
Hispanic Americans—Fiction. | High schools—Fiction. | Schools—Fiction. |
Abused women—Fiction. | Habitat for Humanity International, Inc.—Fiction.
Classification: LCC PZ7.P1325 How 2020 | DDC [Fic]—dc23
LC record available at https://lccn.loc.gov/2019007625

10 9 8 7 6 5 4 3 2 1
First Edition

For my mother

How to

Build

a

Heart

1

"You do realize you're a stalker, right?"

One corner of Roz's mouth curls up, her version of a smile. A full-on smile is rare from Roz. Not that I'd see one now. I speak to her profile as she powers her mother's rust bucket of a car along the winding roads of McMansion Land. She's intent on her target and keeps her eyes focused forward.

"Yeah, Izzy?" she says. "So what does that make you?"

Great question. And not without a little edge. Roz's comebacks are razors.

I'm not half as sharp, so I don't say what pops into my head. Mami's voice. In Spanish. She always doles out her wisdom—and warnings—in Spanish. Even though she knows *my* Spanish sucks.

"Dime con quién andas y te diré quién eres."

In other words, "Tell me who you're hanging out with and I'll tell you who you are."

Which is code for, "I don't like your friends, Isabella."

Which translates to, "Especially Roz Jenkins."

Which is muy inconvenient since Roz is my best friend and lives across the road from us.

Instead of a comeback, I make my best innocent face. "Me? Just along for the ride."

Roz laughs, this quick punch of sound. Like the smile, a full-on laugh from her is rare. "Accessory to crime, more like," she says.

I throw my hands up in surrender. "Honestly, Officer, she said she was just giving me a lift home from school! I had no idea she was hunting hot guys!"

The corner of Roz's mouth curls down. "These guys are not hot. They're douchebags," she corrects me.

"Right," I say.

"I'm just curious is all."

Obsessed, more like, I don't bother to argue. What else would you call our latest detour into the outer reaches of Clayton, Virginia? Miles from lovely Meadowbrook Gardens Mobile Home Park, where we live?

I've cruised these back roads with her seven times, occasionally catching a glimpse of a huge house with a three-car garage set back in the trees. There's not much else to see in McMansion Land—Roz's term for where the "rich, superficial, fake assholes" from her high school live. *Seven* times.

And that's not counting how many trips I'll bet she's made out here by herself.

"These people fascinate me," Roz continues. "Admit it, don't you love when you lift a rock and all the bugs scuttle?"

"Totally. Love doing that," I agree. "But we're not lifting anything here with these drive-bys. It's more like we're sitting three feet from the rock, staring at it, waiting for bugs."

"We'll see bugs tonight," she assures me.

I smile, but glance down at my watch. I can only be so late before Mami suspects something. She knows I had a cappella practice after school today, so I would have had to catch the late bus or else wrangle a lift with one of the other St. Veronica's girls driving back to Clayton. She doesn't know Roz pulled up as I was leaving the building. Lured me in with her irresistible, "Hey, chica. Going my way?"

I'm not supposed to be driving with Roz. I'm not supposed to be hanging out alone with Roz. There are actually a whole bunch of Mami-imposed Roz Rules, and while this scenario has never been specifically forbidden, cruising the back roads where Clayton's millionaires live is probably a violation.

"Tell me again how *this* time is different?" I ask her.

Roz sighs her let-me-explain-it-to-you-again-stupid sigh. "The boys' basketball team has made it into the playoffs. They're having a celebration pasta party at the Shackeltons' house."

For a second I'm not sure who she means. Roz usually refers to her crush simply as Hot Sam. She never uses his last name.

And would never admit he's her crush. But I've heard enough about Sam Shackelton's hair (dark brown with red highlights) and eyes (sky blue) and hook shot (Sam is leading scorer) and friends (all douchey) and car (Jeep Cherokee) and *bee-atch* of a girlfriend (Awful Melissa) to know my friend is way into him.

"Cool," I say. "I love pasta. But couldn't we have swung home first so I could change?"

Roz pulls her eyes from the road for one moment so she can strafe the length of my school uniform—white cotton blouse, green and navy pleated skirt, navy knee socks—with a withering glance. "You know, that getup is so retro it's practically *in*," she comments.

"Vintage," I agree. "I think my mother wore something just like it when she was in high school."

"It screams 'Future Nun.' Does it come with a chastity belt?"

"No, but they do require matching underwear."

Roz's eyes widen.

"Green and navy thongs with the St. Veronica Catholic School seal on the back," I deadpan.

There's a long moment before Roz gets the joke. When she does, she releases one hand from the steering wheel to flick my knee. The polish on her blunt nails is blue-black and chipped.

"I'll bet at your school it's a sin to *say* 'thong,' never mind wear one," she says.

"You got that right."

"We're not invited, Izzy."

"Duh."

"But I know how we can see what's going on," she adds.

"Why does that make me nervous?" I say, glancing out the passenger-side window. We're passing the hilly, horsey part of Clayton, officially known as Clayton County, with fields that extend for miles, crisscrossed by white fences. A few massive brick houses are scattered in the distance, ringed with trees. I know from past excursions that Hot Sam lives in the more woodsy, less horsey part. Where each home is hidden at the end of a street-long driveway . . . except there's no street sign. Only mailboxes with a single number.

"You're nervous because you're a dork," Roz tells me.

"Really?" I say. Not about my dorkiness: we both agree that I am the complete dork inverse to Roz's total badassedness. "I think I'm nervous because you haven't let me in on the plan. Is there a plan?"

Upward curl of the mouth corner again. "Oh yeah," she says. That's all.

We reach the section of road where Hot Sam lives; Roz always points it out when we drive past. About a quarter mile before his driveway, however, she turns off, onto a packed dirt entrance. It extends unevenly into the woods, and we bounce in the suspension-challenged car. Tree stumps, freshly hacked, line the way, and it smells like wet pine.

This dirtway eventually opens into a construction site and the skeleton of a half-built McMansion. A porta potty and a carpenter's trailer are the dead giveaways that this is a work in progress. But it's long after hours, so no one's here.

Except us.

Roz pulls alongside the porta potty and cuts the engine.

"Well. This is fun," I say.

She swivels in her seat so I can see her face-on. The thin wire ring that loops through her left nostril. The blue highlights in her not-quite-blond hair, verging on purple in the dusk.

"A few hundred yards through the woods, that way," she says, tilting her head in the intended direction, "is Sam's backyard." An unpleasant chill begins at the base of my skull and runs down the length of my spine. "There's a little pool house and a rock wall, close to the back deck. From there you can see right in. They have a huge flat-screen on one wall. I could pretty much watch a whole movie on Netflix the other night. Without the sound, of course."

I feel my heart pick up the pace. "Wait, you *spy* on his *house*? Geez, Roz, I was kidding about the stalker thing!" I don't know what else to say. This is creepy. And a little sad.

And okay, I'll admit it: kind of badass.

She waves her hand, batting away my shock like it's an annoying mosquito. "Please. It's not like I'm taking photos or anything. Just . . . observing the Douche in his native habitat."

I can't help it: I laugh. Only Roz could blur the lines between a scientist studying primates and a nosy teen spying.

"C'mon." She nudges me. "You know you want to look."

"No way."

"Chicken."

"Totally. That's my middle name. Isabella 'Chicken' Crawford."

Roz shrugs. She swings open her car door. "Suit yourself," she replies. And heads into the woods in the direction of the Shackelton house.

I watch as she disappears into the shadowy arch of branches. It's very quiet out here by the porta potty. The eyeless, gaping holes of the McMansion's window frames remind me of this painting I learned about in art class. It's called *The Scream*.

"What the hell," I hear myself mutter as I climb out of the car.

I dodge low limbs and pick my way between fallen trees in pursuit of Roz. There's no clear path and I can only guess which way she went. I trudge maybe a hundred feet when I hear this soft tapping sound: rain, on the leaves. Great. I really don't want to get soaked. And lost. What is it they say about wandering in the woods? You walk in circles? I have zero outdoor survival skills. I'm not even a Girl Scout.

I turn back toward the car. But then, a twig snaps.

"*Izzy!*" A fierce whisper, not far away. I peer into the gloom and can just make out Roz's outline alongside a tree.

When I reach her, she yanks me close.

"Geez, make a little more noise why don't you?" she hisses in my ear. "You're like an elephant crashing through."

"Sorry. I don't have your creeper skills."

She points. Just ahead, we can make out a brightening through the trees. Voices. Music.

"Stay close," Roz whispers. "And be quiet!"

The sound and light increase as we approach the edge of the Shackeltons' backyard. The woods end and become lawn. Become a patio, with lots of furniture. Those wicker-and-cushion couches that look like indoor furniture someone hauled outside. How does that stuff not get totally ruined in the rain? Of course, there's a pool. Rock walls and gardens. A grill.

Actually, it's not a "grill." It's an Outdoor Cooking and Party Mecca. At one end is a brick oven, neat pieces of wood packed in an iron ring to one side. At the other end, there's a massive metal meat-cooking contraption that looks big enough to roast a pig. A couple of burners, in case you want to boil corn. Stone counters.

My father would have loved it.

Charlie Crawford: Grill King. Who liked nothing better than loading his Weber with charcoal briquettes, his cooler with bottled drinks, and his backyard with buddies from his unit. Although it was never "his" backyard. Just the patch of grass we shared with all the other families that lived in base housing.

But that was ages ago. And Charlie Crawford is long gone.

A poke in the ribs from Roz pulls me back into the reality of wet woods and a party in progress. Beyond the patio is a huge house that seems to be all windows and glass doors. We can see into bright rooms filled with laughing boys. Watching some sports thing on TV.

Roz was right: that is one seriously huge flat-screen.

She whispers in my ear. "On the right. Pool house." She points to a small wooden building at the edge of the patio. A low rock wall extends along one side. "We can see great from there." She takes off, skirting the border of the lawn just inside the cover of the trees. I follow.

When we near the little house, Roz darts to the rock wall. She dives behind it, lies flat on her belly, then twists her head around, signaling me with one hand to follow. I pause. I really don't want to leave my safe cover in the trees. Roz waves again, her brow furrowing in this "C'mon, move it!" expression.

A unison male cry from inside the house startles me. The whole roomful of boys is shouting and fist-pumping at the flat-screen. Someone must have scored.

It's my chance. As the entire team faces in the opposite direction, I race from the woods and hurl myself into the dirt alongside Roz. The ground is damp and soft; I'm going to have to get really creative explaining to Mami what happened to my white cotton blouse.

Roz and I lock eyes behind the protection of the rock wall. Hers are round. Bright. I've never seen her look so . . . alive. She winks at me, then pulls herself into a crouch and peers over. I do the same.

I can practically read the labels on the soda bottles lining the kitchen counters—that's how close we are. I count a dozen guys either strewn on sofas or shoveling food onto plates, while a low background pulse of music competes with the sports commentator's voice on the television. Two adults—a mom? A dad?—weave among them passing out napkins, laughing at something one of them says.

"What a bunch of assholes," I hear Roz mutter. Not for the first time.

I don't respond. I don't know these people. And even when I have given her some pushback, wondering how it's possible that every person at Clayton County High School could be an asshole, she just says, "You're new here."

Which is true.

"Skinny guy on the couch with the Kawhi Leonard corn-rows? Green shirt?" she begins. I have no idea who Kawhi Leonard is, but I see a boy in a green T-shirt eating spaghetti. "That's Darius Jones. He's cocaptain with Sam. What a jerk . . ." And she's off. Filling my ear with all of Ned Perkins's/Isaiah Green's/John Mayhew's damning qualities, from their expensive cars to their outrageous sneakers to their terrible girlfriends. Especially their girlfriends. With Hot Sam's Awful Melissa ranking as undeniable Queen of the Worst.

It's amazing what she knows, and what I know, second-hand, about these people. I live in fear that if I do eventually cross paths with one of them, I'll slip and say, "Oh my god, you're Cassie who cheats on the vocab tests!" or "You're Eric who asked nine girls to homecoming!"

I mean, not really. I wouldn't say something *that* stupid. But all this info I shouldn't know would be screaming around my head and something might pop from my mouth. Who *are* you? they'd wonder. Dark-haired, green-eyed girl I've never met but seems to know me?

Sometimes I think I should tell Roz not to tell me any more. Fascinating as it all is, I don't want to slip.

I hate slipping.

Before she points out anyone else, a shadow falls across the deck. Someone stands at the sliding door, about to open it.

"Frank! Here, boy!" we hear through the glass. A dog, one of those little bug-eyed dudes that are so ugly they're actually cute, appears at his heel.

"Uh-oh," Roz whispers as the door opens and the dog skitters out.

I'm too busy thinking Frank is a completely hilarious name for a dog to realize: this is not good.

Frank lifts his leg and is about halfway through his whiz on one of the Shackeltons' bushes when he aims his nose in our direction. I can see his nostrils quiver: our scent is a balloon floating inches from his smushy face. Whiz over, he takes two steps toward us and growls.

The boy who let him out calls, "C'mon, Frank. Inside!"

I feel Roz squeeze my arm.

"That's Sam," she says.

Frank barks.

"Frank!" Sam insists, clapping. Frank ignores him, his toenails scraping the flagstones as he advances.

"Go, go, go!" Roz hisses in my ear. She doesn't stand: she rolls, away from the wall, until she's at the edge of the woods. Then, at a half crouch, she bolts. She doesn't slink quietly now: she crashes through the underbrush like a *herd* of elephants. Frank, with a full-throated yap, tears after her.

Leaving me, Isabella Chicken Crawford, frozen in the mud behind the Shackeltons' garden wall.

"Damn," I hear. Way too close. Hot Sam has crossed the patio and now sounds like he's about five feet away. Not that I'm about to lift my head and confirm that distance. "Frank!" He claps again. He whistles, loudly. One of those two-fingers-in-your-mouth dog whistles. Then, a woman's voice, from the house.

"Honey, what's wrong?"

"I think Frank is chasing something. He just ran off."

"Oh no. I hope it's not a porcupine again!"

"Serve him right. Dumb dog," Sam mutters. He claps again. "Here, boy!"

I can tell from the sound that he's crossed the lawn. And his back is to me. Which means this is my moment. Before I second-guess myself, I roll, Roz-like, only toward the little pool house. As soon as I reach it, I duck behind it. I peer around the side.

I guessed right: Sam stands at the edge of the woods and isn't looking anywhere in my direction. "Frank!" he yells into the darkness.

"Sam, c'mon in, it's raining," I hear the woman say. "He always comes back." I read hesitation in the boy's shoulders, but he turns. The light from the house falls on his face and for one second, before I pull back behind the protection of the shadows, I get a look at the most gorgeous boy I have ever imagined.

Not seen: *imagined*. Because that's how incredibly well God constructed Sam Shackelton. You almost can't believe it.

I wait until I hear his steps on the deck and the sliding glass door open and shut. The coast is clear, but it's full-on dark now. No way am I heading back into those woods: I *will* get lost. Or run into Frank. My best option is to get to the main road and walk to the construction site where Roz parked.

And where she's—hopefully—waiting for me.

The Shackeltons' long driveway is lined with cars from the basketball boys, and I duck behind each of them as I make my way toward the road. The rain has picked up, and my blouse clings to me like plastic wrap. My soaked skirt winds wetly against my knees; my waterlogged sneakers squinch.

There is no way I'm going to be able to explain this to Mami.

At the end of the driveway, I turn left . . . and am blinded by headlights from a car parked a few feet from the Shackeltons' mailbox. I almost fall backwards.

Then I hear, "Izzy! Get in!"

Roz. She's pulled the car just off to one side, so it's half on the road, half in the ditch. The passenger door swings wide. I scramble in, still blinking from the light. I land on something warm and wet.

Frank. He whimpers and jumps into the back seat.

"Oh my god! What's *he* doing here?"

Roz reaches back and scratches the top of the dog's head. "He caught up with me in the woods, and the only way I could get him to shut up was to pick him up. He's actually very friendly."

"What are *you* doing here?" I demand. *Why aren't you waiting for me back where we parked?* I don't add.

"Do I have perfect timing, or what?" she says. Frank barks. As if he's agreeing with her.

"So what happens next?" I ask. "We add dog nabbing to the list of this evening's entertainments?"

"You want him?" Roz asks. "The Rodent might get jealous."

Roz isn't a fan of our dog, Paquito Schultz. "Paco" for short. A dachshund-Chihuahua mix, he once nipped her when she accidentally stepped on his tail. Since then, she only refers to him as the Rodent.

"Seriously, Roz."

"Take him back, I guess."

"Oh? And how's that? Knock on the door and say, 'Hey, while we were trespassing on your property and stalking your son, we stole your dog! Here he is! Bye!'"

Roz does one of her sort-of laughs. But I wasn't trying to be funny. "Nah. You can just carry him to their yard and let him go. He'll probably scratch at the door and they'll let him in." She looks at me. Waiting.

"Hold on, what 'you' are you talking about?"

"They know me, Izzy. I can't carry Frank back."

"I didn't steal him!"

"Neither did I. It was a rescue. He followed me and would have gotten lost."

"Oh, that's a pile of—"

"Don't! Don't swear, Isabella!" Roz interrupts. Frank barks again. "You know swearing is a sin."

For some reason this pisses me off more than anything else. It's not like she doesn't make Catholic jokes 24/7. But right now, in my wet, muddy uniform—way late getting home and facing a tirade from Mami about violating the Roz Rules—I'm in no mood for jokes about sin.

I reach behind the seat, grab Frank by his collar, and pull him into my lap. He gazes at me with his bulging bug eyes and licks the tip of my nose.

"You're lucky I like pugs," I tell him. I turn to Roz. "Just so you know, I'm doing this because if we leave the dog out here, he might get hit by a car."

"You're so good, Izzy. Or should I call you Saint Isabella?"

"And for the record, I'm not the one who's chicken. *You* are."

No retort. I got her there.

I climb out of the car, dog in my arms, and retrace my steps down the long, dark driveway. When the lights of the house come into view, Frank begins to squirm. I let him down and he rockets off. I treat myself to one last look at the Shackeltons' glowing house, then hustle back to the car.

Roz has the engine running, and pulls away the moment I close the door. Neither of us speaks for a while.

"I told you we'd see bugs," Roz says, finally breaking the stalemate.

"I saw Sam," I tell her. She glances at me, waiting. "One hell of a bug."

"*Hell*uva bug," she agrees.

Another moment of silence, and then the two of us give in to the adrenaline and begin laughing hysterically.

It's amazing how quickly I forgive her.

2

THE WHOLE DRIVE BACK FROM THE SHACKELTONS' I'M WONDERING what story I'm going to come up with that might save me from the Wrath of Mami. As we pull alongside the Jenkinses' home, I notice an unfamiliar car parked across the road next to ours.

"You got company," Roz comments.

I can't help but glance at the dark windows where she lives. "You don't," I say, swinging open the car door.

"Surprise, surprise," she remarks. "Let's see if my dear mother left anything for dinner before she hit the bars."

"How could she 'hit the bars'? You have the car."

Roz hesitates, narrows her eyes before answering. "Shawn's back," she says. Which is all she needs to say. Shawn Shifflett is the latest—and not greatest—in her mom's revolving door of boyfriends. His most recent expulsion came in the middle of the night and involved yelling, cops called, and objects hurled at his black pickup as he roared off. Somewhere in all that, there was pounding on our door. Mami opened it while I huddled on the bed with my little brother, Jack, who was freaked out by the noise.

It was Roz, shaking, in her pajamas. Mami wrapped her in a blanket off her own bed, made her tea, and let her stay the night. The next morning, when everything was quiet, Roz went home.

No one had ever come looking for her. I don't think Gloria even noticed that her daughter had gone missing.

"You okay?" I ask her.

"Sure," she answers. "Whatever." She opens her door. The rain has picked up. "See ya." Roz quick-steps away from the car. Only when I see her lights flick on do I grab my backpack and trudge to our door.

And there's Narthex Lady, the woman who passes out bulletins every Sunday in our church lobby (aka the narthex), perched on one of the high three-legged stools at the kitchen counter. She and Mami hold coffee mugs.

"Ay, Dios mío!" Mami exclaims when she gets a look at me. She always emotes in Spanish.

"Sorry I'm late," I begin, ever so lamely. I still don't have an alibi.

"Whoa," says Jack from the Scrouch, aka the scratchy excuse for a couch Mami picked up at a yard sale, upholstered in some faux-tweedy, highly flammable material. He's watching television, Paco on his lap. "What happened to *you?*"

"Hi," I say instead, smiling at Narthex Lady while I try to wrestle my feet from my soaked sneakers.

Mami, tsk-tsking, approaches me with a dry dish towel. "Isabella, you know Mrs. May from church, right?" She begins daubing my head with the towel; I'm dripping on the entry mat. Anyone who has ever attended Sunday Mass at St. Bernadette Roman Catholic Church knows Narthex Lady, with the beehive hairdo and radioactive smile.

"Call me Brenda," Mrs. May says.

"Mrs. Brenda," Mami prompts.

I grab the towel from her annoying patting hands. "Sure. Hi," I repeat.

Now Mami is frowning and examining the brown stains on my wet blouse. I cover them with the towel, pretending to dry myself off. Meanwhile, Paco has bounded off Jack's lap and sniffs me with great interest. I must be coated in pug residue.

"You're *soaked!*" Jack observes with delight. My little brother is relentless.

"Yeah," I agree. "I had a cappella, and instead of the late bus I got a ride home. She took the long way, we got caught in the rain, and . . . I'm sorry, would you excuse me?" I look at Narthex Lady. "I'm just going to go dry off."

She smiles. "Of course, dear, don't mind me. I was just leaving."

Before Mami can press the issue, I beat it down the hall to my room, Paco panting at my heels. I've barely peeled off my soaked blouse and bra and yanked a dry T-shirt over my head when Jack bangs my door open.

"Hey! Privacy?" I tell him. "Out."

He throws himself on my bed, which takes up most of the tiny room. Paco is curled in the center of the comforter like a little bagel. Jack rests his head on the dog's tummy, and the two of them grin at me.

"Oh whatever," I grumble, pulling on gray sweats. "What's Narthex Lady doing here?"

"You mean *Mrs. Brenda*?" he says with exaggerated emphasis. Even my six-year-old brother recognizes the humor in Mami's attempts to teach us some manners. "I want her to go, I'm hungry," he complains.

"What's for dinner?" I ask.

"Arroz con pollo," he whines. His favorite. And my little brother is not good at waiting, especially not for food.

I join them on the bed. "She'll be gone soon," I tell Jack. "How was your day?"

He bounces up, startling Paco. "Awesome!" He's revving up. Dude needs protein. I listen through the door: Mami and Mrs. Brenda are still chatting.

"Yeah? What made it so awesome?" I ask.

"Well," Jack says, squinching his nose in concentration. It's this very cute thing he does, as if his brain is wired to his nasal passages. Wiggle the nose and thought happens. "First, lunch was *awesome*."

"What'd they have?"

"Italian dunkers!" he exclaims, bouncing just a little.

"No way. They had those last week."

He straightens up to display telltale marinara stains streaking the front of his shirt, the result of "dunking" fried mozzarella in red sauce.

"Okay, I believe you. What else made today awesome?"

"My team won four square at recess," Jack continues. "And we had library! I got to pick a book. Can we read tonight?"

"Did you get something new?" I ask.

He holds his breath and doesn't answer.

"Oh no, Jack. Not again. Please tell me you *didn't* . . ."

He's trying not to smile. But then he giggles. Then laughs. I glare at him, which only makes it worse, until finally he explodes with, *"Piggie Pie!"* In a screechy baby-voice. The one he uses when he's upset or uncomfortable.

Piggie Pie is his favorite book and he keeps checking it out. Every week. Even though there are hundreds of books in his school library, and *Piggie Pie* is a picture book from the little-kids section. Jack should be checking out books from the Easy Readers shelf. Mami spoke to his teacher about this.

Correction: *confronted* his teacher about this. I lose count of all my mother's epic takedowns, but that one I remember. We were driving home from Jack's school after her first conference with his very young, just-hired teacher.

"Do you know what that imbécil said to me?" Mami's voice shook, even though she was trying to keep it low. Jack was seated in the back.

I remember feeling my heart sink. Would Miss Mahaney, la imbécil in question, be another person in town I'd have to avoid following a "conversation" with Mami?

"She said," Mami continued, "sometimes children who don't own many, if any, books of their own become attached to one in the library's collection. She said they keep checking it out so others can't take it home. That way it feels like theirs." Mami shot me a can-you-believe-it? look. "She said not to worry, let him have his 'comfort' book, he'll eventually move on. So I said, 'Really? Like, when he's fourteen?'"

My heart sank further.

"I said to her, 'Sweetheart, let me ask you something. If I had driven to this conference in a Lexus instead of a rusty Ford, wearing yoga pants instead of my nurse's aide uniform, would you still think it's okay that my son, the little brown boy, chooses books below his reading level?'"

"Oh god," I groaned. I couldn't help it. It escaped me, like gas. Which only spurred her on.

"No, Isabella. Escúchame. I'm not wrong. Then she starts to get all, 'Now, Mrs. Crawford, that's not fair,' and I say to her, 'You bet I know it's not fair. So here's what's going to happen. No more *Piggie Pie*. *Unless* he comes home with a chapter book, too.' Well, then she starts in on how that's not fair to the other children because they are only allowed one book each. So I said, 'You know what? I think we should continue this conversation with your principal.' And like that!" Mami snapped her fingers. She has this crazy loud snap that sounds like a whip cracking. "Jack is allowed two books."

Here's the thing: you don't mess around with Margarita Garcia Crawford. Miss Mahaney learned that fast.

"Jack. Jack!"

He settles down. A bit.

"Did you get a second book?"

His smile fades. "Yes," he says. Sighs. "*Sam the Minuteman*."

I hold up my hand. He gives me a reluctant high five. "Awesome. We'll read about Sam *and* piggies tonight."

There's a tap at my door. Mami.

"Mrs. Brenda is leaving. Come say goodbye," she orders.

Jack bounds up. "Dinner!" He races down the hall. I'm about to follow him, but Mami puts a restraining hand on my arm.

"Who drove you home?" she asks, voice low.

She knows. She's like a witch. I need to search her closet and find her crystal ball.

"Lindsey," I lie. I force myself to look her in the eye. Lindsey Hale is a St. Veronica's girl who lives on the other side of town, not far from the medical center where Mami works. Whenever she gives me a ride back to Clayton after school, I have her drop me there, claiming my mother's shift is almost over and I can drive home with her. Sometimes that's actually true.

Most times it's not. But it's only two miles between the medical center and Meadowbrook Gardens, so not much of a walk. I just wait until Lindsey pulls away, waving bye, see you tomorrow.

In the six months we've lived here, no one from St. Veronica's has ever driven me all the way home. I always tell Mami they drop me at the Meadowbrook entrance to save time. I've already inconvenienced them, I explain. And we live so far in, all these little winding roads.

She's never really bought that line, and sure doesn't buy it now. She frowns. "I did not see a car pull up."

I shrug, pushing past her and heading down the hall to the arroz con pollo. My mother's chicken rocks and my stomach is complaining.

"What, it is pouring and she can't take you to the door?" Mami demands, following me.

Jack has already perched himself on the stool vacated by Narthex Lady, a fork in one fist and a knife in the other. I sit on the one next to him.

"It's fine," I say, trying to put an end to the interrogation. "I don't melt. What did *Mrs. Brenda* want?" I kick Jack under the counter. His face reddens as he fights to hold back giggles.

Mami doesn't answer right away. She turns to the stove and begins shoveling steaming rice and chunks of chicken onto plates from her cast-iron pot. The kitchen smells like garlic and onions, peppers and olives.

"She is helping me fill out some papers," Mami finally says, sliding very generous servings before us.

Jack attacks. I grab his arm.

"Wait, buddy," I say.

He groans, but holds off until our mother hands us glasses of milk and fills a plate for herself. Then she stands, on the other side of the counter. There are only two stools.

"Okay," she says. The three of us hold hands. Bow heads. "Bless us, O Lord, and these Thy gifts, which we are about to receive from Thy bounty, through Christ, our Lord. Amen." Release hands.

"Good Lord good meat good God let's eat!" Jack roars, then shovels a massive forkful into his mouth.

Mami doesn't react; he does this every night. Like it's a tic. Ever since I told him it's the prayer Daddy taught me.

Jack never met our father. Mami was five months pregnant with him when we got word that Charlie Crawford had been killed in action. The only memories Jack has of him are the ones we share. Mami was pretty annoyed when I shared the good meat prayer.

She seems to have moved on from the wet-uniform-ride-home issue, but I'm not taking any chances.

"What sort of papers?" I ask. "Chicken's great, by the way. D'you use the sazón?"

Mami shakes her head. "I think that MSG gives me headaches."

"Mrs. Brenda was talking about the new house," Jack says, mouth full.

I'm not sure I hear him right. "Whose new house?" I ask.

Mami suddenly seems very interested in separating a bay leaf from her pile of rice.

"Ummphf!" he exclaims. He's added another forkful. At this point his mouth is so stuffed, he's beyond intelligible sound.

"Jack, slow down," Mami says. "You'll choke."

Jack's jaws work the food, chewing methodically until he clears his throat. "That's the other thing! That made today *awesome!*" he exclaims.

I'm confused.

"Our house!" Jack cries. "Izzy, we're moving! To a *real* house!"

I feel my head snap up, my muscles seize. I look at my mother, but she's turned her back to me while she fumbles around with something under the sink. She's not making eye contact.

What. The. Hell.

3

DESPITE WHAT SHE THINKS, ROZ'S TIMING IS ANYTHING BUT PERFECT.

Especially this afternoon. Mami and Jack are due home soon, then we're heading to the Mystery Location. And here's Roz at the door.

I'm just off the bus, home for maybe thirty seconds, when she knocks, calling out "Hey, Izzy!" as she walks in. I'm in the kitchen hunting snacks, haven't even changed clothes yet. Does she watch for me out her window?

I glance at the wall clock over the stove. We have a little time.

I pull a Sprite from the fridge and toss the can to her. I check out the options in the cupboard. "Cheetos or Doritos?"

"Both," she says, wandering into the living room.

I join her, two bags and my own can in hand. I crack the pop top and take a long draw. The bubbles rush and recede in my stomach like an ocean wave. "Mami and Jack will be here in, like, half an hour," I tell her.

She flops on the Scrouch. Roz thinks I'm not supposed to have *any* friends over when Mami is out. She doesn't know this is a Roz Rule, specific to *her*. In any case, she thinks it's stupid and likes to tell me I'm a dork for letting my mother push me around. Still, she always slips out the back door when Mami pulls up.

Roz doesn't bother asking why they're coming home early today. Which is good. I'm not sure what I'd tell her.

Because it's such a long shot. Like winning the lottery and getting struck by lightning simultaneously. This House Thing, which Mami finally revealed last night. After I freaked out.

"Is he kidding right now?" I demanded when Jack spilled the beans that we were moving. Again. "We had a deal—"

But she cut me off. "Isabella. It is not what you think."

"It's never what I think! Or want. Mami, we've been over this! I *hate* moving and you told me I could stay for high school!" The tears rose. So unfair. I'm so *sick* of things being unfair.

Which made what I said next even worse because it was totally unfair.

"If Daddy was alive, we'd never have lived like this. Moving all the time. From one crap place to another."

Jack gasped and clapped a hand over his mouth. "Izzy swore!"

I braced myself. Mami has some serious rules about bad language. But instead of berating me with a Gatling gun of Spanglish, she stared into her plate, picking at a very large bay leaf in her rice.

"That's right, Isabella," she finally said, placing her fork on the counter and abandoning any pretense of eating. "So much would be different if your father were still with us. But don't kid yourself: we moved a lot when Charlie was alive. That's the military."

"We stopped being military years ago," I shot back. *Explain all the moves since then*, I didn't add. But I didn't need to. Mami pressed her mouth into a thin line. She couldn't argue with me.

Jack tugged at my sleeve. "Izzy! It's okay! We're not moving far!"

I shook him off. I wasn't in a mood to humor him. "Oh yeah? How not far, Jack? Do you even know what 'far' is? Which is more far, Alaska or . . . your school? The Meadowbrook Market or . . . Grandma Crawford's house?"

Jack didn't answer. He's never been to Grandma Crawford's house. Instead, he turned to Mami. "Tell her!" he insisted.

Mami reached atop the fridge and pulled down a folder. She handed it to me. Across the top it read: Habitat for Humanity of Greater Clayton. At the bottom was this logo with little blue people beneath a green roof. Their arms were raised as if in some happy prayer, some "Say Amen!" chorus I haven't heard since my last Crawford family reunion, back when Daddy was alive and we went once a year to North Carolina to see the relatives.

"I didn't tell you because I didn't want you to get your hopes up," she said. "But I applied for us to get a house. Every night for the last few weeks, after you two went to bed, I've been filling out papers. I had to show them all my records and pay stubs and get references . . . But the people at church have been helping me, and that's why Mrs. Brenda was here. She says we passed the first part. She says that's very good. It means we are close to being picked."

My head spun. The only thing I knew about Habitat for Humanity was that they built houses with smiling volunteers who looked like they'd never held a hammer before.

"I'm sorry . . . what?" I said. "Picked for a house where?" I tried to imagine some alternate universe where free houses were doled out to Puerto Rican widows and their children.

That's when she told me about the Mystery Location. Some place in Clayton where Habitat had recently been given land. Mami had applied for us to be one of the first families to move there.

She is taking me and Jack to see it this afternoon.

I pop the Doritos bag and grab a handful. Roz does the same with the Cheetos. We munch in silence for a while.

"So. 'Dyou get in trouble for being late last night?" she finally asks.

"Nope. 'Dyour mom leave you anything to eat?"

She flashes me the are-you-kidding? look.

"How long has Shawn been back?"

Roz reaches for the Doritos. "Three days."

"I thought you said she pressed charges and had an order against him."

"She did. Then she dropped them. After he begged her for-giveness and swore he'd never hit her again."

"Isn't that what he said the last time?"

"Too bad Mom doesn't have *your* memory," Roz remarks. She rises from the Scrouch and crosses the room to the television case. There's a framed eight-by-ten of my dad there, and Roz picks it up. "You look like him, you know."

"Bald?" I comment. She's holding the formal headshot of my father in his dress uniform: blue-black jacket with red trim and brass buttons, white hat with black brim and Marine insignia. Buzzed hair. Sticking-out ears. Unsmiling. And even though he's my dad and parents always seem old, he's young in that picture. Too young to look so serious.

Roz actually smiles. "The eyes," she says. "The same green eyes. But with your mom's dark hair."

"Mami says I have Crawford eyes."

She places the photo back on its shelf.

No matter how many times we move and how much stuff we lose, break, or toss each time, that picture of Master Sergeant Charles Lee Crawford is preserved in Bubble Wrap, carefully unpacked, dusted, and displayed by my mother. Front and center. It's the photo everyone thinks of when his name is mentioned. Besides our parents' wedding picture and a few random snapshots, it's Jack's only image of him.

And I don't like it. As a matter of fact, I sort of hate it. I have my own personal picture of my dad (I'm the only one in the family who even knows it exists), and it's nothing like that stiff military one.

Roz has been in our place a gazillion times and never commented on the photo before. I'm wondering if maybe I should show her the *good* picture of Charlie Crawford, finally break down and share it with someone. But then, she stops me cold.

"Did your dad have a gun?" she asks.

The Dorito I was about to pop in my mouth lands on my lap. "He was a Marine, Roz. Of course he had a gun."

"No, I mean his own gun. A personal weapon."

"I don't know. I mean, if he did, he never told me." I try to make my voice sound matter-of-fact. But she's actually freaking me out a little. "Why?"

She runs her finger over the top of the television, almost like she's checking for dust. "Shawn has a gun."

"Please tell me you're kidding right now."

"I wouldn't kid about that."

"He showed it to you?"

She doesn't answer right away. "He didn't *show* me. He just . . . has it. Pretty much all the time. The other night he was watching television and pulled it out and laid it on the coffee table. Like it was a pack of cigarettes or his car keys."

"Is it *loaded?*"

She finally turns to me, her expression incredulous. "Izzy. It's not a toy. Of course it's loaded. Except when I take the bullets out. Sometimes when he's asleep. Pisses him off, but it helps *me* sleep."

My mind races. This is bad. Bad bad bad. Shawn Shifflett is a mean drunk. The cops have been called for more than one of his benders, and Roz's mom almost got thrown out of Meadowbrook Gardens because of him. Now he's got a gun?

There's a lot to say, but that's the exact moment we hear the wheels of Mami's car grinding on the gravel outside. Roz flashes me a knowing look and heads for the back door. She grabs the Cheetos *and* Doritos on her way out.

"Hasta luego, chica," she says.

No sooner has she closed the back door than the front one swings open.

My mother pokes her face in. "Isabella? Vamos!"

My head is officially spinning.

When I climb into the passenger seat, I find Jack sitting in the back, *Piggie Pie* open on his lap. He looks at me with an expectant smile.

"'Dyou bring the Cheetos?" he asks.

"Sorry, they're gone," I tell him, without getting into where they went. He begins to whine as Mami backs out. Every nerve in my body is agitated by the sound he's making. "So. Do I *finally* get to know where this place is?" I ask Mami, trying to talk over him. For some reason she refused to get specific last night. Even though she knows I hate surprises.

"Stop it, Jack. We'll get something for you to eat on the way," she tells my brother as she hands me a map.

He opts for swinging his leg instead of whining, so now I'm getting kicked through my seat.

"How do you stand him?" I mutter.

"Tus propios pedos no huelen y tus hijos no son feos," she replies, smiling.

From the back seat, Jack bursts out laughing. "Your farts do too smell, Mami!" he shrieks.

Typical. Jack always understands all her little Spanish words of wisdom, while I'm clueless. My annoyance deepens.

I glance at the map. It's one of those foldouts of Clayton, and she's scribbled directions on it. Also drawn a big circle on a point outside the main city, with arrows leading to it. Like the Mystery Location is a buried treasure.

"You know, if you upgraded to a smartphone like the rest of the world, instead of your antique flip phone, you could use Google Maps," I inform her as I scan the roads leading to her circle.

Mami frowns. She is so not tech savvy; she's only just figured out texting. And I'm not a great map reader. But as I run my finger along the arrowed route, I get this funny feeling in my gut.

"So use the map google on *your* phone!" she prods.

"It's home charging," I tell her. *And I wouldn't want to waste my precious data*, I don't add. Last Christmas she got me the cheapest "smart" Tracfone possible, with the understanding that I would buy my own airtime and data cards. I'm super-careful about when I use them, always worried I'll run out of minutes.

"It probably wouldn't help anyway," Mami says. "There is no address yet. No street. Right now, it is just land."

I look out the window. We are definitely retracing the trip I took with Roz last night.

This can't be right.

"I still don't get why anyone would just give us a house," I tell her.

"Oh, they don't give them away!" Mami laughs. "You pay. But here is the difference." She counts on her fingers. "One: it is a very low mortgage and there is no interest. Two, you don't need money up front, what they call a down payment. Three, instead of a down payment, you give them *hours*. Every family has to work so many hours building their own house. They call it *sweat equity*."

"Will I get my own hammer?" Jack wants to know. I try not to wince at the thought of Jack running around swinging metal tools.

"Sure," Mami tells him, winking at me.

"Yes!" he exclaims, and fist-pumps.

"But Mami, we don't know anything about building," I tell her. "We can barely screw picture hooks into the walls."

"They teach you," she says. Simple as that. She glances at the map in my lap. "What do my directions say? Exit twenty-four A or B?"

"I thought you said you've been to this place already!"

"Yes, but I don't remember if it was A or B."

"Wow, how awesome is this? Not only do we know nothing about building anything, but you don't even know where we're going!"

"Ay, Dios mío, Isabella! A or B?!"

I glance at her scribbles, then look up to see the exit looming. "B! B! B!" I shout.

Mami swerves, and we practically two-wheel it onto the exit. More than one driver behind us lays on the horn. My mother glares at me. "Why are you so negative?" she demands.

"Did you eat all the Cheetos?" Jack asks from the back.

I decide I'm sick of both of them, so I shut my mouth and stare out the window.

Mami leans forward and presses the odometer setting. "Our turnoff is seven miles from the exit," she says.

I glance at the map, and with my finger trace what I imagine is seven miles.

"I've been once with Mrs. Brenda. It's very pretty."

I decide not to let it slip that I know exactly how pretty this part of Clayton is.

At mile six we pass the Shackeltons' mailbox. At six and a half, we pass the entrance to the construction site where Roz and I parked. At seven, Mami slows, then turns onto a packed-dirt road. It's mostly wooded. We pass one sketch house with a sad stable and even sadder bony horse standing in mostly mud. Finally, the woods recede and we dead-end into a field and a view I can only describe as Drop Dead Gorgeous.

Horses graze on soft mounded hills, crisscrossed by miles of wooden fencing. At the horizon, a ridge of mountains glows blue in the afternoon light. It's the sort of view you could stare at for a lifetime and never tire of it.

The three of us climb out.

Mami leads us a few dozen feet from the car, and we gaze out over the field. That's when I notice the flags: little neon-orange flags, affixed to thin wires and stuck in the ground everywhere. There are tire-wide depressions in the soft earth where the grass is laid flat, as if trucks, and many feet, preceded us. Off to one side there's a large wooden sign that reads FUTURE SITE: HABITAT FOR HUMANITY OF GREATER CLAYTON. At the bottom are the little blue raised-arm people.

"In your mind," Mami says, "picture four houses out here. A paved road, maybe in a circle." She gestures with her whole arm, tracing an imaginary cul-de-sac. "Nothing fancy. Three bedrooms. One bathroom. A kitchen big enough for a table where you can sit and eat." Her voice trembles a little. "In my family, we always ate meals together. At one table. Not some counter, you know?"

I nod. Mami never ceases to complain that we have no room for a dining table. And to remind me and Jack that growing up in Puerto Rico, it didn't matter that they didn't have a lot of money. They washed their hands, used cloth napkins, and said grace before every meal. At. One. Table. All. Three. Meals.

This is more standing around talking than Jack can bear, so he begins to do laps, airplane-style, his arms outstretched like wings, around the field of flattened grass. Mami and I watch him run against the backdrop of slanting light and navy-blue mountains. I allow myself the fantasy: that this is the view out my very own bedroom window for as long as . . . I want.

A soft breeze stirs the grass. I shiver, even though it's not cold.

"What are our chances, Mami?" I have to know. I hate to be negative, like she said—but just like Jack doesn't do waiting, I don't do disappointment. Not anymore. I've used up my lifetime's quotient, and to be perfectly honest, I'd rather not get my hopes up.

"The next part is they visit us at home," she says. "They have to meet all of us, and see that where we're living isn't good."

I snort. "That shouldn't be too hard." Mami doesn't laugh. "When?"

"Three days," she says. She counts on her fingers. "Jueves."

"I have a cappella tryouts Thursday."

She stares at me like I've just sprouted a Christmas tree on the top of my head. "Isabella! We have to *all* be there for this home visit!"

"Well, I have to be there for tryouts." *I want to be there*, I don't add. The St. Veronica's a cappella group is the coolest thing—actually, the only thing—I've ever belonged to at a school.

"They make you try out again? I thought you made it already." She staggers a bit; Airplane Jack has just crash-landed at her hip.

"We're auditioning new members. We have two spots open."

Jack stares at us, squinting.

"Tell them you can't make it. This is more important."

"Mami! You tell me all the time to get involved. Make commitments. Follow through. So, that's what I'm doing! Now you want me to blow this off?"

"They will understand," she says. "Especially when you tell them what it's for."

Yeah. Somehow I'm not loving the idea of telling the girls at my private school that some charity group is interviewing me and my family.

"Are you two fighting *again*?" Jack has had enough. "Can we go home? I'm hungry!"

Mami doesn't answer but begins marching toward the car. Jack trots behind.

No one speaks as we pile in. Mami throws the car into reverse and glances at the gas gauge.

"We need to make one quick stop. I'm on empty," she says.

Jack moans and hurls himself against the back seat. "I have to pee!" he wails.

"You can pee and get a snack when I stop for gas," Mami tells him. "*If* you are quiet now."

Jack sniffles. He's close to tears. But the whining stops.

In all of McMansion Land, there is only one place where you can buy anything: a little "country" store called Four Corners. It has two gas pumps. Roz and I stopped here once, and it's actually decent. It's the complete opposite from the Meadowbrook Market (located just outside lovely Meadowbrook Gardens Mobile Home Park), where I work a few hours a week. The Four Corners restroom isn't gross, it doesn't smell like spilled Everclear, and there's a deli counter where they sell good sandwiches. There's also a wide snack rack, so as Mami pulls up to the pumps, I hand Jack two dollars from the glove compartment, where we usually keep loose change and a couple of spare bills. He darts out before she's put the car in park.

As I step out of the car to follow him, she puts one hand on my arm.

"Mija, wait." I hear her take a deep breath. "I don't want us to fight."

"Me neither," I agree. *So why do you?* I don't add.

"I will see if the Habitat people can come after your try-outs. What time will you be done?"

"Probably . . . four? So I could be home by . . . five? Let me check the bus schedule."

"We will both check," Mami says. "Okay?"

"Okay," I agree.

Her expression relaxes. She leans over and kisses my forehead.

I decide to ask her again. "Mami, what are the chances we're actually going to be picked?"

"I have no idea, Isabella. But I do know this, we should pray." Her hand instinctively goes to her neck, and the small gold disk that hangs there. It's her Mother Cabrini medal. Patron saint of immigrants.

Dios mío. Time to rescue the store clerk from Jack.

It takes me all of three seconds to locate my brother in front of the snack rack, trying to choose between Funyons and Fritos.

"Definitely go for the onion breath," I suggest.

He replaces the Fritos, then bolts toward the checkout to pay. Unfortunately, that's the precise moment the one other customer in the store turns into our aisle, and Jack crashes headfirst into him. And bounces off. Like he hit a wall.

It turns out that Sam Shackelton is not only beautiful: he's rock solid.

"Whoa! Are you okay?" the Adonis of Clayton asks my hyperactive brother.

Jack gazes up at him, dazed but grinning. Like he wants to try that again. "Fine! Sorry!" he replies, then dashes off with his Funyons and his two dollar bills.

Leaving me. Standing in the aisle. With Hot Sam.

Whose eyes are *not* sky blue, like Roz says. They're stormy blue. Darkish, flecked with gray.

Those eyes flit over the length of me and the brows contract. He looks puzzled.

"Do you go to St. V's?" he asks. Then he, unbelievably, turns red. Like he's embarrassed. Him!

That's when I remember I'm still wearing my school uniform. With the knee socks. I realize this is the time to follow my mother's advice, and pray. *Dear God, please let a giant hole open in the ground beneath me right now.* I struggle to think of some not-dorky response, but Sam speaks again.

"Sorry, dumb question." He sort of smiles. "I mean . . . obviously, right?"

Here's the thing about prayer: Most times, instead of getting what you want? You get what you need. So while a giant hole does not appear, a miracle does occur.

I manage to do cute instead of dorky.

I spin once, and the plaid pleated skirt swirls. "Can't mistake this St. Veronica's style."

His face reddens a little more. "My sister goes there," he says. "Aubrey Shackelton?"

Knock me down with a feather. He's *Catholic*?

"Really?" I worry I've just shrieked the word. "What year is she?"

"Freshman," Sam says. "Well, kind of. She transferred in second term. She's really only been at St. V's for a few months."

"This is my first year, too," I say. Then stop.

Before I slip and tell Sam Shackelton too much.

Luckily, Jack reappears and saves me from myself.

"Izzy! I paid *and* I peed! Let's go!" he demands.

Hot Sam smiles. "Let me guess, little brother?"

A second miracle. People rarely get that we're related. As much as I lean Crawford, he leans Garcia.

I smile back. "You're two for two."

"I know. Genius, right?"

Jack heads for the door. I'm supposed to follow. I take one step in that direction.

"I'm Sam, by the way," he continues. "Sam Shackelton."

"Right. Aubrey's brother," I say. Another step toward the exit. "I'll keep an eye out for her." Jack has run outside. I really need to go.

"Nice meeting you. Izzy. See you around!"

I manage this half-assed goodbye wave before I peel out after Jack, but I treat myself to one last backwards look at Sam. He's standing there with both hands jammed in his pockets, watching me, smiling with his mouth closed, head tilted. Like he's trying to figure something out.

It's completely adorable. Dios mío.

Mami stands outside the car, urging us to hurry, and Jack waves his Funyons over his head as he darts toward her. A breeze lifts the hair off the back of my neck as I climb into the car. Something occurs to me: I didn't tell him my name. But he said it. *Nice meeting you. Izzy.* He was paying attention when Jack spoke to me.

I shiver for the second time that evening.

4

Roz thinks it's hilarious when I tell her a cappella is cool.

But she's never heard Veronic Convergence. And she's not here to see this: the long line of nervousness snaking down the hallway from the choir-room door, all the way around the corner toward the gym. It's Tryout Day and the girls are forty-deep for only two open spots. Everyone wants to be a VC girl.

Which makes me wonder: how the hell did I, Izzy Crawford, who scores off the charts on the Dork Meter, get in?

As I quick-step past the gauntlet of hopefuls on my way to the audition room, I can't help feeling like a fraud. These girls eye me like I'm some sort of rock star, but it seems like yesterday I stood on this line.

It sucks to want something this bad and know your chances of getting it are almost nonexistent.

I remember the first time I heard Veronic Convergence. It was the opening-day-of-school assembly, and the VC girls sang the national anthem. I remember I felt a little sick.

They were like something out of a Pitch Perfect movie. *That* good. *That* fun. And cute. Even though each girl was a different shape, size, and color, they were all some version of . . . confident. Cool. And they made it look easy.

When they followed the anthem with a kick-ass rendition of Lorde's "Royals," the auditorium exploded in applause and my misery was complete. I felt like a starving person viewing a banquet from the other side of a glass wall. But when you've never taken voice lessons (*not* in Mami's budget) and attended six different schools in six years (none of which had decent choirs), you don't get your hopes up. No matter how much you love to sing.

After the assembly, as I wove through the crowded halls alone with eyes glued to my schedule and a map of the school, I felt someone link an arm through mine. My new guidance counselor, Mrs. Enriques.

"Isabella! Just the young lady I was thinking about! ¿Qué tal?" Mrs. Enriques, una puertorriqueña by way of Nueva York, had bonded with Mami big-time when we came in to register me at St. V's. Despite my best efforts to convince her I really wouldn't speak Spanish with her, the two of them had settled in like two old amigas while I sat there, understanding about 25 percent of their heartfelt, rapid-fire conversation.

"I'm fine, Mrs. Enriques. How are you?"

"Wasn't that wonderful? The girls' a cappella group?" she asked, tilting her head toward the auditorium we'd just exited.

"They're awesome," I agreed.

She smiled and pulled me in closer, like we were sharing a secret. "You should try out. They have auditions next week."

I laughed. "That would be an utter fail, Mrs. Enriques. I can't sing like that."

She narrowed her eyes and smiled. "Your mami told me you are a great singer."

"Mami is musically challenged. Probably also tone deaf," I informed her.

"Still. You need some extracurriculars, Isabella," she continued, her voice bordering on a purr. There was something Mami-like about her single-mindedness. "I put your name in for the audition list."

Brakes. Kids walking behind almost crashed into us.

"Wait . . . *what?*" My voice loud in my own ears. "Mrs. Enriques, I wish you hadn't done that!"

She patted my hand. "I know, I should have asked first. But sometimes we need a little push, you know? To do something that scares us? Give it a try! You have nothing to lose."

Before I had a chance to detail the long list of my likely losses (dignity, pride, and reputation for starters), she spied another hapless student she had been "thinking about," uncoupled from my arm, and sped off down the hall.

That morning—and my outrage at the meddling Mrs. Enriques—comes rushing back like some post-traumatic stress trigger as I step into the audition room, where I find all the other VCs assembled. I've never gotten over my suspicion that some back-room-guidance-office deal had been cut to land me a spot in Veronic Convergence.

"Miss Izz!" a few of them cry. I settle into a chair, and our leader, a senior named Min Yee, hands me a sheet. It's got the list of auditionees, with boxes to check (or not) for various categories, plus an overall rating from 1 to 5, with 1 being "not ready for VC" and 5 for "outstanding." As I scan the categories, Min explains to everyone how this will work.

"Each girl will tell us a little about herself and why she wants to be in a cappella," Min begins. "Then she'll sing one verse and the chorus from a song of her choice. She'll exit, and before the next comes in, I want you all to do your ratings. Right away, gut reaction. Questions?"

I raise my hand. "This last box, 'Presence.' What exactly is that?"

"Great question," she says. "Anyone want to explain?"

Jamila Hooper, who is also the pitcher on the St. Veronica's softball team, dives in.

"Demeanor," she explains. "How she projects. Not just her voice but her personality. We're performing up there, so is she having fun? Do we want to watch her?" Jamila looks around the group. "Do y'all want to add to that?"

"Don't confuse it with looks. This is not a beauty contest," someone adds.

"Hell no! I wouldn't be here."

Laughter and snaps.

"Gotcha," I tell them. It occurs to me that it's a good thing I had no clue about this scoring system when I auditioned in the fall. I was too busy trying to sing in tune and keep breathing.

As if reading my mind, Min offers one last comment as she walks to the door to admit the first girl. "And just so you know,

Miss Izz?" She pauses, hand on knob. "You scored a perfect five for Presence."

Snaps.

Hold on. Izzy Crawford has presence?

Before I can wrap my mind around this concept, the first girl enters.

Here's what I quickly learn about auditions: they are as excruciating for the auditioners as for the auditionees. Everyone is so nervous. The stress and desire, even from the confident-seeming girls, is exhausting. You can't help but feel all the feels right along with them.

What makes it worse: most aren't very good. After the sixth pitchy rendition of "Let It Go" (mental note: future auditionees will be forbidden from singing Disney tunes), the smile muscles in my face ache from too much bright, friendly encouragement. Three becomes my new favorite number as each girl fades into the next, and more than a few of their answers to why they want to be in a cappella are fairly stupid. ("I couldn't decide between this and volleyball, so I tossed a coin and this won!") Plus the clock is running. I glance at my watch.

I need to be home for the Habitat people by five, which means getting on the late bus by four. Which, judging from the way this is going, isn't happening. I have two choices: ditch the rest of the auditions or call in reinforcements.

Since ditching isn't an attractive option, I text Roz as Girl #33 enters.

Me: **SOS!**
Roz: **Sup?**

Me: **Need a ride home from school. Got the car?**

Roz: **I can make that happen**

Me: **430 out front?**

Roz: **k**

Me: **You're the best luv you!**

Roz: **I rock**

When I look up from my phone, Girl #33 is standing at the front of the room. She's a knobby-kneed blonde with a sprinkling of acne on her forehead. Her shoulders slump in that bad-posture way from growing too fast and not knowing what to do with your weird new body. She still has braces. Her cheeks flame with two bright red patches.

I glance down at my sheet, pencil already hovering between "1" and "2" next to "Presence." Which is when I notice her name. My head snaps up.

"Hi, I'm Aubrey Shackelton," she says.

"Hi, Aubrey," everyone sing-says.

Her cheeks burn brighter. "Um, today I'm going to sing—"

Min cuts her off. "Ooh, before that, Aubrey, could you tell us a little about yourself and why you want to be in a cappella?"

Aubrey looks mortified. Like she's already blown it. She takes a deep breath. "Right. Sorry. Okay. Well, I'm a freshman. I'm from East Clayton and just transferred here from Clayton County High School. I was in chorus there. I love to sing." She stops.

I see Min's eyes widen, her head tilt forward in encouragement.

46

"And . . . were you in a cappella at your old school?" she presses.

Aubrey shakes her head. "They don't have it. I've never sung a cappella. I'm not sure I even like a cappella."

Every eye in the room widens. The thirty-two girls who preceded her proclaimed their undying love for a cappella. Aubrey is not doing herself any favors.

"But I do know I need to sing with all of you."

There's a pause, broken by Min. "Could you expand on that?"

Aubrey hesitates. She glances at the door as if she's considering making a run for it. "Last Christmas I saw you all singing at the mall," she begins. "I was shopping with my mom. We could hear you from the food court."

Everyone laughs. I remember that day. It was my first time performing with the VCs. We'd been invited to sing carols alongside this pathetic fake Santa. (Not only was the dude *thin*, but kids kept snapping the elastic on his beard.)

"Anyway, you all looked like you were having so much fun. I wasn't having any fun at my high school at the time. I actually sort of hated it." Aubrey pauses, her eyes widening in surprise. As if she hadn't intended to say that. She clears her throat. "So. Here I am."

A long awkward silence signals that Aubrey is finished.

Min steps into the breach. "Excellent! Thanks. So, what are you going to sing for us today?"

"'Stand by You,'" Aubrey says. "I love Rachel Platten."

Oh god no, I manage not to say. I glance at the sheet again. She's a Soprano I. But you'd have to be a Super Soprano I to pull off Platten-esque high notes. Disastrous choice. I press my lips in a tight, clenched smile. I want to stop her, beg her to sing something—anything—else.

Aubrey Shackelton is about to flush her audition. I don't know why I particularly care. But I don't want to see her fail.

"Can I have a C?" she asks.

She's the first to ask for the pitch pipe. Min gives her the note. Aubrey begins.

And within five seconds, it's obvious that we're in the company of an extraordinary talent. It's not just that Aubrey lures us in with the husky low notes of the opening. She convinces us that whatever pain inspired Rachel Platten to write this song is her pain, too. As the song grows louder and the notes climb higher, becoming, finally, a victory anthem, we forget that Aubrey was only supposed to sing one verse and the chorus. She sings the whole thing and we don't stop her. Not only that: near the end, where Platten's instrumentation backs down and it's just singing and clapping, all of us start clapping along.

Aubrey has just turned her audition into a performance.

When she's done, there's another long silence. But nothing like the first. We look around the room at each other, eyes round, until Jamila breaks the stalemate with an explosive "Hot *damn!*" Everyone laughs, a few whoop, and we all applaud. It's hard not to stand, give the girl an ovation or something. But Min is frowning, making the slashing "cut" gesture at us across her throat because we are supposed to be fair and not indicate, one way or another, how we feel.

Too late for that.

Aubrey, meanwhile, has blushed herself into a shade approaching purple. But there's a hint of relief on her face. And more than relief from the barely suppressed smiles throughout the room: People are pumped. Veronic Convergence is about to add one kick-ass soprano. And she's only a freshman.

Aubrey hustles out, and the rest of the girls blow by in a whirl. There are three more "Let It Go"s (unbelievable) and a really sweet "Over the Rainbow," but otherwise no one stands out for me. I've scribbled in all my ratings, and it's pretty clear who will fill our two spots: Aubrey and Rainbow Girl. I glance at my watch: 4:15. Phew. This will definitely wrap in fifteen minutes.

"Okay," Min begins. "Anybody want to start?"

Lindsey jumps in. "Am I wrong or do we have a three-way tie?"

"Shoot. I thought it was just me," says Simone.

"Uh, me three," adds Jamila.

Other heads nod. My surprise feels bright, almost comical. What—or rather, who—did I miss?

Min steps up to the whiteboard at the front of the room. "Okay, let's each of us name our top five, and their scores. I'll total them here, we'll see what we've got, then talk."

As the VCs call out their picks, a pattern emerges. Rainbow Girl (#38) and Aubrey (#33) are clear front-runners. But so is #24. A girl named Sarah. I scan my ratings: next to #24 I've scrawled *gahhhhh* and a line of exclamation points. Which nudges my memory. Sarah was the fourth "Let It Go."

After we've all reported in, Min does the addition, and sure enough: Aubrey, Sarah, and Rainbow Girl (whose name is Ann) each have 210 points. The closest score after that is 191.

We have a three-way tie.

Min sighs and settles herself into the choir director's chair up front. Like she's in it for the long haul. Not good.

"Talk to me, ladies."

"Take all three?" Lindsey suggests.

I suppress the urge to jump up and kiss her. Yes! I think, glancing at the clock over Min's head: 4:37.

"Bad precedent," Simone declares. "We go to thirteen now, what'll be next? Fifteen? Twenty?"

"Well, we *need* Ann," one girl asserts. "There's a spot for one alto and one soprano, and she's the highest-scoring alto."

"Great point," Min says, jumping up. She grabs a marker. "Are we agreed, Ann's our alto?" Snaps all around. Min draws an emphatic circle around Ann's name.

"So, now we have to choose between Aubrey and Sarah?" Lindsey says. "I don't know if I can."

"I don't think this is even a close call." Simone again. "I know we were all blown away by Aubrey's sound. But—how can I put this kindly—she is not a performer. Hers is the first zero I've ever given for Presence. Sarah, on the other hand, is . . ."

"Gorgeous?" Jamila suggests. Which doesn't sound like a compliment. It's the first time I've heard a VC girl get testy.

"Not that we'd hold that against her, Jamila," Min remarks.

"Poised," Simone continues, meeting Jamila's eyes. "As opposed to terrified."

"Uh, singing in front of you people *is* terrifying," I say.

Everyone laughs, breaking the tension.

But Simone isn't done. "Listen, everyone's nervous. But we can't appear nervous. We have to appear totally relaxed. I don't think Aubrey can pull that off. But hey, she's only a freshman! Sarah's a junior. I think given the tie in their overall scores and the gap in their stage presence, we should go with the more mature girl."

I see nods, hear a couple of snaps. Lindsey is frowning and Jamila looks downright pissed. Min, meanwhile, is heading for the whiteboard, ready to circle a name . . .

"Whoa. Hold up there." The words emerge from my throat. Everyone turns to me. I think they're as surprised as I am.

"Umm . . . this isn't so clear cut. To me, anyway," I manage.

Min looks interested. "Go on," she says.

My mind whirls. I have to be careful. I know things I shouldn't and I have questions they don't. Questions that have nothing to do with this tryout. Like, why is rich, popular, athletic Hot Sam's sister the Queen of Cringe?

How could you have the talent of a diva and the confidence of a mouse?

Here's what I do know (because she pretty much said it): Aubrey Shackelton needs this.

Not wants. *Needs.* There's a huge difference. You *want* the cute top you saw at the store; you *need* air and water. You *want* to be invited to the party; you *need* friends. A friend. Any friend.

I'm not sure the other VC girls know about needing.

"I didn't score Sarah nearly as high as the rest of you," I begin. "Maybe all the 'Let It Go's started to blur for me?" That draws a few snickers. "At any rate, I think Aubrey is gives-me-chills amazing."

"No one argues with that—" Simone begins, but I cut her off.

"Sarah isn't amazing. She's good. She's got stage presence. She's a very put-together person. And I predict if she doesn't make VC, she'll get on with her life just fine. But not Aubrey.

"Aubrey is painfully shy. She's so clueless, she didn't know how to sell herself to us. But she's crazy talented, and Veronic Convergence will sound better with her. And . . . maybe it's not just about what she brings. Maybe it's about what we give. I think Aubrey will be good for this group, and we'll be good for her."

A long silence follows my little speech.

Finally, Lindsey says, "I agree."

"Me too." Jamila.

"Me three. And thanks, Izzy," says another. Snaps.

Min looks around the room. "Let's see a show of hands," she says. "All those for Sarah . . . ?"

The tradition is for all the VCs and auditionees to gather in the auditorium after the tryouts. Min thanks everyone, tells them what a hard choice this was, encourages the girls to try again next time there are openings . . . then announces the new members. It's the excruciating cherry on top of the awful sundae, because thirty-eight of the girls are in tears while two are trying not to shriek with excitement.

I tell Min my ride is waiting for me and I need to skip this finale. Which is true, but also a great excuse. I don't do other people's disappointment if I can help it.

When I emerge from the building, Roz is out front with the car idling. I jump in.

"Thank you thank you thank you," I begin. "I owe you big-time."

Roz acts like she doesn't hear me. She peers at something in her rearview mirror, her nose wrinkled as if she smells something bad.

"Don't turn around," she says. "Look in the side mirror. See behind us?"

I adjust the side mirror, and see a navy Range Rover parked about three lengths away. A slim blond girl leans against it, arms folded across her chest. She appears to be waiting for someone. She wears leggings and leather riding boots.

"What?" I ask.

"That's Melissa. Sam's girlfriend," Roz says.

I suppress the urge to whip my head around. "*Awful* Melissa?" I lean forward to get a better look.

"The one and only," Roz confirms. "What the hell is she doing here?"

"Damned if I know," I reply. "Are you sure it's her?"

"Can't mistake those bad highlights. Or her daddy's car," Roz says. "Let's wait a minute to see who she's picking up."

I glance at my watch. 4:46. Even if Roz guns it, I'm late. "Roz, can we please just go? I'm already going to be in it so deep with my mother." I make my best pathetic face. Which is pretty pathetic.

Roz does the disgruntled growly noise. The one for when she's annoyed with me. "Where's the fire, Izzy? One minute?"

I shake my head. "There's these people I'm supposed to

meet," I begin.

She flashes me the are-you-kidding? look.

"Church people."

"Oh. Well. 'Church people,'" she says. She rolls her eyes. Roz isn't big on church. "Why didn't you say that in the first place?" She glances in the rearview one last time, then shifts the car into drive.

"Thank you," I repeat. "I promise I'll make it up to you. Fan you and feed you grapes, buy you endless bags of Cheetos, massage your feet with oil . . ."

"Ew. Stop right there. I don't like people touching my feet."

We pull out from the curb and head down the winding driveway. Roz keeps her eyes on the road, but I glance back before we exit the school grounds. The front doors yawn open and girls spill out. One approaches the Range Rover. I see Melissa straighten, see the girl practically skip toward her. See words exchanged, an excited embrace.

As Roz turns onto the main road, Aubrey gets into Melissa's car. I try to imagine her voice as she tells her brother's girlfriend that she's been chosen for the most amazing a cappella group ever.

I know why I don't tell Roz about the Habitat meeting. For one thing, I don't want to jinx it. For another, why upset her and make her think we're moving? It's such a long shot.

I have no idea why I don't tell her about Aubrey.

5

I show up twenty-five minutes late, in spite of Roz breaking every speed limit posted between St. V's and lovely Meadowbrook Gardens. Our place smells like a Pine-Sol factory—Mami spent the last two days scrubbing it into submission—and everyone is already gathered in the living room. A woman with silvery hair sits perched on one of our Walmart folding chairs while Mami and Jack take up two-thirds of the Scrouch (with a notably vacant third reserved for me). In the pleather recliner, a man cradles Paco in his lap.

His face is creased with smile lines that deepen when he sees me. Which is a welcome contrast to the if-looks-could-kill glance I get from Mami. Or Jack's agonized expression. He's wearing his khaki Church Pants, which are pretty much a little boy's version of a Hair Shirt. Not that they hurt in any way. They're just not supposed to get dirty. Which, for Jack the Hyperactive Stain Magnet, involves not moving. Which is torture.

"Finally!" Jack exclaims when I make my grand entrance. Mami places a restraining hand on his arm. Paco stands, balancing on the Smiley Guy knees, his curlicue of a tail whipping him in the chest.

"Yes, here she is," Mami says. "Finally." Her eyes glitter. Her mouth forms a tight smile. "This is my daughter, Isabella."

I am so doomed.

"Sorry I'm late," I begin, crossing the room with hand extended. Smiley Dude rises, propping Paco on his left forearm and shaking my hand with his right. I brave a glance at Mami. "Auditions ran long," I explain. "I managed to get a ride, but then we got behind a bus . . ."

Smiley Guy is all forgiving.

"No worries," he says. "We started with the walk-through. And just now we were hearing all about Jack's day. Plus getting to know this little fellow!" He scratches Paco between the ears. "Who looks very happy to see you! Aren't you? Aren't you happy to see Isabella?" Paco, as if on cue, bares his teeth and grins. He's clearly in Chiweenie heaven: they adore attention. "I'm Lyle Cole. And this is Clare Danvers." I shake Silver-Haired Lady's hand and settle on the Scrouch next to Mami.

"Your mother was telling us you sing?" Smiley Guy begins.

"I'm in an a cappella group at my school, St. Veronica's. We had auditions today for new members, which is why I'm late."

He nods encouragingly. It's an expression I recognize. Which is when it hits me.

This is an audition, too.

"What sorts of songs do you sing?" he asks. "Back when I was in school—"

I cut him off. "Mr. Cole—"

"Call me Lyle," he urges.

"Mr. Lyle," Mami prompts. Of course. I try to contain my irritation.

"Mr. Lyle. Ms. Clare. We don't know the first thing about building."

The room falls silent. Even Paco freezes. The only sound I hear is my own heartbeat, blood pounding in my ears.

If sitting through forty stress-filled auditions taught me anything, though, it's this: don't beat around the bush.

"But we're not afraid of hard work. Especially my mother. There is no harder worker than her. So whatever it takes, if you show us what to do, we'll do it."

I see the two of them exchange glances. Mr. Lyle places Paco on the floor. Carefully, like his skinny legs are bird bones.

"Building with Habitat is quite a commitment," he says. "A lot of hours."

"I'd do anything for a real home," I tell him. "To stay put and not move? Name how many hours. I'll do it."

"Isabella, if you didn't have to move but could stay here, would that be all right?" Ms. Clare asks.

I know she's supposed to ask, but . . . really? Do they not *see* this place?

"I guess it's all right if you're tuna. And like living in a can."

The frozen expression on Ms. Clare's face tells me she doesn't get the joke. Neither does Mami. Who looks . . . murderous?

Only Jack appreciates me. He whoops. "Ha! Tuna! And it's smelly, too!" he piles on.

"What I mean is," I quickly amend, "we freeze in the winter and bake on hot days. Every time we cook, the smoke alarm goes off—that's how little air circulation there is. And it's . . . gross. Look at this carpet! We tried washing it but those stains are permanent." *One of them looks like a massive bloodstain*, I don't add. No need to freak Jack out.

"It sounds like you've moved a lot," Mr. Lyle prompts. "Tell us about that."

Before I can answer, there's smashing at our front door. Not knocking: repeated, double-fisted pounding that threatens to pop the flimsy aluminum hinges. Accompanied by a man's deep-throated cursing. And a familiar voice screaming my name.

"Good god, what's that?" Ms. Clare exclaims.

Mr. Lyle startles like he's been poked with something sharp.

"Roz," I say, but Mami is already racing to the door, Paco close on her heels, yapping. I stand to follow when I'm brought up short by a whimper.

Jack. Knees curled to his chest as he presses back into the Scrouch. As if he's trying to disappear into the cushions. His face has gone white.

I hadn't told them Shawn was back. Hadn't wanted to break it to my six-year-old brother that the scary man who yells at Roz and drives too fast and curses at Mami when she calls the police was living across the road again.

I drop to my brother's side and wrap my arms around him.

"Shh, shh, shh," I murmur, pressing my cheek against the top of his head. "It's okay, buddy. I'm right here." His little shoulders tremble.

Mami opens the door and Roz stumble-bursts inside like she'd been leaning her full weight against it.

"Mrs. Crawford, help please!" She's panting, her face red and tear streaked. She dives into my mother like she's home base and there's two out. Except Roz isn't playing; she's running for her life. With one arm, Mami maneuvers Roz back and behind her, putting her body between my frightened friend and whoever is chasing her.

"Yeah, you try 'n' run! I know where you are!" we hear.

Jack sinks further into himself. There's no mistaking Shawn.

"You stay away from me! Stay away!" Roz shrieks. "I will call the police and they will lock your ass away this time!"

"Say that to my face, girl!" Shawn's furious reply sounds closer. Too close.

Then, Gloria: "Rosaline Jenkins, you get yourself out here!"

Mami steps into the doorframe. She's only five foot two, but for some reason she seems to fill the space.

"Gloria. Shawn. Get away from my house," she says clearly.

"This ain't none of your business, Margarita!" we hear Gloria yell. "Tell my daughter to get out of there."

"You're right, it's none of my business. Unless you bring it into my home. Scaring my children. Then it's my business." Mami doesn't shout. But her voice is steel.

"So send her out!" Shawn, slurring. But he doesn't sound any closer.

59

"Lyle?" Ms. Clare's eyes are round. "Should we call nine-one-one?"

Mr. Lyle shakes his head. He rises from the chair and squeezes Ms. Clare's shoulder as he brushes past her. He joins Mami at the front door. "Why don't we all take a deep breath right now?" he says, addressing the cool air outside. "Let's not escalate this and do something anyone regrets."

"Who the hell are you?" Gloria demands. "Roz! I know you hear me!"

Roz has seated herself on the edge of the Scrouch and covered her ears with her hands, now rocking back and forth, humming. Like some little kid, playing the I-don't-hear-you game.

"I am a friend of Mrs. Crawford's," Mr. Lyle continues. "I don't mean any disrespect to you, but I suggest—"

"I'm gonna count to ten!" Gloria screams. "And you better be out!" The woman sounds deranged.

A sob escapes Jack. It cuts through the bedlam. Even Roz lifts her head, her face swollen from crying. Mami casts one furious glance at us, then steps into the night and closes the door behind her. We can still hear through the walls.

"No, *I* am going to count to ten," she says. "I am going to count, and you two are going to leave. You are going to stop screaming outside my door and you are going to stop scaring my children. That is what is going to happen. If you are smart. But if you are not smart, then I'm going to call the police. Again. And Gloria, this time? Schiavo will throw you out. When he realizes *he* is back."

Roz's eyes meet mine. Dominic Schiavo is the manager at

Meadowbrook. The last time Shawn caused trouble and police were called, he threatened Gloria with eviction if the dude moved back.

"Know what you are?" Gloria shouts. "A Mexican *whore!*"

"One," Mami replies.

"Screw it," we hear Shawn say. "Let her stay. No one wants her sorry ass back!" This last bit he yells for Roz's sake.

"Two," Mami continues. "Three." We hear gravel skitter as Gloria and Shawn retreat. "Four."

The counting continues until the Jenkinses' front door slams shut across the road. Mami comes back inside. Her eyes, blazing, go straight to Roz. "Are you hurt?"

Roz shakes her head, then throws herself into my mother's arms. Mami holds her tight as Roz's shoulders heave with sobs.

The home visit is pretty much over after that. Poor Mr. Lyle can't seem to figure out what to do with himself: reassure Jack (who has curled into a catatonic human ball on the Scrouch) or comfort Roz or talk down terrified Ms. Clare (who still wants to call 9-1-1, even though Mami tells her that would be the wrong move right now). He ends up herding us all into the living room for a prayer.

As we stand in a circle, arms linked around each other's shoulders, I can't help feeling ridiculous. We look like we're in a football huddle. Playing some game of Touchdown Jesus while we keep our ears open to sounds of a possibly returning wolf outside our door.

The wolf Roz lives with now. As we stand there, I see her working to control her breathing, still too shaken to flash me the smirky, rolled-eyes glance all the praying would normally prompt. I want to ask her what the hell happened to set him off this time, although it doesn't matter. In the past, anything from Roz drinking the last of the orange juice to Roz (supposedly) swiping twenty bucks from his wallet sparked a scene. Mr. Lyle's words wash over me, barely registering ("Lord, bless and protect this family . . .") as I wonder how long it'll be this time before Roz can go home.

By the time Mr. Lyle and Ms. Clare finally leave—the obligatory we'll-be-in-touch and please-don't-worry-we'll-be-fine exchanged as the adults walk outside—Mami has set us up with grilled cheese and tomato soup at the counter. Food has returned a sense of normalcy to Jack, who munches, wiping his butter-greased fingers on his Church Pants. Roz stirs her soup in distracted circles.

"You'll stay here tonight," I tell her. I know I don't need to ask Mami.

"Thanks," she says, not looking up.

"You could just stay all the time," Jack suggests. Then burps. "The Scrouch pulls out, you know. Into a bed."

Roz glances at me over his head. One corner of her mouth curls up. A bit. "Yeah? I'll bet it's full of Pringles crumbs and dog hair."

"Paco doesn't shed!" Jack insists.

"He's right," I tell her. "So just crumbs. But they're all yours."

Roz ruffles Jack's hair. "Tempting. I'll think about it."

He smiles, taking her word for it.

Mami returns. "How is everything? Okay?" she asks. "I'm sorry I didn't have anything better for dinner. After I cleaned the kitchen this afternoon, I didn't want to cook." She peeks into the pot. There's barely any soup left.

"This would be a gourmet meal at my house," Roz comments. Mami and I exchange a glance. "It's delicious. Thank you."

"Roz is sleeping over!" Jack announces. He slips down from his stool. "I'm done!"

Mami deposits his empty bowl in the sink. "Izzy, help Jack brush teeth and get into pajamas?"

Roz gets down as well. "Can I do that? I'd like to help."

"Yippee!" Jack exclaims. He takes off down the hall. "And then we'll read! Roz, I got a book from the library today . . ."

"Let me guess," she says as she follows him.

Mami and I watch them disappear. She continues clearing dishes, but I take them from her hands.

"Make yourself a grilled cheese," I tell her.

She exhales deeply, shaking her head. "I'm not very hungry," she says, but lets me clear. As I scrape and rinse, she allows herself to sit on one of the stools. She leans her head against one hand.

"What must they think of us?" I hear her say. For a moment, I'm not sure who she means. Gloria and Shawn? Who cares what they think?

But of course, that's not who she means. I see her then, my brave little mami facing down the bad guy with the gun (does she even know he has a gun?), her hands raw from scrubbing, her clothes and her hair smelling like cleaning products. Dressing my brother in his good clothes, hoping, praying, that we make a nice impression and prove that we are a respectable family. A worthy family. People who deserve something better than this.

She doesn't look so brave right now.

"I'm sorry I was late!" The guilty words spring from my throat. I had one job, one thing I was supposed to do. And I screwed it up.

Mami's eyes fill. I never see her cry. She pulls me in close, presses me to her chest. It's strange, but I can't remember the last time my mother held me. When does that stop? As a little kid, it's hard to know where you begin and your mother ends, you feel so intertwined. Jack is usually wrapped around her like a vine each night at bedtime when they read. But somewhere, at some point, that all changes. It's like we float away from each other, bobbing on our own flimsy life rafts, without even a rope connecting us. I miss touching my mother.

"Oh, mija," she breathes into my hair. "Te quiero."

6

THE FACT THAT MY FIRST THOUGHT THE NEXT MORNING IS WHETHER Roz can sneak home to grab the top I was hoping to borrow probably doesn't say much about my character. But it's 'Form-Free Friday, the one day of the month we can wear normal clothes instead of uniforms to school, and I really don't want to outfit-repeat. I've managed to come up with fairly cute stuff the past six times, but at this point the pickings in my closet are getting slim.

I suspect I'm the only girl at St. Veronica's who doesn't live for 'Form-Free Fridays.

As I dump milk over my Cheerios, I peer through the kitchen window and across the road. Shawn's truck is nowhere in sight.

"Coast is clear," I comment as Roz emerges from the bathroom. She'd fallen asleep on Jack's bed, the two of them knotted in the blankets, *Piggie Pie* on the floor. She plops onto a stool next to Jack. I shove the cereal boxes to her side of the counter, but she makes this face like I've offered her a bowl of bait worms.

"Just coffee," she says. "Black." I fill a cup. "Actually, I heard him pull out an hour ago. He has the early shift this week."

"Breakfast is the most important meal of the day," Jack informs us through a mouthful of cornflakes.

Roz nods in agreement, sipping. "True. That's why God invented donuts," she tells him. "Speaking of God, this is amazing."

"Mami likes her coffee strong," I say. Just as Mami walks in. She's already dressed for work, in the cute top I got her for Christmas. It has little pandas all over it. She must be assigned to the children's wing today.

"No, not strong," she corrects as she brushes past Roz on her way to the coffee maker. "I like it so when you put a spoon in the cup it stands straight up."

Jack squinches his nose. "God didn't invent donuts," he finally decides. "That's silly."

"No, but he *did* invent the food pyramid. And donuts are definitely on the pyramid," Roz says. "Pit stop at Dunkin' this morning?" she suggests to me.

I can feel my mother's eyes lasering a hole in my back. I glance at my watch. "Uh, I don't think I have time," I tell her. "I need to be at the bus stop in twenty minutes."

She shrugs. At Roz-miles-per-hour, twenty minutes is an eternity.

Mami steps up to the counter, her hands wrapped around a steaming mug. "Did you sleep, mija?" she asks. For a second,

I think she's talking to me. I've never heard her address Roz with a term of endearment.

"I did, thanks," she says, then turns to my brother. "Even though you kick. And steal the covers."

"Do not!" he retorts.

"Do."

"Oh yeah? Well, you snore!" he fires back, giggling.

"And you fart," she adds. "In your sleep."

"Do not!" he says, laughing.

"It was like poison gas, blasting from your butt," she continues. "I could barely breathe."

Jack shrieks. And spits out his cereal. Roz doesn't fully appreciate how easy it is to rev him. Or, maybe she does?

"Okay, let's finish up," Mami warns. She sees where this is headed.

Roz covers her mouth with her forearm and blows farty noises. They sound very authentic. This causes my brother to pretty much dissolve on the floor in hysterics. Paco yaps in approval.

Mami scoops Jack up by the armpits and replaces him on the stool. She shoots him her that's-enough look, and he semisettles down. Starts in on the flakes again.

"So." She refocuses on Roz. "What will you do today?"

Roz stares into her cup. "Same's I always do, I guess," she says. "Get dressed. Go to school. They sleep it off, we go around as if nothing much happened. Until it happens again." She shrugs. "That's pretty much all I *can* do."

"The pickup's gone," I murmur to Mami. She doesn't answer. She seems to be thinking.

Roz clears her throat. "Mrs. Crawford, I know I said sorry last night, but . . . I really mean it. I didn't know where else to go or what to do . . ."

"Shh, shh, shh," Mami says. "You did the right thing." She glances at Jack and shakes her head, signaling Roz not to get into it right now.

But Roz misses the signal. "Thank you for not calling the police," she continues. "I know, I threatened to do it. But that would have really messed things up. Not just because of Schiavo. But the cops would've called social services again. And I can't. I just can't."

Mami nods. We know about this. Bad as Gloria is, Roz would still rather live with her instead of the random foster families she got stuck with last time her mom went off the deep end.

The issue isn't really her and Gloria. They do okay when it's just the two of them and Gloria isn't drinking. It's the sorry-ass guys she drags in. With Shawn being the sorriest of all.

"How're you doing, buddy?" I say to Jack. Hoping Roz picks up on my attempt to change the subject.

"He was just visiting," Jack answers. Between bites.

"Huh?" I say.

He shovels in another mouthful. "The scary guy," he mumbles. No one responds. "He doesn't live here anymore, so he was just visiting. Right, Roz?" He aims his enormous brown eyes at her.

Mami doesn't wait for Roz to say the wrong thing. To tell him the truth, instead of give him the reassurance he wants.

"Time is up! We need to go to school," she announces, suddenly all business. "Go get your backpack and your sweater."

Still chewing, Jack scooches off the stool and races off. We wait until he's out of earshot.

"It is not safe for you with that man there," Mami begins, stating the obvious.

"Ya think?" Roz replies. Which doesn't sound nearly as sarcastic as it does defeated.

"I want to help you," Mami continues. "But I can't have him chasing you here. You know?" Roz nods, frowning into her cup. I see her bite her lip. "Do you have someplace to stay? Family?"

"I have a friend I could crash with for a few days," she says. She looks at me. "Marliese." Marliese is Roz's one friend from school. She dropped out earlier this year, landed a job bussing at Applebee's, and now has an apartment over her stepfather's garage. Roz knows I'm not a fan. Marliese parties. Hard. Which, honestly, is her business. I don't care. But she gives me crap for boycotting that scene.

Mami doesn't know about Marliese. I don't think I've ever mentioned her name. But her witchy-perception-powers tell her this is not good.

"A few days to let things cool off is okay," she says. "But that is not a permanent solution. You need to talk to your mother. When he is not there."

Roz rolls her eyes.

"No mother wants to lose her child," Mami says. "She will hear you." Roz doesn't answer. I'm not sure she shares Mami's convictions about mother love. "Do you want me to come with you? Would that help?"

"No," Roz answers straightaway. Then adds, "Thank you. That's really nice, Mrs. Crawford. You're right. I should talk to her. But I'll do it myself."

Mami nods. She dumps her coffee into her to-go car mug and collects her bag lunch from the fridge.

"I'm also sorry about what she said last night," Roz adds. Hesitates. "What she called you."

Mami waves her hand. "That was the drink talking," she says. "Just make sure you correct her." Roz looks puzzled. Mami glances at her watch and sweeps past us as she heads down the hall to find out what happened to Jack. "I'm Puerto Rican. Not Mexican. Big difference. Isabella? Vamos."

"I'll give Izzy a lift to the stop," Roz offers. "Least I can do."

I see Mami break stride for a moment. But even she doesn't have the heart to impose the Roz Rule against driving. Not this morning. She manages a polite smile for Roz and a knowing look at me before shouting threatening hurry-ups to my brother.

When Mami finally drags him out the door (trailing his backpack by a strap, his sweater buttons misaligned), Roz gets right down to business. She knocks back the rest of her coffee and slips from the stool. "You need that top," she says.

I feel relief spread across my face. I wasn't sure how to bring it up. I'm sort of amazed she remembers. "Thank you! You are a goddess."

She snorts, letting me know what she thinks of goddesses. "Give me ten minutes," she says. "I also need to get my stuff and text Marliese. Then, donuts."

"Dude, no! I have to go to school!"

"Don't worry, I'm driving you. Screw the bus."

"But what about you?"

She flashes me her you-can't-be-serious-right-now look as she swings open the front door. "No freakin' way I'm going to school. I need a mental health day," she announces. "Back in ten." She skips out, and I watch until she crosses the road and disappears behind her own door.

As I rinse the breakfast dishes and put the cereal away, my phone buzzes. I don't recognize the number but answer anyway.

"Hello, is this Isabella?" I hear. "This is Lyle Cole."

I'm wondering how he got my number, but then I remember: it's on our paperwork. Every shred of information we had to give, we gave. "Hey, Mr. Lyle. How are you?"

"I'm actually calling to check on *you*, dear. I tried your mother but there was no answer. How did everything go last night?"

"Mami is taking Jack to school right now. She's one of those responsible drivers who shuts off her phone when she's behind the wheel."

He chuckles. "Well, good for her. I'll confess I'm calling from my car."

"I won't tell on you," I say.

He laughs again. He's a friendly guy, even if he is useless in the face of drunk-ass maniacs. "Did you have any other problems last night?"

"No problems," I tell him. "And things are quiet this morning."

71

I can hear Mr. Lyle exhale. He really was worried. "That's good news, Isabella. I'm very relieved."

I manage to not say *Me too*. I don't want to give him the impression we live in some war zone, constantly battling with neighbors.

"Could you give your mother a message from me?" he says.

"Sure."

"I know she was concerned that last night's disruption interfered with our home visit. I wanted to reassure her that your neighbors aside, Clare and I both agreed that we very much enjoyed meeting you all and that we have everything we need."

"Okay." Then I stop. I really don't want to say the wrong thing to this guy.

"Isabella, please tell your mother not to worry."

Pause. I wonder if I should say okay again?

But then Mr. Lyle repeats himself. "You folks have nothing to worry about." I hear a smile behind his words.

"Thanks, Mr. Lyle," I manage. "Bye."

"Bye."

Outside, I see Roz loading bags into their car. Stuff she's taking to Marliese's, I guess. She slams the door shut, then heads back in our direction. In one hand she carries her "accessories bag," which is basically this fanny pack filled with some of the cool fake jewelry she makes herself. Draped over her arm, there's the shirt she promised. I glance at my watch. We've got time, especially if she's driving me all the way to St. V's. Plenty of time for a donut. Hell, maybe two. A little celebration is in order.

Because unlike Roz, I get signals. And Mr. Lyle basically just signaled to me that despite last night's disaster: we're still in it.

7

FORGET SINGING: EVEN WHEN SHE'S ONLY TALKING, AUBREY Shackelton's voice is full of music. Tinkling glass and wind chimes. Like God attached angel bells to her vocal cords.

Some people are just born lucky.

I'm at my locker when I hear her. The crowded hall is loud with students switching from sixth to seventh period, but Aubrey's unmistakable sound slices through the background noise.

Or maybe it's just that she's standing twelve inches away. Speaking to *me*.

"That's a great shirt," she says.

Roz called it Southwestern Hipster. It's basically this long-sleeved, white crinkle-top blouse with a high-low hem that falls to the hips in the back. She "paired it" (her words) with my one pair of skinny jeans and favorite scuffed leather ankle boots. Over donuts and more coffee at Dunkin', she instructed me to pull my hair into a loose side braid, insisted I wear these silver hoop earrings she dug out of her pouch of "accessories," and draped one of her Crazy Bead Creations around my neck. It's strung with colorful glass and assorted metal. There's a thick fake-gem-studded silver cross at the bottom.

Even though her own look falls in this no-man's-land between goth and grunge, Roz says she wants to be a stylist. Which makes no sense, given her claim to hate rich, superficial assholes. Who I imagine are the sort of people who pay stylists, but whatever. Meanwhile, she experiments on me.

Which keeps me in the game on 'Form-Free Fridays since my closet is pretty bare compared to Roz's, a bursting clown car of clothes. I stopped asking where she gets it all, even though she insists Goodwill, flea markets, and the Salvation Army store are treasure troves for anyone willing to hunt.

I pivot to face Aubrey. She's wearing a University of Virginia hoodie and jeans. "Thanks," I say.

Her gaze drops to the Crazy Beads. "Ooh. And *that's* cool." Without asking, she reaches for the cross and rubs her thumb along the rough stones. "Where did you get it?"

"My friend made it."

Aubrey's eyes widen.

"The shirt's hers, too. I'm fashion challenged, so she pretty much dresses me."

She laughs. "Me too. Fashion challenged, that is. Does she go here? I could use a consult."

Our eyes meet. Which is when she appreciates the too-much-too-soonishness of this moment. We'd never spoken one word to each other before, even if we recognize each other from yesterday's tryout. But since I ducked out before winners were announced, we haven't actually met.

She drops the cross like it's red-hot and her cheeks begin to burn. Aubrey Shackelton might be the most talented as well as the most socially awkward person ever.

I decide to toss her a lifeline.

"Nah, she doesn't go here," I say, smiling. "She'd never survive the uniform."

Aubrey laughs, a tad loud. It startles, like a blast from a silver cornet. Girls rushing to class aim curious glances at us.

"I'm Izzy, by the way."

"I'm Aubrey," she says. "But you know that." Her cheeks glow a little brighter. Yikes.

Just then, the bell rings, signaling two minutes before the next period begins. I slam my locker shut.

"I had to leave early yesterday," I say, "so I didn't get a chance to tell you, you *crushed* your audition."

"Thanks." She fixes her eyes on her shoes, but I catch a glimpse of a smile.

"Seriously, we were blown away. And *very* pumped that you'll be singing with us."

"Yeah. Me too," she replies, raising her head. "I mean, pumped to sing with all of you. You guys are amazing." We stand there looking at each other as the hall empties. I wonder if I'm wearing the same panicky grin as her. Like she can't decide whether to hug me or run.

"I'm going this way," I say, pointing toward the history wing.

Aubrey falls into step beside me. "I had to leave early, too," she says. "Yesterday. My ride was in a super hurry to get home, so I couldn't stay to meet everyone."

I arrange my expression in a way to indicate that I am *not* dying to know why Awful Melissa was in such a super hurry. "No worries," I tell her. "Everyone's really nice. After the first rehearsal, you'll feel like you've known them forever."

Aubrey nods. "That's what everyone kept telling me about the VCs. God. This place is so different from County!" She shudders, as if she's a war zone survivor trying to shake off haunting memories.

"That good, huh?" I comment. "I haven't lived here very long, but you're the second person I know who doesn't love that place."

"Who's the other?"

"My stylist," I say, winking at her.

She laughs. "Now you've given me two reasons to want to meet her."

Even if she stalks your brother, hates all his friends, and despises the girl who picks you up after school? I manage to not say. This conversation is starting to feel a little surreal. Come to think of it, just walking down the hall chatting with Hot Sam's sister feels a little surreal.

Okay: a lot surreal. I'm trying not to imagine the *WTF??* look on Roz's face if she could see me right now.

"Are you from Clayton, too?" she asks.

I feel my shoulders stiffen. I can't help it. Whenever people I don't know start asking personal questions, I clench.

Breathe, I remind myself. Keep it simple.

Don't slip.

"Yes," I say. That's all.

"So why'd *you* decide to bypass County High and come here? I mean, it's a thirty-minute drive."

I give her my standard answer. "We're Catholic," I say. "And my mom's a big believer in parochial schools."

Aubrey seems satisfied. "Do you have your license?"

I nod.

Aubrey groans. "I still have a year and a half before I get mine!" She looks as if this will be time sentenced to hard labor. "After that I'll have my own car. But in the meantime, if I can't find a ride, I'm stuck on the bus! Which takes *forever.*"

I don't know how to respond to this. I'm unfamiliar with a world in which a driver's license automatically comes with a car of one's own.

It's the sort of thing that infuriates Roz. Not just the *fact* of it—kids with rich parents who can buy them cars, or whatever, whenever—but the *So what?* of it. Like stocking the garage with cars is no different than stocking the bathroom with toilet paper.

Chances are Aubrey Shackelton probably knows a few people who don't get a personal vehicle when they pass their driver's tests. But chances are even better that I'm the first person she's met whose family doesn't have a garage.

Not that I'm about to tell her that.

"You weren't stuck on the bus yesterday," I comment instead.

"That was my brother Sam's girlfriend. He was going to get me after the tryout, but he had basketball practice, so she helped out. But it's not an everyday thing, you know?"

I don't, actually. I don't know anything about any of these people, and right here, this, now, is the moment Isabella Crawford walks away. Or should walk away. Not only because the final bell is about to ring and we've reached the door to my next class but also because the art of avoiding slippage means saying—and doing—nothing that shows your hand. Hold your cards close to your chest and put on that poker face. It's not as hard as you'd think. People love to talk about themselves, and if you keep directing the conversation and questions back to them, they leave the interaction with the impression you're the absolute best. Even though you haven't told them a damn thing.

I'm crazy good at this game. And I've had years of practice. So what I say next makes no sense.

"Your brother's name is Sam? You know, I think I met him. At that little country store, Four Corners?"

Her face lights up. You'd think I'd just offered her a Pez from a Santa dispenser. "That's right near our house! Do you live out there, too?"

The bell rings. I should go. Retreat, escape into class. Quit while I'm ahead.

But some people, even when they're literally being "saved by the bell," can't help themselves.

"No, we were just stopping for gas," I tell her. "I met him by the snack rack. Tall, right? Brown hair, blue eyes?"

"Goofy grin? Chipped tooth?" she adds with a hint of glee. Like a true kid sister.

"He said his name was Sam and he had a sister at St. V's," I say. "I didn't make the connection until just now."

Flat. Out. Lie.

I am so going to hell.

Okay, not really. But it's definitely a sin. And I'll pay. Somehow.

Meanwhile, Aubrey is backing down the hall toward her next class.

"Oh my god!" she enthuses. "Small world, right?"

"Right," I agree, hand on knob. *Too small, maybe*, I don't add.

As I swing the door open, Aubrey tosses one last comment my way.

"Hey, Sam's picking me up today. We could totally give you a lift."

I should say no. I should pretend I didn't hear her, and head into class. I should say, *Oh, that'd be great, but I need to stay late today.* I should say pretty much anything but what I do say:

"Sure. Thanks!"

Aubrey does this little skip, waves at me, then disappears down the hall. I step into class, where, luckily, my teacher is having trouble with his overhead projector and is too busy futzing with it to fuss at me for being tardy. I slip into my seat, pull out my notebook, and try a deep, calming breath.

But I'm anything except calm. My heart races.

What am I doing?

8

I AM THE WORLD'S BEST SECRET KEEPER. BUT EVEN I DON'T KNOW how I'm going to not tell Roz that I drove home in Hot Sam's Jeep Cherokee.

For anyone who wants to fight me on my World's Best Secret Keeper status, I would show them this: a four-by-six photo of my father, Charlie Crawford, which I stow in an envelope, tucked between the pages of my journal, at the back of my night table drawer. In spite of years of moves and objects broken, lost, and tossed, I've never misplaced that photo.

And I'm the only one in our family who even knows it exists. I'm like Frodo, in *The Fellowship of the Ring*. I've kept it secret, and safe.

I've had it since I was ten. It came in the box with my father's stuff after he died. They do that. Send the widow the "personal effects." I remember the box arrived not long after the memorial service because my Tía Blanca was still with us and she answered the door for the deliveryman. Mami wasn't expecting anything, so she and Tía Blanca cut right through the packing tape to see what was inside.

As soon as they looked, Mami made this choking sound and ran from the room. Tía Blanca followed, leaving me alone with it. Of course, I peeked.

I remember thinking it was strange to see my father's clothes folded in a cardboard box. Even stranger were the sheets of colored-pencil drawings at the top of the heap: galloping horses, sandy beaches with blue oceans, gnarly trees studded with round red apples. Why were the pictures I had drawn for Daddy and mailed to him . . . here? The last time we'd Skyped, he'd told me he decorated the walls right next to his bunk with them. He said all the guys told him I was going to be a great artist.

Kids aren't stupid. I wasn't stupid. They'd told me my father wasn't coming home again. They'd said the word—"dead"—and I knew what it meant. I'd seen dead birds and car-smushed squirrels. The boy who lived next door had a dog that died. But the idea that my daddy had left the world forever and was never again going to walk through that door booming *Where's my Izzy?* was still so fresh.

I tried to take the drawings out of the box, but they wouldn't stay in my hands. Like they were mine . . . but not. They floated from my fingers, scattered like colorful leaves on the floor. And as they fell, something that had been tucked between them slipped out. The photo.

I recognized him right off. He was wearing desert-colored cammies and posing with a few other guys dressed the same way. You can't see his green eyes because he's wearing sunglasses, or his blond hair because he's wearing his helmet. But he's grinning that Big Charlie Crawford grin, that I-am-so-up-to-no-good cute-guy expression that you just know broke a million hearts before he fell, head over heels, for my mother.

That "Hey, Mom's working late, let's eat Cocoa Puffs for dinner" grin that made *me* fall head over heels for *him*.

I love that he's saved, in that moment, looking like that. Not unsmiling and uncomfortable in the formal picture Mami displays. Not like he ended up. His vehicle tripped an IED planted in a road outside Ramadi. All the guys with him died. Grandma Crawford got the flag at the memorial service, folded into a stiff triangle by robotic Marines in perfect uniforms. Mami got the box with all the stuff from his bunk. And I got that picture. Because before Tía Blanca returned to the room, I decided it was mine. As if Charlie Crawford himself had hidden it between the pictures I had sent to him. Our little secret. Like Cocoa Puffs for dinner. Six years ago I claimed it, and haven't shown it to anyone.

Compared to that, a lift home is nothing. But it will be way harder to hide.

For one thing, you can't stick it in a drawer.

To my credit, I try to stop it from happening. I wait a full five minutes following the dismissal bell, the last possible second I can wait before the late bus to Clayton pulls out of the St. V's lot. Any longer and I'll be stranded. They're gone now, I think, as I race for the exit. Aubrey will assume I'm not coming, and she and her beautiful brother will drive off into the sunset.

But no such luck. The moment I step outside, the Hallelujah Chorus of Aubrey—which, from any normal human being, would be yelling—reaches my ears.

"Izzy! Woo-hoo! We're over here!"

Woo-hoo? God, help this kid.

There's no pretending not to hear her: everyone in the parking lot can hear her. She's standing alongside Sam's Jeep, which is idling near the exit, in front of the line of buses poised to pull out. Smart move. If you get stuck behind the buses, you wait. And kill brain cells breathing diesel exhaust.

This is the moment. The point of no return. I can choose: wave them on and climb aboard the usual bus, the predictable bus, the bus of rejecting Aubrey's friendly offer and thirty minutes chatting with her and Sam and having to figure out how I'll tell Roz later . . . or step into the what-if of that Jeep Cherokee.

I go with what-if. And damn if Aubrey doesn't swing open the front passenger-side door as I trot toward them.

"You sit here," she says, smiling like someone who knows she's letting you have the biggest piece of birthday cake. With a whole frosting flower.

"Ooh, shotgun," I say before slipping in. "Thanks."

And there he is, with that lopsided smile. His hands grasping the steering wheel, Clayton County High letterman's jacket partially unzipped, foot on the brake. Twelve inches between his shoulder and mine. I concentrate on not staring at his knees and the angle formed by his long legs, folded into the space between the gas pedal and the driver's seat.

"Hey," I say, as casually as any semihysterical person can.

"We meet again." He smiles at me with his perfectly aligned teeth.

What chip was Aubrey talking about? Give me a break. He's Adonis. Gods don't have chipped teeth.

Oh help. Help help help.

Aubrey climbs into the back and slams the door shut, and Sam takes off. Just in time. The buses are starting to move.

"So, Sam remembered you, too!" she starts right in. "I told him one of the VC girls met him at the Four Corners market, and he was like, 'Izzy with the green eyes?' And I was like, 'Yes! That's her!'"

Oh my. Oh my oh *my*. Did your socially awkward little sister just reveal to this girl you don't know that you noticed, remembered, and commented on her eyes, Sam?

Moments like this are rare in my life. I decide not to waste this one. So I shoot Hot Sam a sideways glance that says in no uncertain terms: *Gotcha*. Aim these emerald orbs at him and watch as that signature Shackelton blush ignites the base of his neck and slowly creeps north. Who knew a tendency to insane blushing was genetic?

I decide to toss this Shackelton a lifeline as well.

"Well, I'm glad you remembered me as Izzy-with-the-green-eyes instead of Izzy-with-the-crash-and-burn-brother," I say.

Before Sam can reply, Aubrey pounces. "Oh, do you have a brother, too?" She's right up near our heads.

"Bree, buckle up," Sam orders.

She flops back, and he looks at me and rolls his eyes. Not in a mean way. More in a see-what-I-put-up-with? way.

Hot Sam is also an All-Star Older Sib.

I twist in my seat to face Aubrey. "I do," I tell her. "Little brother. He's six. He met Sam, too. Actually, it was more like a head-on collision. I'm afraid he's a menace."

Sam laughs. "Nah. He's just got a lot of energy," he says. "I was that kid."

"Still are," Aubrey says.

"Hey. Let's not give Izzy here the wrong impression," Sam counters, smiling at her through the rearview mirror.

"Oh? And what impression would that be?" I ask her.

Aubrey takes the bait. "Well, Sam's not exactly a menace," she begins.

"Hey!" he repeats. But there's a smile in his voice.

"But he is hyper. I mean, when we were growing up? Our parents couldn't keep him busy enough. Sometimes he'd be signed up for three different sports at once! It was insane."

"I needed outlets," he explains.

"Kind of like the human version of an electrical plug?" I suggest.

They both burst out laughing.

"Pretty much," he says.

"What sports do you play now?" I ask. "I mean, that's a letterman's jacket, right?"

"Basketball," Aubrey chimes in. "And he's a cocaptain. *And* their team is in the playoffs."

I try to look like this is all news to me. "So. You don't suck," I say to him.

"I don't suck," he admits, grinning. "But enough about me. Aubrey says you sing?"

"Not like her. Your sister has an amazing voice." Quick pivot.

"Hey. Hear that?" Sam shoots her another rearview glance. "That's what we've been telling you. Maybe now you'll finally believe it."

"What about you, Captain Sam?" I continue. "Do you sing, too?"

"He's completely tone deaf!" Aubrey exclaims. "It's, like, the *one* thing he can't do!"

I feel my eyebrows arch, Mami-like. My mother can pull a pretty skeptical expression. I'm a close second to her. "One thing?"

"There are lots of things I can't do," he assures me.

"Such as?" I ask.

He hesitates, for just a second.

"Oh my god. You can't think of anything. How do you live in the same house with such perfection, Aubrey?"

"It's superhard, let me tell you. Sam is good at *everything*. He's even the best at being tone deaf. No one sings as badly!"

He nods. "You should see me do karaoke," he says. "I get standing ovations. It's world-class awful."

The three of us laugh. I can feel myself falling in like with the Shackeltons.

There isn't a trace of asshole-ishness about them.

"So. Where are we taking you, Izzy Green Eyes?" Sam asks.

I turn my head to the passenger-side window. I don't want him to see my own cheek-glowing reaction to his teasing. "Could you drop me at the hospital? My mom's shift is almost over and she can give me a lift from there."

"Is your mom a doctor?" Aubrey asks.

"Nurse," I reply, conveniently leaving out the "aide" part.

The rest of the ride flies by. It's the quickest thirty minutes I've ever spent in a car and possibly one of my best efforts at redirecting the conversation away from myself. By the time Sam pulls into the circular drive at the hospital entrance, I've heard all about Frank ("You have a dog? I love pugs!"), their mom's pasta-party lasagna ("She hosts the entire team? Really?"), and what chance his basketball team has against the opponents next weekend.

"You should come," Sam says as I open the door. "Friday night at seven. We need all the fans we can get."

"Oh, would you?" Aubrey exclaims. A hint of begging. "Otherwise I'm stuck sitting with my parents."

Sam frowns. "You know you could always sit with Melissa and her crew."

Aubrey grimaces like someone about to get a tetanus shot. "They're only nice to me because I'm *your* sister."

"That's not true—" he begins.

"My brother is so nice," Aubrey interrupts, "he doesn't realize how mean other people can be."

I look full-on at Sam. Who just happens to look full-on at me. It's the strangest moment. Like we're both asking each other the same question. Although I can't tell you what the hell that question is.

"I've never met anyone that nice," I say.

"I'm not," he insists, as if being nice is the last nail in his coffin of perfection.

"Let me see what I can do," I tell Aubrey. Then, to Sam, "Thanks for the lift. That was . . . really nice." I swing the door of the Cherokee shut before I can see his reaction, then turn on my heel and head straight through the revolving door of the medical center. Once inside, I peek to see if they're still there, but the Shackeltons are gone.

Here's what I know: you don't let yourself catch feelings for the same guy your best friend likes. Even if she swears that he, and everyone who breathes the same oxygen as he does, is a superficial, fake asshole. Roz needs to say that. Even if deep down she doesn't believe it.

You don't allow yourself the fantasy that not only is that guy not an asshole . . . he might actually be a decent person. A good brother. You don't let yourself become friends with that guy. You don't step into his world. Not only because you don't belong there but also, and most importantly, because it would pretty much be like sticking a dagger into your best friend's back.

I am the World's Best Secret Keeper. But even I don't know how I'm going to keep this from Roz.

9

It's Friday. Game Day. I've just gotten off the bus, and I'm trudging the last few hundred feet of road leading home when I spot someone's car parked outside our front door. Mrs. Brenda sits in one of the plastic chairs Mami planted on our minuscule patch of sort-of grass. My sun-and-flower-loving mother pulled those chairs from lovely Meadowbrook Gardens Mobile Home Park's communal storage shed the first warm day this month. She steals minutes, when she's not working or cooking or wrangling us, to sit in one of them and point her face toward the light, eyes closed.

Sometimes I ask her what she's doing out there, and without opening her eyes she'll say, "Thinking."

Which is code for: "Don't bother me right now, Isabella."

Which translates to: "I need some alone time."

Which is muy annoying. I mean, I get that she needs

alone time. We all do. But when it's your mom, it doesn't seem like alone time. It seems like she's got secrets. Stuff she doesn't tell.

I guess deep down I feel like only the child is allowed to have secrets. Not the parent.

At any rate, they make me sad, those cheap chairs. Especially now, seeing Mrs. Brenda spilling out the sides of the one she's squeezed herself into.

"Isabella!" Her smile plumps her cheeks into two round red apples. "How are you, sweetheart?"

"Fine," I auto-reply. Which is code for: "You don't want to know." I flop alongside her in the other awful chair.

Basically, the long list of what I have not dealt with has grown to an intolerable length. For starters:

1. I still have Roz's shirt and necklace. That's because I haven't seen or heard from her in a week. Not since she texted me that she was crashing at Marliese's for the foreseeable future.
2. I still haven't figured out how—or whether—to tell her about Aubrey. Or Sam. Or tonight's game. Speaking of which . . .
3. I still haven't figured out how I'm getting there. Or even solidly decided that I'm going. Even though Aubrey is counting on it. Actually, all the VCs are counting on it. Which is a whole other story.
4. I still don't know whether to tell Roz about Habitat. I mean, why tell her I'm moving if I'm not? Hell,

for all I know this Marliese thing is permanent and *she's* moved!

5. I don't know how to handle Aubrey. Since the Day of the Lift Home, I have become her new BFF. Or girl crush. Hard to tell which. In either case, she follows me through the halls like a rescue pup that recently escaped euthanasia. Only to find itself placed with a new owner who prefers cats.

I mean, I don't. Prefer cats, that is. But geez, she's driving me crazy. And just the way a dog always sniffs out the cat lover in a room and cozies right up to her, convinced that a few loving glances and big wet licks will win her over? Aubrey is convinced that total slobbering will win *me* over. A couple of the other VC girls even noticed. We were finishing our lunch the other day when Jamila nudged me.

"You've got a fan," she said, pointing over my shoulder. I turned, and there was Aubrey, filing in with the freshmen for the next lunch period, trying to get our attention. Not quite at the Wacky Waving Inflatable Arm-Flailing Tube Man level. But close.

"I know, right?" I murmured, smiling between clenched teeth and aiming one quick royal wrist pivot at Aubrey before we ducked out.

Jamila laughed. "She's just excited. It'll wear off. But honestly? Feel free to call in reinforcements if you need help."

Which gave me an idea.

"Hey. Do you want to go to a basketball game?" I asked.

Jamila shook her head like someone who has turned

on the radio to hear the same bad song played for the thousandth time. "Just because I'm black doesn't mean I'm into basketball."

"And just because I'm Puerto Rican doesn't mean I like flan," I shot right back. Which I could tell surprised her. The VCs aren't used to edge from me. Or any mention of my being Puerto Rican.

But Jamila got the point. "Fair enough," she said. "What's flan?"

"It's this slimy egg custard. Think vanilla snot."

She burst out laughing. And eyed me with fresh respect.

"Jamila. You just said I should ask for help. Well, Aubrey is bugging me to go with her to watch her brother's basketball team. They're in some playoffs and it's important to her. So, why don't we get a group and go together?"

She wrinkled her nose. "You want me to spend a weekend night watching white boys play a sport I don't care about? You gotta do better than that."

"Who says they're all white? I know for a fact one of the captains is black." I crossed my fingers behind my back, praying she wouldn't ask me how I know that.

"You ever actually *been* to East Clayton?" she asked, her voice rising.

I decided not to tell her about my multiple trips through McMansion Land, so I shook my head.

"Everyone there goes to the county school. Clayton *County* High. The people who live in Clayton city? And look like me? They go to plain old Clayton High."

"Please. Black people live outside Clayton city, Jamila."

"Not many. Listen, I don't have a problem with Aubrey. She's a good kid. I'm just saying . . . East Clayton? Really?"

"Just because they're white doesn't mean they aren't hot," I countered.

Which got her attention. "And you know all this how?"

"Trust me," I said.

"I'll think about it," she replied.

She did more than think about it. She jumped on the VC group text and proposed we all go. "Let's support our newest member's big brother!" was how she put it. Which fooled absolutely no one. Because if there's one thing lacking in a Catholic girls' high school, it's . . . boys. "Support" was code for a whole lot of things missing from our education.

Here was the problem: everybody wanted to carpool.

Which meant I needed to convince Mami to give me the car. No small feat since she'd already planned to have me stay in and babysit Jack while she went to her single parents' support group at church. When I made my case that I hardly ever went out with the girls from school and this was a one-time thing whereas she went to her group every Friday, she relented . . . but said she'd take Jack to group. So one of the girls could pick me up for the game and drop me off afterward.

A fairly epic battle followed, with me insisting that wouldn't work, I needed the car, and Mami telling me I was being completely unreasonable and wondering aloud if I was about to get my period. Because how else to explain such insanity?

I hate the way Mami attributes our disagreements to my menstrual cycle. As if she's always right and I'm quarterly crazy one week out of four.

So now it's five o'clock, two hours before tip-off, and my phone has been buzzing nonstop as the VC girls confirm who's driving as well as who's getting picked up and where. I've been radio silent, hoping against hope that I'll be able to change Mami's mind.

Because I really want to go to this game. Of course, at this point, that'd probably take a miracle. Where's a guardian angel when you need one? I look at Mrs. Brenda seated in the horrible chair. She's a religious woman. Maybe she knows one?

"You don't seem fine," she comments after watching me for a long moment. Not unkindly. "Long week?"

"No longer than usual," I tell her. "I've just got some plans I'm trying to work out. How are you?"

Mrs. Brenda sits up as if she's been waiting all her life for someone to ask her this question. "I'm very well, Isabella," she says. "As a matter of fact, today has been one of the best days I can remember in a long time." She aims a meaningful smile at me that feels like a laser pointer boring into my skull.

"You know, everyone calls me Izzy," I tell her. "Except Mami. When she's mad."

Mrs. Brenda laughs. "I can't imagine your mother ever getting mad at *you*," she says.

Think again, I don't say. It occurs to me this might be rude, keeping her out here on the weedy patch.

"Want to come inside?" I ask. "Mami and Jack should be home any minute."

Mrs. Brenda shakes her head, beaming. "I'm enjoying this early spring sunshine," she informs me.

I nod, resigned to my chair. From my pocket, the phone vibrates like it's radioactive. I need Mami to get home so I can convince her to give me the car, so I can text everyone I'm coming, so I can go watch Sam's game . . .

"Yes, this is one of the best days I can remember!" Mrs. Brenda repeats.

Dios mío. Please, help. Save me from this very nice, very annoying woman. Because I'm teetering on the brink of headed-to-hell rudeness I know I'll later regret.

For some reason, the Lord has a free moment, and my prayer is answered that instant: Mami's car appears, winding along the narrow road. Mrs. Brenda pulls herself out of the plastic chair and stands as the tires grind to a halt before us.

Judging from the mixture of surprise and concern on my mother's face as she emerges from the car, she wasn't expecting company.

"Did we have a meeting? I'm so sorry—" Mami begins.

But Mrs. Brenda cuts her off. She stretches out her arms and wraps Mami in a tight hug. She whispers something in her ear. Mami startles, steps back, like the words are electric. Her hand flies to her mouth. She begins to cry.

"Izzy. What's wrong?" Jack's small voice beside me. I hadn't even noticed him get out of the car.

But Mrs. Brenda hears him and turns. "Nothing's wrong, sweetheart," she tells him, her eyes brimming as well. "I was just telling your mother that Habitat has accepted your family's application. You're getting a house."

For some reason, at this very huge, very important, fairly

incredible moment, all I can focus on are these two dumb plastic chairs. Mami tsk-tsking weeks ago when she hauled them from storage and discovered black mold and fresh scratches on their legs. Scrubbing them with bleach and rinsing them with pots of water because we don't have a hose. Placing them on the one spot outside that wasn't gravel or bare dirt or asphalt. Sitting in them like she's some tourist at the beach or reclining, poolside, at a resort.

I hate them. I despise them. Because my mother works so hard. She almost never stops. And it hurts my heart to see that at the end of the day, a few minutes alone, in crap chairs, is all she gets.

But all that is about to change. Everything is about to change.

I don't even realize I'm crying until I feel Mrs. Brenda's arms around me and realize her tears are mixing with mine.

"Yay!" Jack exclaims. "Can we go to Applebee's?"

He leads with his stomach, that boy. And right now, Applebee's is his favorite big-treat-eat-out place.

The four of us head inside, with Mrs. Brenda filling Mami in with all the details—how excited the Habitat people are, what happens next—and Jack freeing Paco from his crate so the poor little guy can pee. In the midst of all the rejoicing, I feel my phone vibrate.

I retreat to my room to check it and sure enough: everyone's weighed in and accounted for except me. The long chain of text messages ends with simple questions from Aubrey:

Aubrey: **Do you need a ride? Or will we meet you there?**

It's now or never, I think as I head back down the hall to the kitchen, where my mother is trying to make tea for Mrs. Brenda, who keeps insisting, "No, thank you."

"Mami?" Everyone turns. "Sorry to interrupt right now, but . . . I still don't have a ride to the game tonight. Are you sure I can't have the car?"

The eyebrows arch, but before she can say anything, Jack dives in.

"I want to go to Applebee's!"

I don't actually believe in guardian angels, although Mami swears by them. But here's the thing: if they exist, I'm guessing Mrs. Brenda might be ours.

And this is when she decides to unfurl her wings.

"I have an idea," she says. "How about we go to Applebee's right now? My treat. We'll both drive there, and after dinner I'll drop you and Jack at church, Margarita. I know a few people there who will give you a ride home, so Izzy can have the car. To go wherever it is she wants. Would that be a good plan?"

And that's how I end up wandering into the Clayton County High School gymnasium only minutes before the starting whistle, my tummy full of Fiesta Lime Chicken, my hair straightened and makeup fresh, wearing the cute white top I still haven't returned to Roz. The bleachers are packed and the air practically pulses, strobe-like, with energy. I scan the crowd for my crew, focusing on the side crammed with people wearing the Clayton County blue and gold, when through the bedlam I hear the familiar "Woo-hoo!"

Aubrey stands in the middle of the mob, waving and jumping up and down like an insane rabbit. All the other VCs are seated around her, waving at me as well. I beeline it to their side and scooch into the space they make for me.

"Yay! You made it!" Aubrey, stating the obvious, in my ear. She's seated behind me and slightly to my right. On the floor, just a few rows below us, the County coach has huddled his five starters close and is giving them final instructions. Sam is bent over, hands on knees, but I can only make out the top of his head because someone's very tall dad, sitting in front of me, blocks my view. My gaze wanders to the visitors' side of the gym. It's packed with equally enthusiastic fans in different school colors. I don't know a soul. Except . . .

At the top, all the way to the right, sit two girls. They're on the far edge, so you wouldn't necessarily notice them. Except they stand out. In all the noise and motion, they are silent and still. Amidst a riot of color, they are muted. In black. From head to toe. Like two crows in a flock of parrots.

Something about them is familiar.

I take out my phone, open the camera app, and aim it at the girls. I zoom in, splay my fingers wide on the screen, and reveal: Marliese. Sitting next to Roz.

Who isn't watching the game, either. Between my finger and thumb, from the dead center of the two-by-three-inch touchscreen, she stares straight at me.

10

I'm pretty much in the Jamila camp, and not much of a basketball fan, but I could watch Sam Shackelton race up and down the court all night.

The only thing more fascinating is watching him guzzle Gatorade. Comb his fingers through his slightly long hair to keep it off his sweaty forehead . . .

Okay. Fine. I'd be willing to sit on these hard bleachers surrounded by screaming fans all night for a chance to watch Sam breathe.

And I'm not alone.

"Which one is Aubrey's brother?" asks Lindsey, who sits next to me.

"Seven," I tell her. I watch her face as she scans the players' numbers. Her expression morphs from curious to surprised to awestruck like in a time-lapse video. A whole lot changes in a matter of seconds.

"Wow."

It's pretty much all she can say.

It doesn't help that he's also the best player out there. Time and again the opposing side tries to shut him down, first double-teaming then triple-teaming him on defense. But Sam is a great passer, so when they swarm him, he simply dishes the ball to an open teammate, who swishes an easy basket. County drives the score way up by doing that over and over, so when the buzzer sounds at halftime they lead 33–8.

Everyone gets up to stretch legs or buy snacks. I get stuck on the endless Lady Line at the restroom, and have to rush to make it back in time for the second half. I'm pumping quarters into a vending machine when I hear "Nice shirt," behind me. Not quite the tinkle bells of Aubrey's shirt compliment. More like a growl. A familiar growl. I wheel around to face the music. No point faking surprise. Roz knows me too well.

"I thought I saw you! How's it goin'? I haven't heard from you all week."

"Ran out of minutes," she says. Like me, Roz has a Tracfone. We live card to card. "What are you doing here?" Roz says "here" as if the hallways of Clayton County High are the deepest pit in Dante's circles of hell.

"I came with some girls from my school," I say. Which is so only partially the whole story that . . . yeah. I lie. To my best friend. "What are *you* doing here?" I continue. "With Marliese? I thought you guys hated this rah-rah stuff."

The pivot works. Roz, suddenly on the answering-instead-of-asking side of the conversation, scrunches her forehead in confusion. "I'm staying with her. You know that."

I pop the tab on my Coke. "So how's it goin'?" I repeat.

"It's fine. Sucks not having a car. I keep bumming rides from Marliese. Which is getting old."

I nod, as if I know. "When do you think you'll come home?"

Roz takes a deep breath, followed by a long exhale. "Probably soon. Mom texted Marliese and said Shawn's chilled out. I think they know they screwed up and now want to make nice with me. Before I go to Schiavo on them."

The buzzer in the gym sounds the beginning of the next half. Most people have returned to the bleachers and the hallway is empty. Except for us. I take a step toward the game.

"We should go back," I say.

Roz shakes her head. "Marliese wants to leave. There's a party at her stepbrother's tonight."

I take another step and concentrate on keeping my expression neutral. Right after we'd arrived in Clayton, Roz took me to one of Marliese's stepbrother's ragers. We pulled up at the same time as the police—three cruisers, swirling neon lights—and managed to speed off in time to see dozens of kids race from the blaring house and duck into the dark woods.

I declined future invitations to accompany her there. For which she gives me endless amounts of grief. Even now, she's smirking.

"It's not *that* bad, Izzy."

"Did I say anything?"

"You don't have to."

So much for my neutral expression. "Okay. Well. Have fun. Just shoot me a text or something. I miss you!" More steps. Then I remember. "Oh, and *thanks*. I know I need to return this." I point to myself. The top.

One corner of her mouth curls up. "Keep it. Looks great on you."

"Thanks," I repeat. I'm about to turn and run back to the gym when she calls out one last question.

"What girls from school?"

There's this pause. This frozen moment in time, before I disappear into the gym and she disappears with Marliese, when we look at each other and both know: this is an ask. The closest thing to an ask you ever get from Roz. Because the girl's just not wired to say she wants—or needs—anything.

Invite me to sit with you, she doesn't say.

So I don't.

"The a cappella girls," I tell her. *The ones you've never met, but you mock*, I don't add. The ones you call the Uncool, as if they're one step removed from the Undead. Catholic zombie dorks. "Turns out they're basketball fans!" That's it.

"I'll text you," Roz finally says before I turn and rejoin the others.

The second half is ugly. County, led by Sam, busts open a massive lead, which prompts its fans to begin celebrating early and the opposing fans to either fall silent or scream insults at the refs for bad calls. Occasionally, they scream insults at the players on the court, and at one point a resource officer has to "escort" two belligerent boys from the visitors' side out of the gym. Finally, with two minutes left in the game, the County coach pulls his starters. It's an act of mercy but also a chance to give his second string some playing time. As Sam and Co. head to the bench, everyone on the County side of the gym rises in a standing ovation.

Which is when I notice Melissa and her friends.

I don't know how I missed them up to this point: they're sitting dead center, behind us and to our right. They shriek like banshees as the starters retire. Dressed head to toe in blue and gold, with ribbons in their hair and faces painted to match, a few wear white T-shirts with numbers scrawled on the front.

Melissa, of course, wears Sam's number.

"I love you, Seven!" she screams. Right before he sits, Sam glances in her direction. This quick shadow of a half smile passes over his face, as if a bird had flown into the gym and flitted past a light. But it's enough to set off giggles, oohs, and meaningful glances from the posse. Melissa blows him a kiss, waves to him, just in case he, and everyone sitting on her side of the gym, didn't notice her. But Sam has already turned his attention back to the floor and the final minutes of the game.

Roz is wrong about this girl. She isn't awful.

She's ridiculous.

Which makes you wonder. What is he thinking? Then again: maybe he's not.

When the final buzzer sounds, it's Clayton County High, 58; the Other Guys, 18. A slaughter. Both teams shake hands and jog off to the locker rooms, leaving half the fans exuberant, half miserable.

Our crew is just hungry. We vote to decamp to this awesome diner Lindsey loves, and after arranging ourselves into various cars, we drive over and squeeze into a corner megabooth. Everybody starts ordering ice cream and fries. Aubrey claims she didn't have dinner and orders a BLT; Jamila goes for a wedge of cheesecake. I do some quick mental math, adding up the total bill plus tip and dividing by the number of VCs, because I only have a ten on me and nobody is asking for separate checks.

Even if all I get is an herbal tea, I don't have enough for a shared bill.

Then, Min announces, "By the way, everyone, Paul's got this."

"Thank you, Paul!" Simone declares.

Everyone snaps—except me, Ann, and Aubrey.

"Somebody tell the new girls about Paul," Jamila says.

"My dad," Min explains, smiling like someone who just hit a tennis ball with the rim of her racket and watches as it clears the net by an inch. It's unearned, but you'll take it. "He keeps me in Visa prepaids."

"Plastic surgeon," Jamila mutters in my ear.

Mental note: my other angel, if they do exist, is a plastic surgeon named Paul.

The interrogation of Aubrey begins as soon as the waitress disappears with our menus. The girls want details about every guy on the team. Especially Sam. Everyone wants the scoop on Sam.

And wants to know if he's single.

"Taken," Aubrey laughs. "And she's pretty much the most popular girl at his school."

"What does that mean, really?" Min wonders aloud. "'Popular.' Most friends? Most liked?"

"Most power," Jamila says.

"Most feared," somebody else suggests. Which draws murmurs of agreement.

"Maybe just . . . the most," I say. "The thing I want to know, Aubrey, is do *you* like her?"

Aubrey's eyes grow round. As if she'd never considered the question. Or no one had bothered to ask her before. "I guess I like her as much as I've liked any of Sam's girlfriends," she finally decides. Which draws a long "Whooooo" from the table.

"And how many of *those* are there?" Jamila asks. "Does he take breaks in between?"

"Or is he a serial monogamist?" suggests Simone.

"I can never decide whether that's good or bad," comments Ann. "Is that someone who likes commitment? Or can't be alone?"

As the conversation veers away from Sam and toward a general debate about guys who can't be alone, I notice Aubrey getting quieter and quieter. By the time the check comes and we're all heading out, she's stone silent. When I offer to drive her home, she simply nods and climbs into the car.

"You okay?" I ask after we've gone a few miles and she's yet to utter a sound. She bears no resemblance to the Energizer Bunny who's been tailing me ever since she made Veronic Convergence.

"Yeah. Actually, no. Not really."

"Want to talk about it?"

"Why did you invite everyone to come to the game? I thought just you and me could go together."

The anger in her voice throws me.

"I'm sorry, Aubrey. I thought you wanted to be part of the whole VC thing. Not just the singing."

She turns her face toward the window, a little patch of it steaming with her breath. We're passing the Four Corners market, which is hopping. It's dark, so I can't be sure, but I think I recognize a familiar Jeep Cherokee in the lot?

"I guess I just wish people liked me for me. Not for being Sam Shackelton's sister," she says to the glass.

I don't know what to say. Especially because I'm not sure I don't fit that description.

Aubrey twists in her seat to face me. "You know why I left County?" she demands. "Because people were either sucking up to me in order to get near Sam, or laughing at me because I'm not . . . like him. Gorgeous. Athletic. Popular. One of his exes actually thought it would be funny to set up a fake Instagram account called If-I-Were-Cool Aubrey. She posted all these pics of big-boobed women in bikinis, then photoshopped my face onto them. It was awful."

"I'm so sorry. That's terrible." I don't know what else to say. She's describing the sort of bullying I've only heard about. Or read about, like in a *People* magazine article.

Poor Aubrey.

"I got really depressed," she says. "That's when my parents thought maybe St. V's might be better for me. So I transferred."

As we near her driveway, I slow and signal. "I hope that girl got into huge trouble," I say, turning in.

Aubrey frowns. "How did you know this was my house?"

Oops. Not good.

"Uh, you told me the number." There was a number on their mailbox. Right?

"No, I don't think so," Aubrey says.

I fix my eyes forward, aiming the car toward the glowing lights ahead. I feel her staring at me.

Pivot, Isabella. Pivot.

"Well, you must have because how else did I know?" I say. Willing lightness into my voice. We reach the wall of massive garage doors, and I shift the car into park. I turn to her. "Aubrey. You didn't make Veronic Convergence because of Sam. The girls came tonight—yeah, because we're boy starved at St. V's, I'll admit it, but mostly to support *you*."

"I know," she says, staring into her lap.

"We like *you*," I tell her.

"I know," she whispers.

"Even though your brother *is* hot AF."

Her head snaps up. "Ha!" she exclaims, and fake-slaps my arm.

We both burst out laughing. I feel my blood pressure drop.

"Hey, you want to come in and meet Frank?" she asks.

"Love to," I tell her.

Mr. and Mrs. Shackelton are cozied up on the couch when we walk in, watching something on that big flat-screen and eating cookies. From the pool house view, this room seemed sharp edged and bright. On this side of the glass, however, it's soft. Pastels. Everything hints at color, but what color exactly? The walls are pale petals, the carpeting ash. The parents blue-eyed and as beautiful as their furniture.

They are also beyond thrilled to meet me. When Mrs. Shackelton realizes I am "the" Izzy from St. Veronica's, she practically straps me to a chair and force-feeds me desserts. She starts a kettle for tea while the dad insists on hanging up my jacket. They pepper us with friendly questions—"Did you girls have fun at the game?" "Where did you all go afterwards?"—then thank me repeatedly for driving "Bree" home, and make it abundantly clear that their daughter walking in the door with a new friend after spending some social time out of the house is a very big deal.

Which makes me feel more than a little guilty for every time I've ever felt annoyed by Aubrey.

Meanwhile, Frank yaps nonstop. He's thrilled to see me again. Probably wondering where I've been. I'm thinking it's a good thing none of us speaks Pug.

I don't stay long, maybe fifteen minutes, then head back to my car. Which is boxed in.

Sam and his friends have just pulled up.

I can't help noticing that they are unloading a case of beer from one of the trunks. I was right: Sam was at the Four Corners market with his crew. Loading up for the night. I wonder who's got the fake ID.

Awful/Ridiculous Melissa spots me first. She nudges Sam, whispering. The surprise on his face when he recognizes me reminds me of Jack. That time Mami walked into the room while we were trying to wrap his birthday present for her.

"Hey. Izzy." A statement, not a greeting. He turns to the guy carrying the case, and I hear him murmur, "Take it round back to the pool house," before focusing on me. "We meet yet again."

"Yes indeed," I say. Three boys from the team and two girls I don't know emerge from another car. "Great game tonight. You guys were awesome."

"Thanks," Sam says.

Melissa slips her arm around his waist and bares her fangs, which I guess is her version of a smile. She's washed off the face paint, which is a good thing because otherwise she would have been terrifying.

"Hi, we haven't met," she says. "I'm Melissa." Her voice is aggressively perky. Like she's daring you to be more upbeat, energetic, and fun, but behind all the singsong? You can hear thunderclouds rumbling in the back of her throat.

"Izzy," I tell her. I look at Sam. "I'm afraid you're blocking me."

"Were you at the game? Izzy?" Melissa asks.

"I went with Aubrey. Just dropped her off."

"That's so sweet of you!" she says.

I shoot her a level look. "Nothing sweet about it. Aubrey's great. Sam?"

He sort of startles. "Yeah. Right. Let me move my car." He extricates himself from Melissa and digs in his pockets for keys. Meanwhile, the group drifts to the backyard. The pool house. With the beer. Melissa sort of waggles her fingers at me in this fake-friendly wave and fades into the shadows with them. Time to get in my car and get out of here. But as I swing my door open, Sam speaks.

"Izzy Green Eyes."

I turn. He's doing it again. Tilt of the head. Hands jammed in his pockets.

"Thanks for taking Aubrey tonight. She was looking forward to going out with you."

I concentrate on smiling in a way that doesn't show my disappointment. I mean, what else did I think he wanted to say? "Sure. It was fun."

He steps closer. "She, uh, doesn't need to know. About the beer?"

Right. Now I get it.

"What beer?" I reply.

He narrows his eyes at me, surprised.

"G'night, Sam." I lower myself into the car. But he's not done.

"I hope you don't mind, but can I get your number? There's something I want to ask you, but now's not a good time. If you know what I mean."

"Hand me your phone," I tell him.

He pulls his iPhone, warm, from his back pocket and I punch in my number.

"See ya," I say, handing it back.

Then Sam moves his car, and I back out of their long driveway without swerving off into the trees. Which is pretty much a miracle, considering how my heart is pounding.

11

MAMI SLAMS THE CAR DOOR SHUT AND STRIDES TO OUR FRONT
door, leaving a path of sharp heel bites in the soft dirt. She
barely acknowledges Roz, sprawled in one of the plastic chairs.
Before Mami disappears inside, she wheels around to hurl one
final command at me.

"And do not forget, Isabella, that you have to be at work at
two today. Jack!"

From the back seat, my brother emerges, head down. He
trudges past Roz, aiming big eyes brimming with misery at
her, before following Mami. She slams that door, too.

"Bad time?" Roz comments as I flop alongside her.

God, I hate these chairs. "You could say."

"I'd suggest we go for a ride, but sounds like you have to
be at the market in . . ." She glances at her phone. "Twenty-
three minutes. And I don't have a car. Still."

I glance across the street. No sign of life at Gloria's.

"How'd you get here?" I ask.

"Walked," she says, swinging one leg like a pendulum, her foot scuffing a trench in the gravel. "Took me an hour, but Marliese never came home last night and I need some stuff out of my closet. I think I've got a blister."

"Will an ice cream from the market help?"

On Saturdays from two to six, I work at Meadowbrook Market. In addition to my whopping minimum-wage salary (which just about keeps me in phone cards), I'm allowed one free "treat" per shift. If Roz is around, I usually give it to her.

She usually makes sure she's around.

If I were a good friend, right now, I would nuke her a plate of leftover arroz con pollo instead of sharing my freezer-burned freebies. But I'm not that good—Mami's in the kitchen, and we've had more than enough "quality time."

Today was our first official meeting with the Habitat for Humanity people.

It didn't go well.

We met at their office. Clayton Area Habitat for Humanity is located in a rabbit warren of creaky rooms upstairs from the ReStore, which is Habitat's version of Goodwill. The whole place smells like used clothing, which is weird because they don't sell used clothing. Only used furniture. Doors. Sinks and toilets. Lights, desks, air conditioners . . . everything you need for a house. And all pretty decent. Like, way nicer than the Scrouch. Although, that's not saying much.

While Jack played downstairs with some ReStore volunteer, Mami and I took our seats at the conference table and were introduced to all the people who would be working with us. Mr. Lyle, Ms. Clare, and Mrs. Brenda, of course. A red-bearded guy from the "board," whatever that is. Some other guy named Chris, who kept saying things like "pouring the slab" and "raising the walls." A woman named Natalie, who had brought her baby and was quietly breastfeeding.

And one badass grandma named Betts, who showed up wearing Carhartt work boots, jeans, and a red flannel shirt. She had a Judge Judy haircut and hard blue eyes. Mr. Lyle introduced her as the site supervisor, and while she didn't say much, she did manage to glare at me every time I looked up from the phone in my lap.

Betts would win, hands down, a Most Likely to Own Her Own Nail Gun contest.

It was hard to concentrate, not only because Mr. Lyle began the meeting by passing out a booklet-thick stack of papers (boring) but also because my phone kept vibrating. It was mostly VC girls on the group text but also messages from Roz.

They were the first texts I'd received from her in a week.

Roz: **We need to talk**

Me: **Are you home?**

Roz: **Sorta. Outside your house. Where are you??**

Me: **With my mother. A meeting. Long story. Back soon**

Roz: **I'll wait**

It was not a friendly *I'll wait*. It was a *WTF?? I'll wait*. Not that you can tell the difference on a phone screen. I just knew.

Unfortunately, as I was texting Roz, Mr. Lyle asked me a question.

"How does that sound to you, Isabella? Hours for A's?"

I had no freakin' clue what he was talking about.

"Um, okay," I said.

Mami shot me one of her glittery-eyed looks. *Pay attention,* those eyes warned.

"What else can Izzy do to earn hours?" Mrs. Brenda asked.

Betts cleared her throat. "Depends on how old she is," she said. Her voice sounded like car keys in a can. Shaken, not stirred.

"I'm sixteen," I said.

Betts cracked her knuckles. "She can work on-site if she has an adult volunteer supervising her one-on-one."

I wondered what was up with her speaking about me as if I weren't in the room.

"Plus you can earn hours helping at the ReStore," suggested Red Beard.

"Or coordinate meals," added Natalie. "We provide snacks and lunch to everyone every building day. That involves getting people to donate, picking up and delivering food, and cleaning up."

"Trading in an A will seem easy by comparison," Mr. Lyle commented.

"Easy for Isabella." Mami didn't bother to hide the pride in her voice. "She is a straight-A student."

Everyone seated around the table beamed at me.

Except Betts.

"Sounds like you Crawfords will reach three hundred in no time," Ms. Clare commented. Which is when I finally got what they were talking about: sweat equity. What we "put down" on our house instead of cold, hard cash.

Every Habitat family has to give a certain number of hours working on its own or another family's home. How many depends on the size of your house and your family, so for us, with Mami being a single parent with two kids . . . we need three hundred. Most of that will come from her; some can come from me. Apparently, every A I earn at St. V's is worth an hour of equity, which is sweet.

The bad news is: it's just me. Jack's too young. And even though relatives can pitch in, we don't have any around. All Mami's people are in Puerto Rico and the Crawfords are in North Carolina. Not that Mami would ask them . . .

"Of course, first things first," Mr. Lyle continued. "We'd like to share the good news about the Crawford family. Introduce you not only to our Habitat community but also to your East Clayton neighbors."

"A little public relations," explained Ms. Clare.

I didn't like the way that sounded. I think the word "public" set off alarm bells in my brain.

"What do you mean?" asked Mami.

"Well, fund raisers, for one thing," Natalie said. "We've got a few dinners planned and even a silent auction, and everyone will want you to be there to meet the donors."

I'd never heard of a silent auction, but dinner sounded good.

It would have been fine if they'd stopped there. A few meetings, with food, to meet people. Yank Jack into his Church Pants, wear a nice dress, and talk to adults for a few hours. I could do that.

But they didn't stop there.

"And we'd like to feature your family in our newsletter. It's distributed to more than twenty thousand people in the greater Clayton area, and you'd be on the front page. With a picture!"

I can't remember who said that. I think I've blocked it. Sort of a post-traumatic stress thing. Because . . . no. No. Way.

No one was mailing my picture and telling my story all over Clayton.

I looked across the room at Mami. She was smiling away. Like this was all fine.

"Do we have to?" I heard myself say.

Every head turned in my direction. Even Betts's.

"It's pretty standard. With every new family," said Natalie.

"And particularly important in your case," added Mr. Lyle.

I saw Red Beard frown at him. "Equally important."

Mr. Lyle looked irritated. "I'm sorry," he said, sounding not one bit sorry. "But Rita needs to know what we're dealing with."

Red Beard sighed. "Very simply," he began, "a small but vocal group of East Clayton residents challenged this project—"

"Why?" Mami interrupted. Her smile had been replaced by the classic Mami Worried Look: three lines creasing her forehead, eyes wide.

Red Beard stepped in. "Your house is the first of four homes we plan to build in that part of town, on land donated to us. Previously, we've built all our homes within the Clayton city limits, so extending our reach into East Clayton is a first. It was challenged by abutters who were worried that putting houses on half-acre lots instead of four- or five-acre lots would hurt property values."

"Abutters?" Mami asked.

"Homeowners whose property shares a boundary with yours," he explained.

Mr. Lyle made this snorting sound, just shy of a laugh. "The Buttheads."

"Lyle," Ms. Clare warned.

Betts ducked her head. I could swear she was grinning.

"The good news," Red Beard said, glaring at Mr. Lyle and Betts, "is that this was a small group of neighbors. Most people support our work."

"But the losers aren't happy," added Mr. Lyle. "Which is why we're launching a Charm Offensive."

"We are not launching a Charm Offensive," Red Beard replied. He sounded tired. Like this was an old argument.

Mr. Lyle sat up straighter. "Sure we are," he fired back. "We're going to beat back their opposition by overwhelming them with positivity. When the newsletter—and the local paper, and the conversation by the water cooler—is all about this wonderful family that is building a house with Habitat, they'll back off."

There was a pause after that. I decided to weigh in again.

"You'll have to count me out."

"Isabella!" Mami didn't sound angry. She sounded surprised. Shocked beyond mad.

"Excuse me?" Red Beard said.

"I'll hammer nails," I told them. "I'll make food, work in the ReStore, and earn straight A-pluses. But I don't want to be photographed and interviewed."

"What's the problem?" Red Beard asked.

"There is no problem! We will all do the interview!" Mami said.

I looked straight at Mr. Lyle. "Parts of my family's story are . . . painful. I don't like talking about it."

"You don't have to share anything painful, Isabella," Mr. Lyle said.

How about personal? I didn't say. *How about embarrassing?*

How about this: appearing in the Habitat newsletter feels like inviting the entire city of Clayton to examine my underwear drawer?

Mr. Lyle and all these nice people might have our best interests at heart, but they don't begin to get how it feels to be me.

"Maybe to the people who read your newsletter, the dead vet dad and the hardworking single mom trying to make a better life for her kids is a great story," I said. "But to us? It's no story. It's reality."

"Isabella." Mami's voice. Quieter. With hairline cracks. Like she couldn't decide whether to cry or yell at me. "We will talk about this later."

"Or not," we all heard. Betts. Who was squinting at her own phone now, then shoving it in her pocket. Like she needed to leave for another appointment. "We can postpone the family feature until your daughter feels more comfortable. The most important thing right now is cash, folks. I need cold, hard cash if I'm going to buy supplies. Can we count on you for dinners, Isabella?" It was the first time she'd said my name and spoken to me directly.

"Sure," I told her.

Betts stood. "Well, that's settled," she said. "Sorry, folks, but I have to go. I know Lyle here will help you work out all the important details in my absence." Mr. Lyle winked at her. "Isabella." She tilted her head in the direction of the door. "Walk with me."

This, I thought, as I pushed back my chair and followed her from the room, is how the condemned feel on their way to the gallows.

Betts didn't waste any time. She spoke as we descended the stairs, her crank-box voice competing with the creaky wood until we reached the ReStore on the ground floor.

"We're going to be seeing a lot more of each other, Isabella," she croaked.

Great, I didn't say.

"I've built houses with a lot of families," she continued. "Each one of them struggling. Each one of them special. In their own way."

I didn't know how to respond to this, so I didn't.

"I like your mother. She's a good woman," she said.

For some reason, this touched a nerve. I could feel the sting of gathering tears.

"Don't make things harder for her, kid." Then Betts turned on her heel without another word and headed out to her car.

It occurs to me now, as Roz and I set off on foot toward the market for my four-hour shift, that I'm exhausted. Like I've been carrying heavy stones for too long. I hardly have the energy even to talk to Roz, which is so not our way. Finally, she decides to poke a stick at the eight-hundred-pound Gorilla of Silence walking between us.

"I feel like something's up with you."

"We're moving," I blurt.

She stops in the middle of the road. She looks at me like she's not sure if I'm teasing or double-crossing her.

It tumbles out of me, as if pieces of a jigsaw puzzle I'd stuffed in my pocket spill, in no apparent order, onto the ground. From Mr. Lyle to sweat equity and the property in East Clayton. The pieces are strewn before her and she fits them together in a flash.

"You're going to live in McMansion Land," she says. As if she can't quite believe it. "Are they building you a mansion?"

This makes me laugh. "Roz, it's Habitat for Humanity. Not Oprah."

"They only build mansions out there, Izzy."

"Guess again." I don't bother telling her a few of the neighbors share that impression.

"Still. Good for you. Getting the hell out of here." She says "here" like . . . it's the halls of Clayton County High. We resume our walk to the store.

"So why is your mom mad?" Roz continues. As if news like this should be a permanent antidote to mad-ness.

"They want to write about our family in their newsletter," I tell her. "I don't want to do it and Mami is furious. She yelled the whole drive home."

"Why don't you want to do it?"

"I just don't."

Roz snorts. "Seriously? You're up for three hundred hours of hard labor, but you won't pose for the camera and say 'cheese'?"

"It's not just that."

"Then what?"

"I don't know. They pissed me off. I don't mind that the Habitat people know us. But our 'story' isn't the whole town's business!"

I'm getting worked up. Again. Like I did with Mami. And Roz's attitude right now doesn't help. She looks at me like I've lost my mind.

"Hell, wanna trade stories? I'll take the cute brother, the mother who cooks, and the war hero dad. You can have drunk Gloria and pistol-packing Shawn. Deal?"

"My father is not a war hero. He's just a dead Marine."

"Sure he is. There's a reason everybody's always saying 'Thank you for your service,'" she continues. "It's freakin' brave to fly over there where everybody's pointing guns at you."

"God, I am so *sick* of that line!" I kick the gravel. "Do you know, when people find out my dad died in Iraq, they say 'Thank you for your sacrifice'?"

Roz grimaces.

"News flash," I continue. "My dad wasn't a hero. He was unlucky. And 'sacrifice'? That's a choice. Nobody gave me a choice. And if they had, I'd choose my dad. Back home and alive. Every time."

We've reached the market, ten minutes before my shift starts. Nobody pays me for working extra minutes, so I signal to Earl, the guy I'm relieving behind the register, to put me down for an extra snack. Roz and I each take a Dove Bar from the freezer case and go around back to eat.

She looks thoughtful as she unwraps her ice cream. "You know, you fight with your mother. But your dad's the one you're really mad at," she says.

I resist the urge to throw my slightly freezer-burned bar at her head. "That's the stupidest thing I've ever heard. How could I be angry with my father? He can't help being dead."

"Same reason I'm mad at mine. For not being here."

"Yours walked out. Mine got blown up. Really not the same." I don't care how this sounds. Roz is pissing me off. Possibly more than the whole Habitat crew. Which is saying something.

Roz takes a big bite. "End result is the same," she says, mouth full.

The fact that she's talking with her mouth full annoys me. I stare at my Dove Bar. I love these things: they make them with good-quality chocolate, decently thick so you get a nice, solid bite. But right now I have no appetite. I flip mine into the dumpster and wipe my hands on my jeans.

Roz looks horrified. "What the hell! I'd have eaten that!"

"I gotta go," I tell her.

She takes one step forward, blocking my way. "Not until you tell me what's *up* with you. And don't say it's you don't want your picture in some newsletter."

"What if it is?" I demand. "Why don't you *get* that I don't want to be the poverty poster child of Clayton, Virginia?"

Roz's eyes narrow. Like she's finally caught on. "Oh, you mean people might find out your single mom makes crap money and you live in a crappy trailer? You have to borrow clothes from your crap friend who lives in an even crappier place? Boo-freakin'-hoo, Izzy. Cry me a river."

She's trying to piss me off with "trailer." Once, when I told her the term was "mobile home," she laughed and said something like, "Yeah? And denial isn't just a river in Egypt."

"You know what? This conversation is over," I say now, trying to step around her, but she puts her body between me and the door. I'm about to push her out of the way when the expression on her face stops me.

It's the first time I've seen her look truly angry at me.

"You think I don't get why you dissed me at the game last night? Afraid I'd blow your cover with your snotty-ass private school friends?" Roz's stare dares me to disagree.

We are so different. Roz wears poor like it's a badge. Like it's her superpower. If she could, she'd display her troubles like trophies. She's right: I *don't* want the St. V's girls to know where I live. I don't want them to see the stained carpet, the beat-up fake-wood kitchen cabinets, the toilet that runs, those plastic chairs . . . But that's not why I blew her off.

She hates those kinds of girls. Calls them Basic. She would've sat there with that constipated expression on her face like she thinks everyone and everything sucks, and if someone had tried to be friendly to her, she'd have shut them right down. I don't need that.

Especially because I like them. And I shouldn't have to apologize for it.

"Why are you so afraid of people finding out you're not perfect?" she demands.

I can't help it: I laugh. Perfection is so not what I'm worried about. "You really don't get it," I repeat.

Roz doesn't answer. Instead, her gaze tracks to her melting ice cream bar, which she stares at in confusion. Like she can't recall how it got there. She considers it for a second, then tosses it in the dumpster with mine. "You want a news flash, Izzy?" she says. "Here's one. Life ain't perfect. Not for anyone. And *real* friends? They don't expect perfection." She turns to walk home but then thinks of one more thing. "But they do expect honesty." Roz doesn't wait for a reply. She quick-steps away from me and back toward Meadowbrook.

As I watch her go my phone buzzes in my pocket. God, I am so sick of the VC thread today. I pull it out to take a quick look before heading inside to relieve Earl.

And what do you know. Speaking of perfection.

Sam: **Got a minute?**

12

IT'S NOT A DATE.

But that doesn't stop me from dressing for one. I shower and straighten my hair. Apply fresh eye makeup. Dig out my one clean, cute top (he's seen the white Roz-shirt already) and squeeze into my best skinny jeans. So by the time I get around to asking Mami for the car keys so I can make a tampons run (a request no mother, however angry, could deny), I'm lookin' gooooood.

Jack isn't fooled.

"Where are you going?" he asks. He and Paco are watching television.

"Grocery store," I tell him.

His brow furrows in that little-wise-kid way, as if he's trying to decide whether the fat guy in the red suit is the *real* Santa or one of the "elves." That's the line we always feed him at Christmas when he gets suspicious.

"With earrings?" he comments, eyeing my big hoops.

"People wear earrings in the grocery store," I say as non-chalantly as possible. "It's allowed."

He scrambles off the Scrouch. "You smell good, too."

"I just took a shower."

"Not like soap. Like . . ."

"Mami? Do we need anything? Milk?" I have to escape before my secret-sensing brother sniffs out my plan.

"No. Thank you." She doesn't even look at me. She's *that* mad. Still.

As I grab a few bills from the change jar on the counter, I toss Jack a bone. Which should shut him up.

"Cheetos?" I whisper, winking.

He jumps up and down, clapping, as I head out to the grocery store/meetup with Sam.

I had given it a full hour before replying to his *Got a minute?* It went down like this:

Me: **What's up?**

Sam (thirty seconds later): **No worries if you're busy.**

Me (thinking I've overplayed my hand and waited too long): **I'm with people—that's all.** (Actually, customers at a fairly awful convenience store, but hoping he'll imagine me with a pack of friends, sipping lattes at some cool place.) **Everything ok?**

Sam: **Yeah. Later?**

Me: **When?** (Trying to appear so incredibly busy, I need to schedule a time to fit him in.)

Sam (immediately): **Whenever**

Me (long pause because it's very complicated figuring out my fake social schedule and pretending to be distracted by all the "people" vying for my attention at an amazing, fun location): **7?**

Sam (two minutes passed, the boy was thinking): **7 mins from now or 7:00?**

Me (duh?): **7:00. P.M.**

Sam (long pause, how complicated could this be?): **k. Perry's?**

I stared at my phone. Perry's actually *is* a latte-sipping location. It's this trying-hard-to-be-Bohemian hangout on Clayton's downtown pedestrian mall, selling beverages for more than I make in an hour. I've walked by its plate-glass front window a zillion times, behind which rich girls cluster in chatty packs around the distressed-wood tables, nursing oversized, steaming mugs.

It's not the sort of place where you find Izzy Crawford.

Sitting with Sam Shackelton.

But that's what he suggested.

I stared at my phone so long, he double-texted.

Sam: **??**

Me: **Sure see you at 7**

Seven is a quiet time at Perry's: the evening crowd hasn't arrived yet, and the late-afternoon caffeine addicts are long gone. But even if the place had been packed, I'd have spotted Sam at the back corner table. He wears this light blue shirt that sort of glows, and raises his hand in a friendly wave when he sees me. Nowhere close to a "Woo-hoo!" but I'd swear there's a genetic similarity.

He stands as I approach. It's sort of old-school and formal.

"Hey," he says, flashing one of his ready-for-prime-time smiles. His eyes flit from my earrings to my blouse. He notices. It was totally worth setting off Jack's alarm bells just to see this reaction. He looks confused. Like he came to play checkers but I pulled out a chess set. Because this isn't a date. Right? "Thanks for coming."

"No problem," I say, slipping into the chair opposite his. There are two full glasses of water on our table.

"Can I get you anything?" Sam asks.

"I'm good, thanks," I say. I've calculated that I have seventy-five cents to spare in my wallet. That's because after Perry's, I need to stop by the grocery store to pick up tampons and Cheetos. Can't return home empty-handed.

"They have awesome steamers here," he says. "Sure you won't let me treat you? They crush the salted caramel."

I love salted caramel.

"Ooh. I may have to let you," I say.

Sam smiles again (I'm sorry, but where is the chipped tooth, Aubrey?) and heads over to the counter to place our order. As Barista Girl #1 works her magic with the espresso machine, Sam chats with Barista Girl #2 behind the register. They know each other. And she seems especially curious about who he's with. More than once I catch her peering around his shoulder toward our table, trying to get a better look.

I'm guessing this sighting of Sam Shackelton sharing steamers at Perry's with someone who is *not* Melissa will make the rounds of East Clayton's info network before the night is over.

Sam returns with two massive mugs filled to the brim. A caramel-colored leaf design adorns the foam atop each. I have no idea how they do that.

"Those are beautiful. And huge!"

He sets them on the table without spilling a drop. "You seem like the type of girl who isn't afraid of a large." Then turns a horrified shade of red when he sees my expression. Like I can't decide between laughing or dumping the entire steamer over his head.

"That did *not* come out right," he tries to explain.

"No, it did not," I agree.

"You are not large. Not by any stretch of the imagination."

I'm not sure how to respond. He's not making things better.

"I was actually trying to compliment you," he continues.

Which confuses me. A compliment . . . how?

"I mean," he tries again. At this point, he's stammering a bit. "I—I hate the way girls don't eat in front of guys. You know? Like, we'll go out in a group, and all the guys order burgers and shakes and the girls share salads?"

I blow on my steamer and take a careful sip. He's right. It's delicious.

"Actually, I have no idea what you're talking about. The girls I hang out with love burgers and shakes. And fries. Don't forget the fries."

"Exactly! You seem like the sort of girl who orders a full portion of real food and eats it."

"Sam, are you trying to tell me I'm fat?"

"Wow." He plants his elbows on the table and buries his face in his hands. When he looks up, his eyes are full of pleading. "I would love to have the last thirty seconds back. Would you do that for me?"

I hesitate. "Fine. You get a do-over. But *only* because this steamer is amazing," I tell him. Which is true: I'm not leaving until I drink the whole thing. Plus torturing him about his awkwardness is way fun. His shoulders slump in relief as I take another sip.

"Thank you," he says. "First, I don't think you're fat."

"Not that it matters," I add. "Or is anyone's business if I was."

"That's right," he says.

"Body shaming is a terrible thing, Sam," I continue. "I hope you're not that guy?"

"I'm not," he assures me. I'm also guessing from his expression that he's never heard the term "body shaming." Ah, Sam.

"What I was trying—and failing—to say is that you seem like a confident, direct sort of girl. Not afraid to say what you want. Or be who you are."

Now it's my turn to be off-balance. I wasn't expecting that. Not only because it actually is an incredible compliment but also because I had no idea Sam Shackelton had *any* impression of me. Let alone such a cool impression.

Let alone such a completely *wrong* impression.

I decide not to correct him.

"Thank you," I tell him instead. "That's a very nice thing to say."

He looks relieved. Like he's just been told his life sentence has been commuted to ten years. With time served. "Well, it's how you come across. And how my sister talks about you. If you haven't already figured it out, she's your number one fan."

"Yeah, I'm kind of getting that."

"Which is what I wanted to talk to you about," he says.

Another surprise. I'd assumed we were here to talk about the beer.

He doesn't know me. He doesn't know if he can trust me. I mean, no one's supposed to be underage drinking, but Sam Shackelton and his friends could blow their entire high school basketball careers out of the water if they get caught violating their athletic pledges against drinking.

He needs me to keep my mouth shut. Steamers and a face-to-face is a thinly veiled attempt at damage control. Or so I thought.

"You want to talk about Aubrey?" I ask him.

He nods. "How's she doing?"

"Fine, I guess. I mean, you live with her. You'd know better than me."

Is it my imagination, or does he wince when I say that? Like I've pressed my thumb into a bruise.

"You'd think that'd be true," he says carefully. "That we know what's going on with the people we live with? Unfortunately, that's not the case with Bree." Something in his tone signals that this conversation has taken a turn for the serious.

"Did she ever tell you why she transferred to St. V's?" he asks.

"She told me she was bullied at County," I say. "By one of your exes." I decide to live up to his expectations that I'm a straight shooter.

But now he definitely winces. "I can't believe I dated her. When we broke up, she chose to get back at me by going after my sister. What's that line from Shakespeare? Something about hell has no fury . . ."

"'Like a woman scorn'd,'" I finish for him. It's not actually Shakespeare who wrote it, but I'm not about to confirm my Dork Status by telling him that. Besides, I get what Sam means. Even in the sixteen hundreds, that's how it went down. Some things never change.

"Problem was," he continues, "Bree didn't tell us. She was getting ripped to shreds on social media, and my parents and I had no clue. Finally, Melissa saw some of the posts and let us know. We got it taken down and the girl responsible got in trouble, but Bree was a mess. At one point she wouldn't get out of bed. Literally, wouldn't move. It was really bad."

I find it interesting that Melissa was the person who alerted the Shackeltons to Aubrey's bullying. Was this before, or after, she started dating Sam?

"Aubrey told me a little about it. I'm so sorry that happened. She's a nice kid."

"It was really bad," he repeats. "We thought we were going to lose her." He stops for a moment. There's something hard in his voice and expression as he reveals this. As if he's working to control his emotions.

"But she got help," he continues. "And meds. Did she tell you that?"

"No, she didn't," I say quietly. I'm guessing she wants to keep that part of her story private.

"We're lucky," he says, taking a deep breath. "She's living her life again. Likes school. Really likes her new friends." Is it my imagination, or does he say that last bit with emphasis?

"Lucky," I repeat.

Sam looks surprised. I guess something in my voice suggests I take issue with the word.

"I'm sorry?" he says.

"It's just . . . I'm not a big fan of luck. It cuts both ways. Plus it's random. And undeserved. I mean, perfectly nice people get hit by drunk drivers. Awful people win the lottery. That's luck for you."

Sam leans back in his chair. He stares at me as if I'm a just-arrived mail-order item he doesn't remember ever buying.

"You sound like you speak from experience," he says.

"My dad," I say. "He was a Marine. He died in Iraq. He had the bad luck to be riding in a Humvee that got blown up by an IED."

"A what?"

"Sorry. I forget not everyone knows military lingo. Improvised explosive device."

Sam doesn't bother to hide his shock. "I'm so sorry. Was this recent?"

I shake my head. "Six years ago. I was ten. Listen, I don't mean to get all morbid on you. It's just . . . well, I guess 'luck' is a trigger for me. I try to avoid it."

"Good luck with that," he says.

We both laugh. Then sit in silence, waiting for the other to pick up where we left off. Sam swirls what's left in his cup, staring at the deflated foam spinning round.

"What was he like?" he asks.

"My dad?"

"Yeah."

The question startles me. I cannot remember the last time anyone asked. Come to think of it, I don't think anyone has *ever* asked. They usually move on. Politely. As if talking about the dead is bad manners. I used to think this was a white people thing, because Latinos practically set a place at the table for their dead relatives. I know Abuela still lights a candle for Daddy at daily Mass (and makes a point of telling Mami). For our Mexican friends, El Día de los Muertos is bigger than Halloween.

I don't get the silence. When you've lost someone, you could talk about them all day.

So even though I should totally know better? I can't resist.

"He was . . . wonderful," I hear myself say.

"Tell me three things that made him wonderful," Sam says.

"Wow. Well. He was big. Like, six five or something. He towered over my mother. She's very petite. So, for a little kid? He was a giant. We'd play this game where he'd let me climb him. Like a tree."

Sam laughs, nodding as if this is something he can picture.

"He was fun. Everything was a game. His pancakes were always animal shapes, and his trips to the grocery store were always scavenger hunts. He had endless positive energy.

"And for three? I guess I'd say he was a people person. He was always throwing parties, especially cookouts. He'd have loved your grill."

Sam does his supercute head-tilt thing.

"My grill?"

Oh damn. Damn. Damnity damn damn. This. Is. Why.

This is why I keep my mouth shut and my story to myself.

I suppress the urge to race from Perry's as if my life depended on it. Forget I ever met Sam—and Aubrey—Shackelton. Maybe convince Mami to homeschool me because I sure can't transfer to the public school now.

All not happening. So instead, I force what I hope is a casual laugh but suspect sounds somewhat maniacal.

"Aubrey pointed it out to me. When I was over at your house the other day?"

He's not convinced. He and I both know it was pitch-dark in their backyard when I dropped Aubrey off the other night, and there is no way in hell I could have seen the grill. Not to mention it would have been totally bizarre for it to come up in conversation.

I need to pivot. Fast.

"Speaking of Aubrey . . . I apologize," I continue. "Here you are, wanting to talk about *her*, and I'm hijacking the conversation!" It's a desperate attempt.

But it works.

"Yes. You think she's doing okay?" Sam says.

"She seems really happy," I say. "Of course, on a scale of one to enthusiastic, she's . . ."

"Over the top?" he suggests.

"Refreshingly exuberant," I offer. We both laugh. "Is she really like that, or is it the meds?"

"She's really like that," he says, his tone somewhere between exhaustion and exasperation.

"Well. She's crazy talented," I say. "I didn't know someone our age could make their vocal cords *do* that."

"I know, right?" he agrees. "What's really crazy is that we

had to *convince* her she was good! I mean, can't she hear herself?"

"That's wild," I say. I glance into my mug, which is almost empty. Which means it's time to vamos. Before I say something else stupid.

"But here's the thing," he continues. "In case something changes with her? We don't want to miss it. Again."

"We." He's talking about his parents. Did they send him on this mission? Ask him to meet me here and gather intelligence about Aubrey?

It's not a date. He has a girlfriend. This wasn't ever anything. But I feel the thrill of this nondate escape my heart like a slow-leaking balloon.

"So would you do something for me, Izzy?"

Name it, Sam. Anything.

"Look out for her? Let me know if something seems off? Any little thing that might be upsetting her?"

"Sure."

"Thanks." He leans back in his chair and exhales deeply. "You know, she really likes you."

"Well, she's an excellent judge of character," I quip. Which earns me another adorable head-tilt and sort-of smile. Sam looks at me like I'm some Rubik's Cube or other puzzle he can't quite figure out. Yeah. Time to go. I gather my bag and stand. "Thanks for the steamer. You were right, best salted caramel ever."

We walk out together. "Thank *you* for coming. I hope I didn't get in the way of any plans you have for tonight." He tosses that out there. Fishing.

"Nope," I tell him. "My plans are intact." A grocery store run, then maybe a few rounds of Uno with my little brother.

It's a big night. But by all means, let your imagination run wild, Sam.

We exit Perry's, but before parting ways he pauses. "I, um, also want to thank you for not saying anything to my sister about the little postgame celebration the other night."

Finally. Took you long enough to get around to the beer.

You're so stupid, Isabella.

"Can I ask you something?" I say.

Sam looks surprised. There's no mistaking the edge in my voice.

"Are a couple of beers in the pool house worth ruining your season? I mean, I'm not going to tell anyone. But most people can't keep their mouths shut. You guys could get caught."

Judging from his reaction, I'm guessing gorgeous Sam Shackelton isn't used to girls talking to him like this. His face sort of locks while his cheeks burn. Like a six-foot five-year-old caught eating cookies before dinner. Who has never gotten in trouble before.

Or never lost anything that mattered to him. If he had, he wouldn't be so careless.

"Wow," he finally says. "Are you always this honest?"

"No," I reply honestly. "Hardly ever, in fact. I should go now. Thanks again for the steamer."

I turn before he can reply, hurrying to the back-alley parking area behind Perry's, the metal-tipped heels of my boots flinting against the very real cobblestones. Kind of like my racing thoughts, kicking up sparks as I head to the grocery store to collect Cheetos and tampons.

Because unlike Sam, I guard my secrets.

13

I HAVE TO HAND IT TO MAMI: SHE PLAYS DIRTY IN THE NICEST WAYS.

She and Jack were reading together when I returned. He jumped off the Scrouch, upending *Piggie Pie*, and cheered when he saw me remove not a snack- but a *big*-size Cheetos from the grocery store bag. Followed by the box of tampons. Which I might have plunked on the counter a bit loudly.

"You've been gone *ages!*" he exclaimed, snatching the Cheetos.

"You're welcome?" I said.

Mami followed him into the kitchen. She seemed unimpressed with the "evidence" of my grocery store run. She also seemed rather pleased. With a side of sneaky. Like someone who's been given the answer sheet to the pop quiz.

Which should have been my first warning.

"Did you get lost?" she asked.

"I ran into someone I know," I told her. "We got talking."

Not a lie. "Ran into" is first cousin to "Met up with."

"Who was that?" she asked.

"This guy named Sam. His sister goes to St. V's."

Jack squeezed the Cheetos bag open with a loud pop that made us all jump.

"We thought you might've had an accident or something!" he said. He plunged his hand into the Cheetos, pulled out a fistful, and crammed them into his mouth.

"Jack, use a bowl," Mami warned.

I grabbed one from the cabinet and slid it across the counter to him.

"Ms. Betts called while you were out."

It took me a second to remember who that was. The "Ms." threw me. "What did Grouchy Grandma want?" I asked.

"Ha! Grouchy Grandma!" Jack repeated. He already had a ring of orange powder circling his lips.

Mami passed him a paper napkin. "She is making window boxes. I told her you would be happy to help her. She will pick you up after Mass tomorrow."

Such a "nice" sneak attack. Because it smelled like generosity (Isabella is so nice to help Ms. Betts!) but tasted like punishment. Mami knew damn well I'd been up to something, because who takes an hour and a half to complete a ten-minute errand? But she didn't know what, and yelling at me never achieves her desired result.

"Sure. Sounds great," I replied.

We smiled at each other between clenched teeth.

Which is how I find myself exiting Mass immediately after communion today, and climbing into Betts's rusty pickup. It coughs greasy fumes and sags beneath the weight of a massive truck-bed tool chest. She's idling in the handicapped spot right outside the entrance.

"Good morning, Isabella," she croaks as I climb in and slam the door shut.

I glance at her rearview mirror: there's no blue-and-white paper tag with the universal wheelchair symbol. "You are the least handicapped person I know," I reply.

Betts throws the truck into reverse. "Thanks. Nicest thing anyone's ever said to me."

"That was a handicapped spot," I tell her.

She nods in agreement. "Yup. But I wasn't parked. I would've moved if someone with a walker needed this space. Here's what you should know about me if we're going to work together."

If? I have a choice?

"I'm not big on rules," Betts says. "I think of them as helpful suggestions."

Great. This should be interesting.

It turns out Betts lives twenty minutes outside Clayton in this little town called Alder. As we drive along State Route Whatever through hilly countryside toward her house, she tells me she grew up here. Went to school out here, kindergarten through twelfth grade.

In a horse and buggy? I manage to not say.

"It's pretty," I comment instead.

Betts looks skeptical. "Used to be," she says. "Used to be mostly farms and country. Now it's all apartment developments and cul-de-sacs full of creepy cookie-cutter houses. You know, they look so perfect they creep you out? Like they're not real homes with actual people, but movie sets filled with actors?"

I smile, although I have no idea what she's talking about. My definition of "creepy" runs more along the lines of falling down in disrepair, and people like Shawn who are, unfortunately, real.

"Del Monte used to have a tomato-processing plant out here," she continues. "That's where a lot of people used to work."

"'Used to,'" I repeat. "So what do they do now?"

"Grow grapes and hops. Make expensive beer. Vineyards, wineries, and breweries are all the rage around here now. Although you wouldn't catch me drinking that micro-swill. Here's one rule I *do* follow—anything that goes in a pie should never go in a beer."

"So no Oktoberfest pumpkin ale for you?" I tease her.

She releases one hand from the steering wheel and pretends to stick a finger down her throat and gag. I can't help it: I laugh.

"We do still make fantastic pizza," she tells me. "Ever eat at Pie in the Sky?"

"Never heard of it," I tell her.

She nods like some venerable Buddha about to impart wisdom. "It's been here longer than me. One of the few things that hasn't been gentrified in Alder."

Her little ranch house is at the end of a long, unpaved driveway, and as we bump up to it, a mournful-looking hound dog unfolds itself from where it's been sleeping on the front porch. The dog takes a few stiff steps toward the approaching truck, then tilts its head back and bays at the treetops. Betts grimaces.

"That's Posey," she informs me, shifting the truck into park. "She's even older than me. In dog years." As we climb out, Posey howls again.

"Shut up, you big lunkhead!" Betts orders. She walks over to Posey and scratches her between the eyes, massaging the loose skin on the dog's skull until she whops her tail on the ground in delight and gazes at Betts in adoration. "Poor thing is deaf as a post," Betts informs me. "But she's gentle. C'mon in."

The living room looks like thieves ransacked the place and didn't find what they were looking for. It smells like just-baked bread and some sort of soup. There are piles of books and newspapers everywhere. The only "clear" space is the far end of the couch, which sags in a shape roughly approximating Betts's.

"You want something to eat?" she asks, striding into the kitchen. I follow close behind. "I made Brunswick stew." She lifts the lid off a cast-iron pot, releasing a cloud of steam. I peer inside. Shredded chicken swims thickly in a tomatoey broth alongside mystery vegetables. I see corn. Something green. My stomach roars in appreciation.

"I've never had Brunswick stew," I tell her.

Which Betts takes as a yes. She instructs me to fill water glasses and dig silverware from her cluttered drawers as she ladles bowls full. She also slides a platter of biscuits on the table alongside a brick of butter.

The biscuits are warm; the stew scalding. I start with the biscuits.

"D'you make these yourself?" I ask, smearing a healthy portion of butter on one half. Betts nods.

"You betcha. I'm all about that slow food life."

"'Slow food'?"

"As opposed to fast," she explains. "Cooked from scratch. Nothing instant or prepackaged. No microwave in this kitchen."

I fill my mouth with butter-soaked carbs. If a bear hug was a taste, this would be it.

"I don't think we could survive without a microwave," I tell her.

"Your mother is a busy woman. I can't imagine doing all she does without a few shortcuts."

I blow on a spoonful of stew and sip. "Okay *that's* incredible."

Betts can't hide a smug smile. "I make it the way my grand-mother did, and she was from the Tidewater," Betts says. "Okra, to thicken it. Lima beans. Chicken. Grams sometimes made it with rabbit. But most Virginians generally use chicken. I can't believe you've never had it, coming from the South."

"Living in the South and coming from the South are two different things," I tell her.

Betts purses her lips and nods grudgingly, as if she's sur-prised but willing to give me credit for at least one intelligent insight.

"Mami doesn't cook Southern. We mostly eat the foods she grew up with."

"Like tacos and burritos?" Betts asks.

I practically spit out my stew. "Oh my god. No! What's with everyone thinking all people who speak Spanish are Mexican?" I can't tell if Betts is teasing me or is truly that uninformed.

"They aren't?" she asks. I see a sly smile. She's egging me on.

"Mami's from Puerto Rico. Think islands. Mangoes and coconuts and plantains. Guava. We don't do all those chiles and tortillas."

Betts laughs. She gets up from the table and refills my bowl without asking. I let her.

"But your dad was a Southern boy, right?"

"Daddy was from North Carolina."

Betts places the full bowl before me. She plucks another biscuit from the platter and rips it in half for herself. "How did the two of them meet?" she asks.

"Daddy was visiting a friend, my 'uncle' Dickie, who was stationed at Fort Buchanan in San Juan. One night they went to a house party thrown by my Tía Blanca, who was friends with Dickie. Mami was there and according to everyone who retells the story, it was like lightning striking. For both of them."

"Love at first sight?" Betts teases.

"You laugh, but it's true! Dickie says he barely saw my dad for the rest of his leave—he was totally whipped. A few months later Mami got herself a job at a hospital in Norfolk. They married within a year, and I was born nine and a half months after that. And yes, I counted."

Betts gathers our now-empty bowls and places them on the floor, and Posey licks them clean. I can tell Betts is interested in my little family tale, and I have to admit: it slipped right out. Maybe too easily. As I scoop up the knives and spoons and empty glasses, it occurs to me that this is the second time in the past twenty-four hours that someone I scarcely know has wheedled information out of me.

"I'll wash these later," she says as we dump everything in the sink. "Ready to get to work?"

Posey and I follow her out back. Separate from the house is this two-story, not-quite-a-shed, not-quite-a-barn building. There's a round window up high, tucked between the sharp angles of the roof. The front-facing wall is a single sliding door, which Betts hauls open.

Light from the gable window streams in, and there's a familiar, church-like hush. Unlike the messy living room, everything is orderly. Tools gleam. Wood is stacked. The floor is swept clean. Instead of warm bread, it smells like fresh lumber and paint.

Even Posey has a place. She eases herself onto a pad in one corner with a little groan, her old doggie bones collapsing around her like sticks.

"This is cool," I say. Betts watches me out of the corner of one eye as I stroll the perimeter, checking out all the dangerous-looking machines she's got stored in here. "Is it weird that I like the smell of paint?"

She's flipped on overhead lights to reveal a long table heaped with boards cut into rectangles and squares. "Nothing weird about it," she assures me. "Paint is the smell I always associate with something clean and fresh. It's right up there with New Car Smell."

"I once saw a can of that! Seriously, it was called New Car Smell."

"I should get some for the truck. C'mon over here."

As she buckles a brown leather belt around me (it has pockets for nails and loops for tools), Betts explains what we're doing. She's already measured and cut the pieces for four window boxes that are destined for a Habitat house in downtown Clayton. All we have to do is assemble and paint them.

"You ever work with a drill before?" she asks as she shakes out a long extension cord and plugs it into the wall. She drapes a pair of plastic safety glasses around her neck and hands me a pair as well.

"Nope," I tell her.

She plugs the other end of the cord into a gunmetal-gray tool that looks like a hair dryer but has a swirly bit at one end. "Get ready for some big fun then," she says. "Glasses on. Safety rules are *not* suggestions."

Betts has marked each board with a little circle wherever we need to drill a hole—the "weep" holes at the bases where water will drain and the screw holes where we'll attach the pieces—like a kit all set up for me. She demonstrates, applying gentle pressure until the bit pops through on the other side, then hands me the drill.

There's something hugely satisfying about boring into wood. Not to mention gluing. Twisting screws and patching their holes. I don't know how much time passes; it could be fifteen minutes, it could be two hours. But before I've even considered checking my watch, we've got . . . window boxes.

I don't know why that surprises me.

As Betts sets us up for the last part—sanding and painting—she asks, "So whatever happened to Uncle Dickie?"

"Nothing," I say. "He just went on being Dickie."

"But he's not your father's real brother?"

"No, he's a friend. Right after Daddy died we saw a lot of him because they were both stationed out of Norfolk. But not so much now. I think Mami hears from him at Christmas. He got married. They have kids."

"What about your dad's people in North Carolina?"

I feel a tightening in my chest. As if my ribs are guitar strings and someone just tuned me too high.

"It's been a long time since we saw any of them," I tell her. I hear how casually I say this awful thing.

Betts hands me this little brick of wood wrapped in fine-grit sandpaper. She shows me how to sand, in a circular motion, to make everything nice and smooth.

She doesn't say anything about the Crawfords. It occurs to me that maybe my awful thing might not be so unfamiliar to her.

"When Daddy was alive," I continue, even though she hasn't asked, "we'd spend Christmas in Puerto Rico with Mami's family and do the Crawfords in the spring. They have this big family reunion every year. They live just outside Gastonia. They raise hogs."

"Hogs?" That gets her attention.

"Yup. That's what Grandma and Grandpa Crawford did. Started up a hog farm, passed it along to their kids. Except my dad didn't want anything to do with hogs. So he joined the Marines instead."

Betts stops sanding for a moment. "I was on a hog farm once," she tells me. "On a hot summer day. The stench damn near killed me."

"Well, being a Marine killed him."

I'm being glib. I don't think I'm actually as bitter as that came out. Or as upset. I'm not at all upset with Betts. As a matter of fact, I'm surprised by how not-upsetting this whole window boxes thing has been. It's been fun.

But she looks stricken. "I'm sorry. That was thoughtless of me."

"It's fine."

"No, it's not fine. I really am very sorry."

"It's *fine*."

"It's okay to say how you feel, Isabella. It's okay to—"

"Jesus!" I throw the little sandpaper brick across the room. It lands near Posey. She raises her head like a drunk who's been woken from a stupor, blinks curiously at the brick, then flops back onto her pad. "If I was mad, I'd say it!"

Betts arches her eyebrows in surprise but doesn't comment. She returns to her sanding. I retrieve my brick and do the same. After a few minutes of this, the only sound the soft sushing of gritty paper on wood, I surrender. I slam the brick down on the table.

"You know what? You're right. I'm mad. But not at you."

Betts keeps sanding. "Then who?"

"Mami," I tell her.

She looks surprised and annoyed at the same time. As if we'd been talking politics and she just learned I'd voted for the other guy.

"She hasn't taken us to North Carolina to see the family since Daddy died. The last time was his funeral. Jack has *never* met them!"

Betts lays her brick down. "Have any of them come to see you?"

"They never came to see us. Even when Daddy was alive. Crawfords generally don't stray far from Queen's Mountain. My father was the exception."

Betts pulls out a couple of soft rags and hands me one. We carefully wipe all traces of wood dust from the boxes.

"Staying in touch cuts both ways," she says. "And it's not all that hard. What with all this social media hoo-ha."

"I know," I tell her. "Listen, it's not a total blackout. We do Christmas cards with some of them. And once in a while Mami calls Aunt Carrie. She's married to Daddy's brother, DeWitt. They have a bunch of boys, all a lot older than me except for one. My cousin Mark." I pause. I'm this close to telling Betts my nickname for him: Devil Spawn.

But in truth, I don't want to get started on Mark. There's too much to say. Back when we were younger we followed each other on Facebook, but one year he just disappeared. Deactivated.

Which sort of describes my relationship with all the Crawfords.

"I just don't get why Mami doesn't take us to see the only family we have within driving distance! I Google-mapped Queen's Mountain the other day? It's only five hours from here."

Betts pops a can of white primer and mixes it in a slow circle. She fixes her concentration on the flat wooden stirrer going round and round, as if she's watching clothes revolve in a front-loading dryer.

"You did that just the other day?" she asks.

"After that meeting when you were all talking about sweat equity," I tell her.

Betts nods. I don't have to explain. She gets it.

"Folks are complicated," she finally says. "And never perfect. That goes for mothers, too."

She hands me a brush, and the two of us begin coating the window boxes. The soft wood drinks in the white primer, which we apply in long, smooth strokes. Betts glances at her watch and announces we'll only do one pass for now; the boxes have to dry. She'll give them another coat tomorrow, and when I return we can paint them.

"You've earned your first two hours today," she says. "Congratulations."

As we clean up I can't help calculating in my mind: 298 to go. This felt fast, but . . . still. Earning these hours is going to be like climbing a mountain. On your hands and knees. Meanwhile, down the road in North Carolina there's an army of Crawfords who know how to run a farm. Know how to mend fences and swing hammers and drive trucks. Who, as family members, could "contribute" sweat equity hours no problem. Some of them know we live in Clayton. But probably no one knows we're building a house.

It occurs to me Mami's not the only one I'm mad at.

14

THE AFTERNOON WITH BETTS GETS ME THINKING ABOUT DEVIL Spawn. Every once in a while, usually when I have nothing better to do, I check to see if he's resurfaced on Facebook.

I guess Roz isn't the only stalker.

She wanders over after school on Monday, knocking as she enters. I'm tucked into a corner of the living room with my Chromebook, the best spot for piggybacking on a neighbor's unsecured wireless account. I don't know who RubyFish_guest is, but thanks to him/her I can access the internet. Intermittently. This afternoon, the connection is good.

"Hey," Roz says.

"Hey," I reply, not looking up, but relieved she's here. We can't stay mad at each other for too long. "You back?"

"I'm back," she sighs.

Paco eyes her from the pleather recliner without attempting a greeting. Dogs just know.

"Mami made a bunch of empanadas last night," I tell her.

"Oh, yes," she says, making a beeline for the kitchen.

"Heat me up one, too," I say. I hear Roz remove tinfoil and punch in heat codes on the microwave. As she fixes us a snack, I refocus on the task at hand: hunting Crawfords.

Here's what I remember about those reunions: the amazing fried chicken. And the awful boy cousins. Not the girls: they were okay. But the boys? Grrr . . .

Every spring the Crawfords gather. Back when Daddy was alive, we would always go. Unless he was deployed. If my father was overseas, Mami skipped the reunion.

It was always the same: everybody would attend Sunday service at Queen's Mountain United Methodist Church, then file into the fellowship hall for a potluck lunch. We'd eat until we were stuffed; the adults would visit and the kids would run around; and when the sun started to slant, we'd all clean up, pack up, hug each other, and go.

Me, Mami, and Daddy always stayed with Aunt Carrie and Uncle DeWitt. And Mark. I liked him least. Not just of the cousins. Or the boys. Of everyone.

He was the worst Crawford.

Speaking of the worst, here's another thing I remember about those reunions: dressing up. Catholics are notoriously casual Sunday dressers, with the exception of Mami, who insists Jack wear khakis instead of his usual sweats, and Easter, when we go full-on spring fashion show with the rest of the Christian world. But the Crawfords? They Dressed to Pray. Like Sunday service was a direct audience with the Lord.

"Just be glad we're not Episcopalians," I remember Daddy telling me one spring as he and Mami yanked a scratchy, ruffly, girly monstrosity over my head. It was the year Reunion fell on Grandma Crawford's sixtieth birthday, and I was expected to look extra good. I was putting up quite a fuss, to which Mami had responded with one of her Spanish sayings.

"Él que quiere presumir, tiene que sufrir," she informed me.

"What's that?" I wailed.

"If you want to show off, you have to suffer."

"I don't want to suffer!" I screamed. So she passed me off to Daddy.

"What's a pisco pail?" I asked him. My face was red and swollen from crying.

"That's the fancy church," he said. "If we were Episcopalians, you'd have to curl your hair and wear high heels and carry a purse. Maybe even put on some lipstick."

The horror of that possibility stilled my writhing and resisting long enough for him to zip my eight-year-old body into the "church dress." I was allowed to wear clean white sneakers, the one concession I'd won because they knew I'd be running amok with the kids after lunch and needed sensible footwear.

"But we're Catholics!" I couldn't help whining when Daddy stepped back to survey his handiwork. I saw him glance over my head and wink at Mami, who was watching us from the doorway.

"Yes, you are," he assured me. "But let's try not to bring that up too much. Okay? We're at my mother's church, so just for today? Let's be Methodists."

"How do we be Methodists?" I remember asking grumpily.

"Sing," he told me.

During the service, I'd size up the other kids. It was the one time of year I saw my cousins, and I was fascinated by how they'd changed from the previous reunion. Generally, the girls were blonder and girlier; the boys bigger and more annoying. Especially Mark. You could count on him to be swinging a leg and kicking the back of a pew, or picking his nose, or pushing another kid . . . something that required parental intervention and whispered threats of dire punishments. His shenanigans were an irresistible distraction: I couldn't keep my eyes off him. And whenever he'd catch me looking, he'd stick his tongue out. Which got him in more trouble.

Roz emerges from the kitchen with two plates stacked with steaming empanadas. I shift the Chromebook aside as she hands me one.

"What're you working on?" she asks, settling into the Scrouch with her plate. Across the room, Paco's nose quivers. He loves empanadas.

"Trying to track down my disreputable cousin from North Carolina."

"Devil Spawn?" she asks as she takes a huge bite. Roz has heard about Mark. "Why? He's obviously off the grid."

"I don't know. He's like a car wreck on the highway. Awful and fascinating at the same time."

Roz kicks me, grinning.

"I've just been thinking about him. Them. The Crawfords," I tell her. "You know, relatives can help us earn hours toward this house we're building?"

"That's cool," Roz says.

"Not if we don't ask them," I say. "The last time I saw these people was my father's funeral."

Roz picks at the crusty bits on her plate. She seems to be weighing something. "Speaking of this house thing. I think it's great. I'm happy for you guys."

"Thanks."

"I don't want you to think I'm jealous or something. I'm not. That's not why I got mad at you the other day."

"Listen, about that," I begin. I take a deep breath. Time to deliver my explanation.

"At the game the other night? I think I was surprised to see you there. I'm kind of surprised I was there myself. It just sort of happened."

Roz moves her plate to a side table and tucks her legs beneath her. "I didn't know you gave a damn about boys' basketball."

"I don't," I say. "One of the VC girls wanted to go and didn't really have anyone to sit with, so we all went to support her."

I'm amazed at how convincing I sound. Maybe it's because I practiced that line. Like an actor, rehearsing in front of the bathroom mirror.

Because I can't tell her the truth. I love badass Roz, but it's like she's from one world and my school friends live in another and them coming together is like planets colliding. An epic disaster. Where yours truly loses everyone and everything.

Including my not-a-thing with Sam. Which I know is pathetic. I mean, he has a girlfriend! But if I tell Roz I've met the Shackeltons, it'll become . . . ours. Jointly owned, requiring constant updates. And I'd be back in the mud behind the stone wall with her . . . instead of in the big living room eating dessert and petting Frank.

I don't want to share this, even if it is fake.

"Yeahhhh," Roz says. Only half buying it. "I'm kind of surprised I was there, too. You're right, I hate that rah-rah stuff. But that doesn't explain why you seemed allergic to me."

I manage a laugh. "I'm sorry, aren't *you* the one who's 'allergic'? To all the assholes at County? Team spirit, a cappella, private schools, Catholics in general . . . Should I keep going? Or am I wrong, and you're dying to become besties with all the VC girls?" This coaxes a half smile out of her.

"Fine, I get it," she concedes. "I'll try not to crap on your school friends anymore. But I'm not wrong about the rah-rah stuff. Or about you being weird that night."

"I'll try not to be weird from now on," I tell her. "But that'll be hard."

"I know," she agrees. She brushes off her hands. She's wolfed down the empanada. "Mind if I use your bathroom?" As she zips off down the hall, I return to my Chromebook.

I haven't had a lot of success finding Mark on Facebook. Other Crawfords: yes, especially the old ones. They post a lot of Bible quotes, cute animal memes, and updates on who's sick. But Mark has disappeared. Frankly, I don't know why I care. He was responsible for our worst—and last—reunion.

That was the birthday year. I remember the service had just ended, and everyone was filing in for lunch. The long buffet tables were heavy with the sort of food Daddy loved: platters of fried chicken, deviled eggs, heaps of biscuits, potato salad.

Coleslaw. Macaroni salad. Sweet tea. Pecan pie. Mami was helping me fill a paper plate when a little gaggle of girl cousins, each just a bit older than me—Amy, Mary, and Ginny—sidled up to us. They were all wearing sweet dresses and hair bows.

"Aunt Rita? Please ma'am, can Izzy eat with us?" they asked Mami, pointing to the children's table near the back.

I remember Mami hesitated. She usually stuck close to me at these gatherings—"like white on rice, those two," I once overheard a couple of the aunties comment, gazing curiously at us—while the other children roamed free in a kid pack, the Bigs looking out for the Littles. I looked at Mami with pleading eyes.

That's when Daddy stepped in.

"G'on," he said, taking my plate from Mami and handing it to me. "She'll be fine," he told her, although it sounded more like "fahn." Whenever he was home, Charlie Crawford's Southern came out.

I was excited to join them but also scared. Even though I ranked as a true first cousin, I was an outsider. They were so intertwined, so in and out of each other's lives and houses. I had trouble keeping track of who belonged to which parents. And as an only child in a family with a father who was often away for months at a time, I was always with my mother. The aunties were right about us.

I remember Daddy giving me a gentle push, and off I marched with my plate of chicken. As Amy, Mary, and Ginny found a seat for me, there was a noticeable quieting from the others.

"Y'all remember Cousin Izzy, right?" Ginny said, to a chorus of "Hey, Izzy" and hesitant smiles.

I smiled back and ducked my head. I prayed that they would let me stay, but also leave me alone.

And they did. For a little while. Then the questions started.

"You still from Virginia, Izzy?" I heard. One of the boys.

"Yes," I said.

"You live on an army base, isn't that right?" Mary said. "Your daddy's a Marine."

I nodded.

"Fool!" someone yelled, laughing. "Marines aren't army! You are so *stupid*!"

Every head turned in the direction of the voice. Which, of course, turned out to be Mark's. He was sitting about five cousins down from me.

I could feel my face grow hot. "He is," I insisted. "My daddy *is* a Marine."

Mark rose from his chair and approached. There was fried chicken grease on his shirt. "Then you live on a *navy* base," he corrected. He poked Mary in the shoulder and she swatted him away. "*You're* the fool," he told her. There was a plate of biscuits on the table in front of me, and he reached over my head to grab one. He took a big bite and grinned at her, a horrible combination. I remember wanting to gag as he chewed with his mouth open.

"Are you a lonely child?" I heard. One of the Littles. A cousin named Grace.

"No," I told her.

"Ha!" Mark whooped, spraying those nearest him with chewed biscuit. "You mean 'only,' not 'lonely'!"

Grace's eyes filled.

"Mark, go away or I'm gonna tell your daddy you're being horrible to the Littles," Ginny warned.

He stuck his biscuit-flecked tongue out at her, prompting appreciative howls of laughter from a few of the bigger boys. I saw Amy gag.

"She wants to know if you have brothers or sisters," Mary explained to me.

"Oh. No. I don't," I told Grace.

"Is your momma black?" I heard.

The silence that followed was instant. Like someone flipped a switch. The question came from a Little. My cousin Jonnie.

It threw me. My mother was across the room. Couldn't he see for himself?

Here's the thing: as a kid growing up in base housing with other military families? We were all some shade of different. And more than a few of my school friends who called themselves black were lighter skinned than Mami. You had to rely on other things to understand who somebody *was*.

"Mami's Puerto Rican," I said. Like that helped.

Jonnie looked confused. "But is she *black*?" he repeated, louder.

"Jonnie, hush!" Amy warned.

Jonnie screwed his face up in annoyance. "But—" he attempted.

"I said *hush!*" The clear threat implied in her tone set his lower lip quivering. Between him and Grace, the Littles verged on full-on meltdown.

Then: Mark.

"Oh, shut *up*! Aunt Rita speaks Spanish. Y'all are *stupid!*"

I was about to tell Mark plenty of black people speak Spanish, but all hell broke loose at the kids' table. Grace dissolved in tears, the Big boys objected to being lumped in with the "stupid" cousins, and Jonnie started bawling "But Ma'am says she might as well be black!" Or something like that. I couldn't quite tell, what with all the noise.

Finally, Mary stood and pointed a finger at Mark.

"I'm tellin' your daddy you made the Littles cry," she declared. A shadow of panic obscured the sneer on Mark's face. He looked like he might run. But then something else occurred to him. His eyes rested on me, and narrowed. I could see a plan hatching in his mind.

"D'you want to see somethin'?" he asked. It was a choice between bad and worse—stay at the table full of crying children and strange questions, or wander off with Terrible Mark—and I truly didn't know which to choose. For some reason, I never considered a third option: look for my parents. So the next thing I knew, I was hustling to keep up as we sped across the room and through a side door.

He'd found a sort of pantry. It was the size of a large closet and had floor-to-ceiling metal shelves. They were stacked with industrial-sized cans of vegetables and lined with fat rolls of paper towels, bales of napkins, and yardstick-long columns of paper cups. As Mark flicked on the overhead fluorescent lights and closed the door behind us, my eyes were immediately drawn to a rolling metal cart at the far end of the pantry.

It held the most enormous, ornately frosted three-layer cake I'd ever seen.

"Ooh," I said, walking toward it as if I was a marionette pulled by fateful strings. The base of each layer was rimmed with yellow-frosting flowers, while swirls of pink gel decorated the sides. At the tippy top was a bouquet of actual flowers: yellow and pink roses and white daisies. Fake spun sugar hummingbirds stuck on the end of thin wires hovered around the flowers. At the slightest touch, they quivered.

"Is this for Grandma Crawford's birthday?" I asked him. I remember thinking it was too beautiful to eat.

"Yup," he said, satisfaction in his voice. As if he'd made it himself. "It's lemon on the inside. That's her favorite flavor." He didn't mean anything by that, but even my eight-year-old self knew to be a little hurt by that revelation. I didn't know my grandmother's favorite flavor. I hardly knew anything about her.

"When do we eat it?" I asked.

"Soon's lunch is over, I guess," he said, frowning. He was looking at the hummingbirds. Something displeased him. He walked to one side of the cart.

"Why d'you call her Grandma Crawford?" he asked. He placed a foot on one of the lower shelves. The hummingbirds trembled.

"'Cause that's her name," I told him. "What do you call her?"

Mark grabbed one edge of the cart to steady himself, then placed his other foot on the lower shelf. The cart rocked slightly; the hummingbirds shook even more. "Meemaw," he said.

A bad feeling was building in my stomach. "What are you doing?"

"That bird's not right," he replied, reaching for the top of the cake with his free hand.

For a second I thought he'd said "That bird's not *rat*." I wanted to correct him, assure him that those birds were most certainly not rats, but I was struck dumb by the horror of what he was attempting. Mark was trying to grab one of the sugar birds: problem was, he wasn't much bigger than me, and couldn't reach them without planting his chest in the cake.

"I'm gon' move it," he explained.

"I don't think . . ." I managed.

But then there was no need for words. Because the cart didn't simply roll: it tipped clean over, upset by Mark's full weight on one side. As the whole thing came crashing down, he managed to jump off and away, avoiding the giant cake, which slid and landed on the floor in a massive buttercream explosion. It splatted spectacularly, coating my ruffly dress, the wall of cans, and my perfect white sneakers. I looked at Mark: his eyes were wide and his mouth formed a horrified O.

Naturally, there was not a speck of frosting on him. He'd jumped in just the right direction.

"We gotta get outta here!" he exclaimed.

Which, of course, is easy enough when you aren't wearing the evidence of your crime. My feet felt frozen. I wanted nothing more than to run away, but how could I step outside the pantry and into the fellowship hall covered in cake? My eyes filled as I watched Mark open the door a crack and peek out.

"C'mon!" He gestured to me with one hand, but I couldn't move. He turned, his face a tortured mix of irritation, fear, and guilt, and insisted, "We gotta *go!*"

Which is when I wailed.

"I can't!" came out in a choked sob as I pointed to my ruined dress. On the floor, I noticed the remains of a smashed hummingbird, half submerged in frosting. For some reason that broke me, and I burst into tears.

"Fine! Be a crybaby!" he hissed. "But I'm goin'!" Mark slipped out, leaving the door open a crack. And my cries audible to anyone on the other side.

To the first witnesses on the scene, it appeared straight-forward enough: Charlie and Rita's little girl had sneaked into the pantry and destroyed Grandma's beautiful (and expensive) sixtieth birthday cake. The cake was to have been a surprise and also the highlight of the reunion lunch, because everyone had planned to sing "Happy Birthday" and make toasts and speeches to Grandma. That was no longer possible.

The grown-ups eyed me like a criminal; the cousins with a strange mixture of pity and curiosity. Like, they didn't know I had it in me (I didn't), and they sure were glad they weren't me.

I tried, through my tears, to explain to my parents what had happened, but they were in a hurry to hustle me out of there. I remember Mami paper-toweling the awful dress as best she could, but there was no wiping the telltale yellow frosting and pink gel completely away. She led me to Grandma Crawford for a quick I'm-sorry-Happy-Birthday and goodbye, and I remember how her old eyes glittered wetly while her lips, cool and papery, brushed my cheek. I remember Daddy drove Mami and me back to Uncle DeWitt's house so I could change, and by the time we got there, I had calmed enough to explain exactly what had gone down.

Mami told him to leave it alone, let things be, but Daddy was angry. He dropped us at the door and drove right back to the church. He was going to hunt down Mark and make him apologize.

Daddy returned with an expression I didn't recognize. He was quiet, and his face seemed frozen. Hard. He told Mami we were leaving, that very minute, no need to wait for Carrie and DeWitt to come home. Mami seemed upset. Confused. She asked him what was wrong, but I never heard his answer. They went into a bedroom and closed the door, speaking in low tones. I heard something about a photographer, and all the grandchildren, and Daddy saying, "She wouldn't wait. She wouldn't wait five minutes."

That was our last Reunion. Even though my father was stateside for two more, we never went back.

Roz returns from the bathroom.

"So've you had any luck?" she asks me.

"Not really," I say. "There are a zillion Mark Crawfords, but none are him."

Roz takes the Chromebook from my lap. I join her on the Scrouch, peering over her shoulder as she works her magic.

"Does his mother do Facebook? Father? Anyone close to him have an account? As long as they have crap privacy settings, we can check their friends and see if he's there."

It takes a while, but eventually she hits on a Crawford with crap privacy and a friend that goes by "MarkyMark." The profile pic is blurry, but something about it looks familiar, and when Roz clicks on it . . . there's my cousin.

"That's him!" I tell Roz. "Devil Spawn!"

"Whoa. You didn't tell me he was *cute*," she says.

"Ew. Gross."

"No, seriously, Izzy. Your evil cousin is hot."

"Makes sense that Satan would be hot," I counter.

She laughs.

Together we scroll through the photos and posts we can access without the benefit of "friendship," but because he has decent privacy settings, we can't see much. Here's what I can see: Mark still lives in Queen's Mountain. He seems to spend a lot of time joyriding around on ATVs. And while he doesn't post all the cute animal memes and Bible quotes the old Crawfords love, he *does* post a few—how can I describe them?—"inspirational" sayings.

"Is he into yoga or something?" Roz asks. "This is pretty trippy stuff."

"No clue," I tell her. "I'd have predicted he'd end up behind bars. Not doing the Down Dog on some mat."

"Well, mission accomplished. Now you can friend him."

"Nah," I say.

She looks surprised.

"I mean, what's the point? We haven't messaged in years. Besides, he unfriended *me*."

Roz looks at me with an expression halfway between puzzled and amused. Like I'm some jackalope. One of those jackrabbits with antelope horns that no one can decide if it's for real.

"What?" I ask.

"I don't get you. Do you want to be in touch with these people or not?"

I pause. Legit question.

"Yes. And no," I concede. "I guess part of me just wants to stalk them. And another part wants to tell them about the house." I stop there. For some reason I'm embarrassed to admit that we could use some help, even to Roz. I'm not very good at asking for help. But that mountain of equity hours . . .

"You should tell them," she says, making her why-the-hell-not? face. "Get a bunch of them to come pitch in. I'll bet Devil Spawn can swing a hammer." She gives the keyboard a few more quick clicks before closing the Chromebook and handing it back to me. "I should go before your mom gets back."

Roz gathers our empty plates, deposits them in the kitchen sink, and grabs a couple of empanadas for the road. The aluminum front door closes with a sharp slap behind her.

We drove all the way home to Norfolk that last reunion night. The next day, while I watched Mami attempt to wash the frosting off the scratchy dress in our kitchen sink, I brought up the question that was bothering me.

"Mami, are we black?" She looked surprised. Then thoughtful. She turned the water off, dried her hands, and pulled up a chair.

"No, Isabella. We are not black. Why do you ask? Do you think you are black?"

"One of the cousins asked me. At lunch the other day."

Mami tilted her head, puzzled. "Who?" she asked.

"One of the Littles. Jonnie," I told her. "He said someone said you might as well be black."

My mother's face was close to mine, and while her

expression didn't change, her eyes did. Like the sky when the weather shifts and the clouds move fast.

She rose from her chair and went to the pot where there was always some coffee at the ready. She poured us both cups: mine mostly milk with sugar; hers straight up.

"How did you answer your cousin?" she asked, carefully arranging our hot cafés on place mats at the table, then sitting.

"I said you were Puerto Rican."

One corner of her mouth curled up. "You didn't say I was brown?"

"No. I didn't. You're not a crayon!"

A startled expression crossed my mother's face. Like I'd just gotten the right answer on a test she hadn't given yet. "No, I am not. No one is. That is very smart of you, Isabella. You understand that no one is just a color, like a crayon. But you know, some people? They see the skin and stop there. Like that's all there is to know."

"That's dumb."

She clicked her tongue disapprovingly at me. "It's *limited*," she corrected. "What's important is: who do *you* think you are?" She stared at me, waiting.

"I'm brown," Mami continued when I didn't speak. "Short. Catholic. Puerto Rican and opinionated."

"Pretty," I added.

She kissed the top of my head. "Your father is tall," she continued. "Southern. White. Brave."

"Funny. Happy," I said. This was fun.

"Kind," she said. Her eyes glistened as she thought of

Daddy. "Very handsome. But mija, who are you? Who is Isabella Crawford?"

It's strange: I don't remember what I said. Probably easy stuff. Like, green eyes and black hair. Light brown skin. Dog lover. Pizza eater. Really, what does an eight-year-old know about herself?

But here's the thing: I'm still trying to answer that question.

15

THE BLEACHERS SHAKE AS PEOPLE STOMP, EACH CRASH OF FEET threatening to collapse the whole thing and dump fans in a tangled heap. Coaches shouting instructions to their players on the court can't be heard above the din of chants. Students have coated their faces in school colors. The dueling pep bands seem to be staging a competition of their own.

And that's twenty minutes *before* tipoff. This semifinal matchup between the Clayton County and Covington High boys' basketball teams is insane.

Aubrey asked me to meet her here, and eventually I spot her waving at me from some prime center seats. If she was woo-hooing I wouldn't know: it's way too loud.

"This is wild!" I say as she scooches over for me. From the corner of my eye, I catch a glimpse of Mr. and Mrs. Shackelton, two rows up. They are seated in a Parent Pack of middle-aged men and women dressed in County's blue and gold. When they notice me take a seat with Aubrey, they wave so hard I half expect them to dislocate their wrists.

"My parents are just a little excited," she says in my ear. "Sam left the house early. They were driving him crazy."

"Is he nervous?" I ask.

She looks at me like I just asked if the pope was Catholic. "Sam doesn't get nervous. He gets focused."

"Oh. Right," I reply. How could I forget? He's perfect.

Speaking of: he's warming up with the team only a few feet away from us. As Aubrey continues to talk into my ear (I can only catch half of what she's saying), I watch the County boys execute this intricate weave of dribbling, passing, shooting, and rebounding. They seem robotic and hardly miss. Least of all Sam. I can't help noticing how smooth, almost cat-like, his move to the basket and easy layup appears.

I also can't help noticing the muscles in his legs. His arms. Sam Shackelton has definitely logged serious gym hours.

As Aubrey says something to me about an after-party, win or lose, at their house tonight, a roundish mom-type with a worried expression approaches us. She's trying to catch Aubrey's attention.

"Uh, Aubrey? Do you know her?"

Aubrey looks where I point. "That's Mrs. Keating, the choir director," she says. "Weird."

Mrs. Keating motions for Aubrey to join her on the floor, which is no small thing. Aubrey has to pick her way between packed bodies, apologizing to people as she steps on their coats and knees them in the back. When she finally reaches the floor, I can't hear what's said, but I see Aubrey's lips compress in a tight line as she listens.

She shakes her head once, then retraces her steps back to me. Mrs. Keating looks frustrated. With a side order of panic. She walks over to the referee's table and begins an earnest conversation with the guy in charge of the buzzer and scoreboard controls.

"What was that about?" I ask after Aubrey picks her way back through the (now annoyed) fans.

"She wanted me to sing the national anthem," she says. "The girl who was supposed to just called in sick."

I look at her with an expression I hope registers the proper level of are-you-kidding-me-right-now. "You said yes, right?"

"I said *no*. No way am I singing the anthem."

"What? You don't know the words?"

She half laughs. "I have no intention of singing by myself in front of all these people."

"Aubrey Shackelton, that is the lamest thing I have ever heard! Climb right back down there and tell her you'll do it!"

Aubrey looks as if she can't decide whether I'm joking or not.

I'm not.

"You have an incredible voice. You will *crush* the anthem." I nudge her. Hard. "Go. Before she recruits some out-of-tune loser who can't hit the high notes."

"Izzy, stop it. I can't." Her lip quivers. Like she's going to cry.

This is what Sam was talking about. This way-talented girl who is afraid of her own shadow.

How do you convince someone to believe in herself?

"C'mon. Half these people are probably tone deaf! You could croak like a bullfrog and they'd still clap. And never forget, you're a VC girl. Singing before all of us was *way* harder."

Aubrey stares down at her knees and shakes her head.

I stand. "C'mon," I repeat. At the ref's table, I see Mrs. Keating looking around the gym. We've got about five seconds before she finds someone else. "I'll come with, and be right in front of you. You pretend it's your tryout again, and you're singing for me, and Min and Jamila—and we love you. You can do this, Aubrey. You're Veronic Convergence."

I don't know which part of my little speech pulls her to her feet, but next thing you know, we're headed down four rows of bleachers again (people are seriously pissed at this point) and walking toward Mrs. Keating. Warm-ups are over and both teams huddle with their coaches, listening to final instructions. I can see the top of Sam's head. He's gotten a haircut since I saw him at Perry's.

"I'll do it," I hear Aubrey say, "as long as my friend stays with me."

"That should be fine," Mrs. Keating says, clearly relieved. She looks like she wants to wrap me in a big grateful hug, but no thanks are necessary.

Because the mike is set up between the ref's table and the County boys' bench. Which is where they put me. At the head of the bench. Where the cocaptains sit.

Right next to Sam.

When the boys break from the huddle and take their seats, he looks very surprised.

"Izzy? What are you doing here?"

"Moral support," I tell him as they ask everyone to rise for the anthem. "Your sister is singing." Our conversation is cut off as Aubrey steps to the mike. But before I turn my attention to her, I check out Sam's expression.

He looks like a little kid confronted by a mountain of presents on Christmas morning: amazed, pleased, and totally unprepared.

Which is how I'd describe the rest of the gym when Aubrey opens her mouth. At first, everyone faces the big American flag draped to the wall near the exit doors. But as Aubrey sings, a few heads turn. Then more than a few. Then I hear the undercurrent of whispers, the Who-is-shes? and the Wow-that's-awesomes. By the time she's done (she keeps her eyes glued to me, like I'm some life raft), people are whooping and hollering like they're at a rock concert. They've probably never before heard anything like it from a high school girl in a high school gym.

I flash her a thumbs-up but she hardly notices. That's because Sam has left the bench and strides over to her. The applause grows even more deafening as people watch the County High captain give his little sister an up-down high five followed by an enormous hug. Perfect. Both of them. I glance into the stands: the Shackeltons are radioactive at this point. This is what they mean by "glowing with pride."

As Aubrey and I turn to climb back to our seats (the fans seem much less annoyed after hearing her sing), I brush past Sam. Who winks at me.

Oh help. Help.

It doesn't matter that I know better. It doesn't matter that he has a girlfriend, and I'm just his kid sister's wingwoman from the dorky Catholic school she attends. It doesn't matter that my best friend saw him first. None of that matters.

He's beautiful and charming and boyish and athletic and . . . yeah. I'm in Crush Hell.

It also doesn't matter—although it should—that just before I lower my butt onto the bleachers and the ref blows the whistle for the tipoff, I happen to notice two girls, a few rows back and to the left, glaring my way. Actually, only one glares. The other has her mouth close to the glaring girl's ear, her lips moving fast, spitting out words. Fightin' words, from the looks of it.

It's Awful Melissa and Barista Girl #2. Who both saw that wink. Who both absolutely recognize me from Beer Night and Steamer (Non)Date respectively. *Of course* those two are friends.

This is exactly what I was telling Sam: luck sucks.

Except when it doesn't.

With seventeen seconds left on the clock and the score tied, Sam intercepts a long pass between two Covington guards. It's been nail-gnawing close the whole game, and we've all screamed ourselves hoarse. But when Sam steals that ball, a roar, like something from Roman Colosseum days and gladiators and blood and gore, shakes the gym. We are all on our feet, shrieking in excitement or anguish, as he hurls it to wide-open John Mayhew, who, instead of taking it in for the easy, open layup, parks himself just outside the three-point line and throws up a prayer. Fans on the Covington side gasp in hopeful disbelief at this stupidity, while on the County side, fans moan in horrified disbelief. Even someone like me, with a very low basketball IQ, knows this was a monumentally bad shot choice. If it misses, Covington gets the ball with enough time left to score and win. Sam's great steal would have been for nothing, and County's season would be finished.

But then . . . the ball swishes through the hoop. Nothing but net. Three points. Covington will have to hit one that good, with only eight seconds left, to tie it up. The moans become cheers; the gasps turn to silence. The clock runs out and it's over.

Talk about luck.

When the buzzer sounds, it's Clayton County 87, Covington 84—and pandemonium erupts. The County boys mob John, the cheerleaders weep, the pep band blares, and the bleachers truly threaten to collapse from the stomping. Aubrey and I hug, scream, laugh, jump. County is headed to the regional finals. Hallelujah.

Eventually, the teams disappear into the locker rooms and fans head out. I'm about to do the same when Aubrey grabs my hand and begins pulling me toward the exit doors.

"So, are you coming? Please say yes. Otherwise I'll have to hide in my room."

It's still pretty noisy, so I can't really hear her. Did she say something about hiding?

But before I can ask her what she's talking about, Melissa materializes. By herself. Barista Girl #2 is nowhere in sight.

"Aubrey!" she trills. "Oh my god, girl, you were *amazing!*" Melissa throws her arms around Aubrey. She narrows her eyes at me over Aubrey's shoulder. "Wasn't she amazing?"

"Amazing," I repeat. Keep it simple, Izzy.

Melissa releases her hold. "I'm sorry," she says. "Remind me, who are you?" It's not lost on me that this is very different from I'm-sorry-I-forgot-your-name.

It's also not lost on me that she damn well knows who I am. "Izzy."

She cocks her head at me. "And . . . how do you know Sam?" The sugar in her voice is almost overwhelming. Especially because it doesn't match the venom in her eyes.

"She doesn't, actually," Aubrey explains, jumping in. "Izzy's my friend from St. V's."

"Right," Melissa says, stretching the word out like a long piece of sweet, sticky taffy. "For some reason I thought you knew him. Someone saw you at Perry's together."

"Must've been my stunt double," I fire back, flashing my biggest fake smile. "I'm constantly confused with her. And she gets in all *sorts* of trouble!"

Melissa hesitates. Maybe because she didn't expect push-back from me. Maybe she has no clue what a stunt double is. Either way: I can't let Aubrey know I met up with Sam. Even though it was to talk about *her*. (Maybe especially because it was to talk about her.) She'd feel betrayed.

For some reason, Melissa backs down. At least for now. She resets her sights on Aubrey. "So, Bree, what's the story tonight? Your brother isn't answering my texts."

Aubrey shrugs. "He's probably in the shower. What do you want to know?"

"People are saying everyone's going to your house? But Sam never told me that."

"Oh, that's because it's just for the team. My parents and the Mayhews are buying pizza for the guys."

I finally realize this is what she's been talking about: the team after-party at the Shackeltons' tonight.

And Aubrey wants me to keep her company so she's not the only girl in a house full of boys.

I can definitely do that.

Melissa is not pleased. She tosses her hair in this "whatever" way that's supposed to signal indifference but reminds me of a lizard displaying its spiky neck collar when it's gearing up for a fight.

"But friends of the team are invited, right?" she says to Aubrey.

Aubrey glances at the clock over the exit door. "Melissa, I honestly don't know. Ask Sam." She places one hand on my arm. "Mom asked me to pick up some more soda on the way. Do you mind?"

"We'll stop at Four Corners," I tell her. I turn to Melissa. "Nice seeing you!"

"Wait! Why are *you* going?" Awful Melissa should have just fake-smiled and said nothing. But she couldn't help herself, not even bothering to hide the pissed-offedness in her voice.

As Aubrey and I walk out, I lean in and manage to whisper into Melissa's ear, "Friend of the sister." I wink.

It's on.

16

WHAT'S WITH LITTLE DUDES AND BIG TRUCKS?

All week, every day after she picks him up from school, Mami has to take Jack to the house site. A crew has been leveling the ground for the foundation, and Jack can't get enough of the heavy machinery. He comes home bursting with details about gravel and sand and backhoes and bulldozers. He's even gotten friendly with the workmen, or trabajadores, as he calls them.

Which is what Mami calls them. My little brother has a very different relationship with Spanish than I do. He speaks English, with an occasional Spanish word mixed in, but unlike me, he understands everything Mami says to him. I don't know if he even realizes when she switches back and forth between languages.

"He doesn't fight it," Mami explains when someone asks her why Jack understands Spanish and I pretty much don't. "He relaxes and lets it sink in. Isabella closes the door."

Which is totally unfair. There was hardly any Spanish spoken in our house when I was little and Daddy was alive. Then for months after he died, when Tía Blanca came to stay with us? She and Mami spoke *only* Spanish to each other. I remember feeling left out of those conversations, the two of them going on and on for hours. One of them would always be holding Jack, their smooth Spanish words slipping easily into his baby ears.

Jack bursts in through the front door now, startling me and Roz in the living room, where we've been waiting for him and Mami. It's Pour Day at the site, which for Jack amounts to Christmas, his birthday, and the Fourth of July rolled into one.

Basically: the concrete trucks are arriving. After weeks of just pushing dirt around, the real action begins. Big vehicles carting rolling cylinders of liquid rock will pour hundreds of gallons of gloppy gray gunk into the wooden forms that outline the footprint of our house. Jack has already informed me this gunk is like sticky oatmeal, and you should never, ever touch it with your bare hands. After the gunk is dumped, he says, the trabajadores will pack it down, then smooth it off. Then let it dry. Long enough for it to become a hard stone slab. Our foundation.

For my brother, it's a not-to-be-missed event and we all have to be there. Including Roz. She had popped over yesterday (at dinnertime, conveniently enough) when Jack invited her.

"C'mon, we have to hurry!" he shouts now, then immediately disappears outside again.

"Slow down, little man," Roz says, laughing. "It's only cement."

"Oh god, don't say that," I warn her. Just the other day I conflated concrete and cement. Jack spent the rest of the evening correcting me: apparently, they are not the same thing.

"Jack, sit in the front," I order him as we head outside. Mami's in the car, the engine idling. Even though he's still a bit too small to be riding shotgun, I want the back seat with Roz. She was on the verge of sharing some hot gossip with me when Jack arrived.

As we pull out of lovely Meadowbrook Gardens and Jack talks to Mami about dump trucks, I nudge Roz.

"You were saying?"

She leans in close. "Sam dumped Awful Melissa."

I do my best to look surprised.

But I'm not.

Things didn't go well the other night for Clayton County High's First Couple. Aubrey's "Ask Sam" about the pizza party resulted in "No," which triggered a public spat outside the boys' locker room. Which led to multiple angry texts after Sam and the guys drove off to the Shackeltons'. Which culminated in an actual phone call between them, with Sam overheard saying, "You're being completely unreasonable right now."

All of which I either witnessed myself or pieced together from comments made by the guys. None of whom, it turns out, are big Melissa fans.

"Whoa," I say to Roz now, in my best fake-surprise voice. "What happened?"

She shakes her head, baffled. "Rumor is he's seeing someone else, but no one knows who."

Her words scramble my settings. He's seeing someone else?

"Really?" I manage. "He doesn't seem like the cheating type."

Roz sits up straighter. "How would you know what type he is?"

Oh god. Here I go again. I should just wire my mouth shut.

"I just got that impression from stuff you've said."

This seems to satisfy her. "Nothing those guys do would surprise me," she comments. "Although you're right. Sam's definitely the least douchey douche." I give her a soft kick and point front-seat forward. The best way to attract Mami's attention is with vocabulary like "douche."

I scroll back in my mind to the after-party. It was well underway by the time Aubrey and I showed up with soda and snacks. When we finally walked in the door, our arms full, the boys were very happy to see us. And the food. More than a few of them made a beeline for me, offering to carry the full bags.

"Who are *you*?" one of them asked. Extreme friendliness in his voice.

Before I could reply, Sam shouldered in between us.

"This is Izzy. She's Aubrey's friend from St. V's."

I detected a little emphasis on *"Aubrey's* friend." Meaning . . . what? I'm off limits? Or not cool enough? Hard to tell.

Sam shifted the bag from my arms to the guy's. "Are there more in the car?"

"Just a few."

"Lead on," he said, and followed me out.

As we stepped into the night air, we both began talking at once. Then we both stopped; then started again. Laughing, Sam gestured for me to go first.

"I just wanted to say, great game! I don't watch much basketball, but that was amazing."

"Thanks."

"I think I caused permanent damage to my vocal cords from screaming."

Sam laughed again. He laughs easily, and often. "You and the rest of the town," he said.

"Especially that last play. When you made the steal?"

"I don't think it was my steal that prompted the shrieks at that point," he said, revealing what he thought about John's Hail Mary shot without being overtly critical.

"I hear you," I agreed.

We were both reaching for the same bag and clunked foreheads midgrab. It actually hurt. A little.

"Oh my god, are you okay?" he exclaimed. He stepped in close and placed his hand for a moment on the spot where his forehead had just whacked me. Like his instinct was to brush away the pain. "I'm sorry!"

"It's okay. Now you know I'm a klutz."

He smiled. Then the two of us just stood there. Probably both afraid to go for the bags again.

"I know you're not into luck," he finally said, "but I think my sister is very lucky to have you as a friend."

The blush that ignited my face at that moment could have set their house on fire. I felt more than a little grateful to be outside in the dark. "That's a nice thing to say," I managed. "Thanks." I reached for a bag, but Sam put one hand on my arm, stopping me.

"It was you, right? You convinced her to sing tonight?

Don't say otherwise, I know Bree would never have done anything like that. Before she met you."

"I might have encouraged her. A little."

Even though we were in shadow, I could see his mouth curve into an amused grin. "Define 'a little,'" he said.

"Catholic thumbscrews of guilt," I said. "I borrowed them from my mother. They work every time."

"What are you guys talking about?" I hear my brother say now from the front seat, jerking me back into the moment.

"People from school," I say honestly. "You don't know them. Talk to Mami."

"This is pretty," Roz comments. We've exited the highway and turned onto the country road that leads into East Clayton. I kick her again. She's been out here . . . what? Fifty times?

"It's *very* pretty," Mami agrees.

"You don't go to the same school," Jack observes. "You don't know the same people."

"You know, it's really okay to mind your own business," I tell him.

He gasps and turns to Mami.

"Dios mío, must you two always fight in the car!" she exclaims. "Sometimes you make me wish I had a little button I could push so you would both fly out the roof!"

Roz bursts out laughing. Like, a belly laugh.

It's a first.

"An ejector button! Yes!" she crows.

Jack looks hurt.

"Why would you shoot *me* out of the car? Izzy was the mean one!"

Roz digs an elbow into my ribs. "You're so mean."

"I hate you all," I mutter.

As Mami tries to reassure Jack that she was (sort of) joking, we approach the Four Corners market.

"What an adorable little store," Roz says with exaggerated enthusiasm.

"You've really got to cool it," I say to her under my breath.

As Sam and I were carrying the last of the Four Corners snacks into the house the other night, his phone rang. He shifted his bag to one arm and pulled the phone from his back pocket. I could see Melissa's photo pop up on the screen.

"What *now*?" he muttered. As if the caller was a solicitor asking for donations, and not the love of his life. He paused. "Go on ahead of me. I need to take this," he said. As I rounded the corner I heard him say, "Hey."

It was not a warm-and-fuzzy "hey." Which explains what I did next. Which I'm not proud of. But I don't know a person on the planet who would have done otherwise.

I stood behind a bush and listened.

There was a long silence. Then, Sam spoke.

"First of all, you are not being shut out from anything. This is a team party. It's okay for me to have the guys over and not include the rest of the world. Second, I am not going to tell my sister she can't invite her friends! Geez, you of all people! You know how huge it is that she's being social. And third, no. I don't have a thing with her."

Another pause. Then a short laugh.

"So what now? You have spies planted all over town? Checking on me?"

Pause. An audible sigh.

"Because I don't need permission from you every time I speak to someone!" Sam was getting louder.

Pause.

"Really? Are you really asking me that? Okay, fine. You're right. She is hot. She's gorgeous, in fact. But she is *my sister's friend*. That's why I was talking to her at Perry's. That's why she's here tonight. End of story, okay? I'm done with this conversation. Actually . . ."

I'd heard enough. And needed to get out of there before Sam found me skulking in the shrubbery. I returned to the party, my heart racing.

The wink and friend-of-the-sister comment had bugged Melissa more than I realized. Launched her into unreasonable heights of paranoia and jealousy.

Which wasn't assuaged by Sam telling her I was gorgeous.

Did that really happen?

"Hello? Earth to Izzy?" Roz speaks to me now.

"I'm sorry, what?"

"Your mother is asking whether you need to stop at the market."

"No. Why?"

"Because we might be at the site for a while," Mami chimes in. "And you know how I hate you to use those portas."

"The what?" Roz asks.

"The porta potties. Mami thinks they're unhygienic."

"They are disgusting," Mami says.

"And the convenience store bathroom is better?" I argue. "Give me a break."

"At least there you can use my wipes," she says.

Now Roz looks completely confused.

"Mami doesn't go anywhere without sanitizing wipes," I explain. "She's a borderline germophobe."

Jack ducks to the floor and I hear him rummaging. When he reappears, he's holding up a cylinder of generic wipes bigger than his head.

"This is them!" he declares.

"Wow," Roz says, impressed. "You know, I don't think my mom has ever even heard of wipes. Let alone carted around an industrial size."

"She'd need an industrial-sized purse," I tell her.

"Like Mami's!" Jack agrees. "Know what else she's got?"

"Enough in my purse!" Mami insists. "Jack, put those away. Look, we are almost there."

I haven't been out to the site since the first time my mother showed me, so I hardly recognize it now. It's crawling with workmen, earth-moving vehicles, and trucks. Most of the grass has been flattened into mud, and the makeshift outline of a cul-de-sac and temporary road have taken shape. Except for our lot, which has wooden forms set up for the foundation, red flags mark the spots where the other houses will eventually go.

Jack jumps out the moment Mami parks the car, tearing off toward a group of men who stand alongside the concrete truck. I see them laughing and high-fiving him; they must be the guys who have been filling his ear about all things construction related. The trabajadores. My little brother is in heaven.

As Mami chases after him, I turn to Roz. She's stepped out of the car and is staring into the distance.

"This is a beautiful spot, Izzy," she says.

"It is," I agree.

"I am really going to enjoy visiting you out here."

For the second time today, it's like Roz scrambles my settings. For all the dreaming I've done since we got the official word about the new house, I have never pictured the two of us hanging out here. Roz in our home is as predictable and ordinary as rice for dinner or Paco on the Scrouch. Why didn't it occur to me she'd be at the new house as well? It's not that I planned to forbid her from coming by.

I just never imagined it.

Jack is jumping up and down and waving at us, so the pouring must be about to begin. As Roz and I walk toward the concrete mixer, she brings up the Sam stuff again.

"Melissa is going around saying people have *seen* Sam with this new girl. But Sam and 'the bros' say she's lying."

"What do you think?" I ask.

Roz considers. She looks like she just took a bite of something disgusting and can't decide whether to swallow it quickly or spit it out. "Not that I'd ever take her side or anything, but why would Melissa lie about that? Sam, on the other hand, has total motivation to lie. If he's seeing someone else."

Good point. But here's what I don't tell Roz: the other night, he didn't seem like someone who had a new girl waiting on the bench. Guys who do that are relieved when they break up with the old girl.

And when he finally came inside, Sam looked upset. Aubrey and I had just nabbed a couple slices of pizza and were escaping with them downstairs to the playroom. The

Four Corners paper bag Sam carried was crushed. The chips were . . . not okay.

"Dude! D'you sit on them?" John Mayhew said as Sam unloaded the contents on the counter. He took it down a notch when he saw Sam's expression. "What?" he asked.

"Might have just broken up with my girlfriend," we heard as Aubrey closed the door behind us. I might have also heard a few cheers?

Aubrey groaned. "Great," she said. "Another one bites the dust." She flicked on the lights to reveal a finished basement, complete with comfy chairs, another big-screen television, and a pool table. As we settled on a couch, I pressed her.

"I thought you liked Melissa."

Aubrey took a big bite of pizza. She considered my question as she chewed. "I like her fine. But I try not to get too attached," she said. "Girlfriends come and go quickly around here."

"Hmm. Is your brother the 'love 'em and leave 'em' type?" I couldn't help asking.

"You'd think," she said, laughing. "But no. He feels bad after breakups. He's the old-fashioned, romantic type. He buys them flowers. Plans nice dates."

I was trying hard not to appear overly interested in this information. "So why all the breakups?" I asked.

"Hasn't found the right one, I guess."

It occurs to me now that the one person in the whole world I would love to talk to about this is the *last* person in the world I can talk to about this. And I sure as hell couldn't do it now: the concrete mixer is louder than a dozen lawn mowers buzzing at once. Roz and I can barely hear each other. As we near Jack, Mami, and the workmen, I can see the first dribs of gray gunk sliding down a long chute and plopping into the area marked off for the foundation. I decide to say one last thing before the noise grows deafening and shuts down all discussion.

"You know," I tell Roz, "I'll bet Melissa's wrong. Why would he bother to cheat? He could just break up with her and move on."

"Yeah, but they've been *seen* together," Roz explains. "She supposedly doesn't go to County."

"How do you know all this?" I ask.

"Everyone knows. Apparently, Sam took her out at that place downtown. Perry's? One of Melissa's friends works there. Everyone's talking about it. They've even given her a hashtag: SteamerGirl."

We've reached the site and can't hear ourselves think, so we stop talking. Mami holds Jack by the shoulders, just for good measure, but she needn't. He's stone-still and staring as gallons of concrete gush into the space where our house will rest. Even Roz seems caught up in the action.

Which is good. Because I don't know what to say. If I told her the truth, she'd just think I've completely lost my mind.

No way would Roz believe I'm Steamer Girl.

17

MAMI HAS A REMARKABLE GIFT FOR CONNECTING ME WITH WORK.

It's Wednesday (a school night!), and I find myself in an apartment in downtown Clayton, babysitting some kid (granted, she's adorable) so her parents (the Jacksons) and Mami can attend the Habitat Homebuyer Education class. It's this thing all new owners have to do, where they learn about everything from sticking to a budget to draining the pipes in a house. I think I'd rather jab pins in my eyeballs than sit through all that, but Mami is into it. She really likes meeting all the other Habitat families.

Jack had to come with me (can't leave him alone), and I'm sandwiched between their warm bodies, reading, on a couch that might be scratchier than ours. Adrienne Jackson has enormous eyes and a head covered in teensy cornrows. She wears Winnie the Pooh pajamas and smells like dryer sheets. She loves being read to, and while the good news is we brought three library books, the bad news is she only likes one.

Piggie Pie.

Betts promised me equity hours for helping the Jacksons, but I'm thinking *Piggie Pie* counts as hard labor and I should get time and a half.

Adrienne's bedtime is eight o'clock, but by seven forty-five, both kids are tucked up against me, fast asleep. I'm trapped. Mrs. Jackson left me this homemade cake—heavily frosted and doused in colorful sprinkles—that calls to me from the kitchen counter, but I don't want to wake the kids by getting up for a piece. The parents aren't due back for another hour. I stare around the cramped living room. The Jacksons seem to use the same home decorator as us: Designs by Cheapass and Castoff. Although they've got the added touch of huge brownish water stains migrating from a crack in the ceiling. It's a brown that pairs nicely with the vomit-colored, patchy carpeting. Accented by the delicately cracked glass in the one (remaining) window frame. The other has been replaced by cardboard that Mr. Jackson inserted with the help of miles of duct tape. Their landlord doesn't think replacing broken windows is a priority.

I turned the sound off my phone, but from its spot where I placed it on the coffee table, I can still hear it buzz as a text comes in. I extend my arm like a selfie stick, trying hard not to jostle Sleeping Beauties #1 and #2 as I reach for it.

It's Sam.

Need some advice

I stare at the screen. It's been radio silence from him since Big Game Saturday, and honestly? I was disappointed. I thought I'd hear *something*. Especially because when I left the other night, I thought something was . . . might be . . . happening.

Aubrey had fallen asleep as we watched a movie in the playroom. The loud boy sounds had faded and I figured it was time to go home. When I climbed the stairs to the kitchen, I found Sam in there. Alone. He was stacking empty pizza boxes and throwing away paper plates. All his friends had left.

"Want some help?" I offered.

He turned, surprised. "You don't have to help."

I saw a crumpled, sauce-stained napkin on the floor, bent to retrieve it, and, as if taking a free throw, tossed it into the garbage can.

"Swish! Nothin' but net!" I exclaimed.

Which coaxed a small smile out of him. "Are you always this nice?" he asked. Like it was a serious question. No hint of joking.

"I'm rarely this nice," I confessed. "I save it for people who *should* be having a great night but instead are having a sucky night."

His eyes narrowed slightly. As if he was wondering what I knew. "Can I ask you something?" he said.

I had no idea what he could possibly want to know. "Sure."

"Do you think I'm an asshole?"

The question was so totally out of the blue I almost laughed. For a second I thought he was joking . . . but his expression was serious. Almost sad.

"Not at all. Why would you even ask that?"

"What you said the other night. About the beer?"

That's when Aubrey appeared, all sleepy eyes and bed head. She squinted curiously at us. "What's going on?"

"Izzy's helping me clean up," Sam said, just as I said, "I was heading out." Awkward.

Aubrey stared at us for a few seconds, finally announced "I'm thirsty," and began fumbling through the cabinets in search of a water glass. Sam grabbed one of the plastic garbage bags and headed for the garage. I retreated to my car and the long drive home. I haven't spoken to a Shackelton since.

Now, this unexpected weird text? Which could use a little punctuation. Is Sam saying he wants advice? Or asking if I need it? Which I don't.

Or do I?

Is something going on?

I decide to answer open-endedly.

Me: **About . . . ?**

Sam: **Girls**

Wow. The last thing I want to do is give him advice about other girls. That would make my crap night epically crappy.

But I also don't want to shut him down. Damn.

Me: **How can I help?**

Sam: **Answer me one question**

Hmm. This should be interesting.

Me: **I'll do my best**

Sam: **Are all the women in my life crazy or am I just an asshole?**

I struggle to stifle a laugh; I don't want to wake Jack and Adrienne. They may demand more *Piggie Pie*.

I decide Sam deserves to suffer. A bit.

Me: **That's actually two questions. And I've already answered the second. But yes to the first and if you keep asking I may change my mind about the second**

A few minutes pass before he replies.

Sam: **Ouch Really?**

Me: **OMG of course not jk**

Sam: **Phew**

Me: **So what's up?**

Sam: **You**

I stare at that one for a little while. I have no idea what he could possibly mean.

Me: **I'm confused**

Sam: **Sorry. I'm being an asshole. You know I broke up with M?**

Me: **Might have heard that**

Sam: **She's telling people I'm seeing you. And Bree's mad I stole you**

I stare at my screen again. I haven't seen or heard from Aubrey since the party. But our schedules don't overlap and we haven't had VC rehearsal since then, so that isn't so strange.

Here's what is strange: Izzy Crawford having this text conversation/flirtation with Sam Shackelton. I give myself a little pinch. But the screen doesn't change.

Me: **Is this cos we met at Perry's?**

Sam: **Yeah**

Me: **So just tell them the truth!**

Tell them I'm not seeing you and hanging out with your kid sister is the high point of my social life. Tell them Godlike Creatures don't see, let alone date, Divas of Obscurity. I'm not on your radar. I'm not of your world. End of subject.

There's another long pause. Seriously, this boy overthinks. Then:

Sam: **What if the truth changes?**

I feel myself squinting at the screen like a person trying to read through smudged glasses. Is he asking what I think he's asking? Because a "change" would mean I *was* dating him and he *did* steal me from his sister.

Before I can think of anything approaching a reasonable response, the key turns in the front door lock. The parents have returned.

"Oh, how sweet!" Mrs. Jackson coos when she spots me draped with sleeping children.

I stifle the urge to shriek at them to wait in the hall because I need to answer the most important text of my entire life.

"I can tell y'all had a good time!"

Mami's eyes laser-track to the cell phone in my hand. It's glowing, so she knows I'm texting right now.

"We should get going. It's late and it's a school night," she says. She slips her arms beneath Jack and lifts him as Mr. Jackson, on my other side, hoists Adrienne. Both kiddoes barely break breath, that's how out of it they are.

"Thank you, Isabella," Mrs. Jackson says as we head out. "I could rest my mind knowing our girl was with you tonight."

"No problem, Mrs. Jackson," I say convincingly. It's an Academy Award–winning performance of a single line because I manage to sound like a normal person even as another text from Sam ignites my phone. Just get to the car, I tell myself. Deep breath. He can wait a couple of minutes.

Mami doesn't say anything as we cross the parking lot, then deposits the unconscious Jack into the back seat. She still doesn't speak as she and I buckle up. I take that as an invitation to finally check my screen.

Sam: **??**

"Who is that?" Mami asks. Nicely enough. She seems tired. Before I can respond, a loud rap on the passenger side makes us both jump.

It's Mrs. Jackson. Holding the entire uneaten cake. I roll down my window.

"Sweetheart, you forgot this!" she says, pushing the cake at me, plate and all.

"Oh, no, Mrs. Jackson, please. That's too much! Really!" Too late. She's already lowered the thing onto my lap. Hard to balance, with a phone in one hand. I turn to Mami for help.

"Not the whole cake! What about George?" Mami exclaims. "Just a slice! A slice is good."

Really? Are we actually going to attempt slicing cake in the car right now? What is my mother thinking? This is not helpful.

Mrs. Jackson takes one step back. I'm trapped. Again.

"George doesn't need all that cake," she confides. "Besides, she's a growing girl. You enjoy that cake, honey." Mrs. Jackson waves goodbye.

"Thank you!" Mami calls through the window. "That is so generous!"

Mrs. Jackson turns to her apartment and I watch her retreating back as I roll up the window. The inside of the car already smells like frosting.

"That was very nice," Mami says as we pull out. "Very generous."

With one hand I hold the rim of the plate; with the other I cradle my phone. Which has stopped buzzing. Not in the Sam-has-stopped-texting way. Not in a dead battery way.

In the your-cheapass-Tracfone-is-out-of-minutes way.

I had forgotten to check. Of course, even if I had checked, I'm out of cash for the month. So I couldn't afford more minutes even if I wanted them. This. This is what I was telling Sam about luck.

For those of us who don't have any, life just sucks.

"So, who was on the phone?" Mami repeats.

"Nobody," I tell her.

Nobody.

18

AUBREY TRACKS ME DOWN IN THE SCHOOL LIBRARY. I'LL GIVE HER that: she goes for a face-to-face. Not that I'd know if she was texting me. I don't get paid until tomorrow, which means el teléfono está muerto. Sucks for me.

"We need to talk," I hear.

I'm at one of the computer carrels, trying to check my assignments on Google Docs. RubyFish_guest must not have paid his/her cable bill this month because I haven't been able to access the internet from my corner of the living room for days.

I've tried explaining that to a couple of my teachers who think it's okay to "update" the homework online. Without getting into too much detail (because frankly, it's none of their business), I've asked that they give us the assignments in person, in class. But for some reason that's beyond them. They keep adding stuff or changing things and then don't seem to get why I miss the changes.

News flash, people: it costs money to be an iConnected Student.

"Hey," I reply without taking my eyes from the screen. "Give me one minute."

Aubrey plunks herself into the chair next to me as I quickly scan the last page. Sure enough: my chemistry teacher added four problem sets. That would've been a big fat zero for me if I hadn't checked. I hit Print, then swivel to face Aubrey.

She wears her serious face. The one you might see on an oral surgeon peering into an open mouth, preparing to extract wisdom teeth.

"Why haven't you answered my texts?" she begins.

"My phone's dead," I reply truthfully.

She frowns. Phones that don't work are not part of Aubrey's worldview.

"Should be fixed tomorrow," I add. I don't explain "fixed."

"Do you have a thing with my brother?"

I can feel my eyes widen. She's not wasting any time. "Define 'thing,'" I auto-reply. Probably not the best idea. Raises all sorts of suspicions. She throws herself back into the chair and releases an exasperated breath.

"I knew it!" she declares. "Sam swore to me you two were just friends. But I had a feeling. And now with all this stuff Melissa is saying—"

"We're *not* friends," I say, cutting her off. "I don't know what we are, but it's definitely not 'friends.'" *He probably hates me*, I don't add. I ghosted him in the middle of a pretty intense text conversation. If he never speaks to me again, I wouldn't blame him.

"Then what?" Aubrey challenges. "Because I thought you were *my* friend. Not another suck-up putting the moves on my brother."

Moves? If only. Izzy Crawford doesn't have moves. The whole idea is so preposterous I almost laugh, but catch myself. She'll think I'm laughing at her.

Which is the last thing I want to do.

"I am your friend," I answer honestly. "And here's what's going on. Sam worries about you. We got together one time because he wanted to know how you're doing. That's it. *One time*. To talk about you."

Aubrey looks taken aback. A little whiplashed, even. She zoomed into this conversation at 120 miles per hour and now someone just slammed on the brakes. And the airbags inflated. "What did you tell him?"

"I told him you seem to be doing fine," I say. "Was I right? Because this doesn't feel fine. It feels paranoid." I don't intend to turn things on her, but pivoting comes naturally.

"Yeah. I mean . . . yeah," she says. "About being fine. Not paranoid." She hesitates. A little crease of worry forms between her eyebrows. "What did he tell you?"

Now I'm stuck. Because I don't want to lie to this girl. But I also don't want to betray Sam's confidence.

Most of all, I don't want to embarrass her. I'm her new friend. Her turning-a-fresh-page-on-life, Veronic Convergence, stand-up-there-and-sing-the-national-anthem-to-crazy-applause friend. She didn't tell me the other stuff. The sad, depressed, medicated, needing help stuff. People are so judgmental and she doesn't know me that well. Yet.

Eventually, she'll trust me. And I'll tell her that I think she's brave. And strong. But for now? She wants to step away from the sad story. She wants to be liked for herself and not because she's Hot Sam's sister. She wants friends who care about her, not pity her. She wants to be accepted because she's worthy, not because she's needy.

I so get all that.

"Sam told me you were really sad and he felt like he missed it. He doesn't ever want to miss it again. That's why he was checking in with me. Because he knows we're friends."

Aubrey's expression hovers somewhere between touched and suspicious. I'm guessing she's wondering what else he might have said, but doesn't want to push it. In case he didn't.

"He's a good brother," she says.

I nod in agreement. That he is.

Then, her expression changes as something else occurs to her. "He's also the dumbest smart person I know!" she exclaims. "Did he meet you at Perry's?"

I nod again.

Aubrey buries her face in her hands. "Unbelievable. Melissa's crew practically lives there. One of her best friends works there!"

So. Barista Girl #2 is a bestie. Note to self.

But Aubrey makes an interesting point. Why choose a

public place where his girlfriend hangs? It was either because the meetup was completely innocent and he had nothing to hide, or . . . he wanted to force an issue with Melissa.

Or he's a complete blockhead. Which seems to be what Aubrey thinks.

"I'd never been to Perry's before," I tell her. "He bought me a salted-caramel steamer."

"Steamer Girl," she says. As if she's been tearing through the pages of a detective novel and finally learned the identity of the killer. "You do know you're a hashtag, right?"

"So I've been told." I sigh.

This earns me a half smile. "Welcome to my world," she says. "You are now an official target of the Sam Shackelton's Avenging Exes Club. Good luck."

I skip telling her about me and luck.

"How bad is it?" I ask.

She looks thoughtful. "Depends," she says. "Do you care about your reputation on social media?"

"I don't really do social media. So I guess the answer is no."

Aubrey looks as if she can't decide whether to be impressed or astonished. "Not even Facebook?" she asks.

"Oh, I mean, yeah, I have a Facebook page, but so does everyone's grandmother. I meant Instagram and Snapchat."

"How do you *survive*?" She's not being sarcastic. So I decide to be honest as well.

"Well, for one thing my mom makes me pay for my phone service, so I'm always running out of data. And for another? Even though it's all totally fake? Those apps make me feel like a loser. Like the whole world is better looking and having more fun than me."

Judging from the expression on Aubrey's face, I'm guessing parents who don't automatically pay for everything isn't part of her worldview, either. She breaks eye contact and picks distractedly at a button on her cardigan before answering.

"My folks pretty much cover everything. Kind of bratty, huh?"

"Kind of lucky," I correct her. I decide not to add what I think of luck.

"And those apps? Sometimes I think the *point* is to make people feel bad."

"Sounds right."

"You're all over both. Hashtag SteamerGirl is pretty much trending at County."

I stare at her. She's got to be exaggerating. "Without a photo? How could I be trending?"

"Libby took a pic of you at Perry's. Thing is, it's from far away and blurry, so you can't tell who it is. Just that it's a girl with dark hair wearing hoop earrings. Which kinda threw me—I didn't know you had hoop earrings . . ."

"Who the hell is Libby?"

"Melissa's friend. Who works at Perry's."

So now Barista Girl #2 has a name. Not that it helps. Is it even legal for her to snap pictures of me and plaster them all over the internet?

"What can I say? People are stupid. And jealous. And paranoid." I give the wheels on her chair a little push and look pointedly at her when I say that, earning me a soft smile. I can tell she's already feeling better.

"You know, my dad has this funny saying," she says. "'Even paranoids have enemies.'"

"Meaning . . . ?"

"Maybe there is something to some of this?" Aubrey holds her gaze steady on mine, waiting for a response.

"I *don't* have a thing with your brother, Aubrey," I tell her. "I'm not cool enough for Sam. But . . . I'm not going to lie to you. He's really hot. And really nice. And I noticed, all right? That doesn't mean I don't like *you*." I let that sink in. The fact is, it's true. She's an immature pain in the ass, but she's also kind and funny and honest. With absolutely no ego, which is amazing in someone so talented *and* rich.

I honestly like her.

Aubrey stands. She reaches into her backpack and pulls out a paper ticket. "He wants you at the championship game at the civic center on Saturday," she says, thrusting it at me. "He said, 'Here, bring a friend.' Each player got four family tickets."

My head spins. These tix cost fifteen dollars I don't have.

"Are you sure? 'A friend' doesn't necessarily mean *me*. He just doesn't want you to be the kid alone with the parents," I tell her.

She eyes me like I'm a rotten lawyer who's just made the most unconvincing case before a jury, and now my client is going to get life in prison. "Yeah, he's not *that* stupid," she says. "He knows I only have one friend."

I don't argue with her there.

"It's general admission seating," she tells me as we walk together to the printing station so I can collect my chemistry sheet. "The place is huge. Want to drive over with me and my parents? I don't think you'll find us otherwise."

"Maybe," I tell her. "Let me check out the car situation with my mother."

"We can pick you up," she offers.

"That's totally inconvenient for you," I say quickly. "No worries, I'll get there. And I'll find you." How big can this place be?

"I'll save you a jersey," she adds.

"A what?"

"*Jersey*. Each player's guest gets a jersey with his name and number on it to wear during the game. Sam'll get four, so . . . one for you."

"Great," I say. Willing myself to breathe in. Breathe out. Keep walking. Is this really happening? "But is that a good idea?"

Aubrey tilts her head, confused.

"Won't me sitting in the stands with you wearing Sam's jersey just confirm everything Melissa's been saying?"

Aubrey links her arm through mine. "Very dangerous," she says. "But since they're going to talk about you anyway— why not give them something really good?"

19

Aubrey was right: the civic center is enormous. And the crowd is huge. The line for ticketholders extends out the front doors, while the line for ticket buyers stretches down the block. Parking in the "event" lot costs twenty dollars, but miraculously enough, I find a metered spot on the street that costs me four quarters.

Also in the miracle category: Earl is covering my shift at the market. It's a huge favor because the manager doesn't like us to take off, and I'm going to miss that cash. (Luckily, I got paid yesterday, so my phone is now juiced with minutes. For now, I'll take the loss.)

Even Mami cooperated. She didn't blink when I asked for the car keys and told her I might be back late. I don't know whether helping the Jacksons is earning me Niña Bien Points or she approves of me hanging out with a friend from St. V's, but whatever—I'll take that, too.

The only hitch in these plans is Roz. Heading out to the game, I passed her. She was on the sidewalk, across the street from the market. She usually wanders over there on Saturdays during my shift, and she seemed more than a little surprised to see me driving off when I should have been ringing up beers, freezer-burned ice cream bars, and bags of pork rinds. She shot me this *WTF?* look as I whizzed by, but I just smiled and waved. Didn't even slow down.

Predictably, my phone buzzed within seconds.

Roz: **Where you goin?**

I waited for the first red light before answering.

Me: **Meeting a St Vs friend**

Roz: **Skipping work to meet a friend????**

Roz isn't stupid.

Me: **Can't text and drive talk later**

I turned off the phone. And the guilt. I mean, I'm just going to a basketball game, right? Not robbing a bank.

The inside of the civic center is a ginormous echo chamber. Even though tons of people have turned out, voices bounce off the walls because the crowd doesn't even begin to fill the seats. I scan the audience: the Clayton County fans are a mass of blue and gold on one side, while the folks from the opposing team are a sea of green and yellow. Way, way down on the floor, the boys warm up, their uniforms strangely bright under the powerful lights. Even though I'm seeing this in real life, the lights make it look like high-def TV.

I aim for the blue. In the center of the stands and fairly close to the floor, a group wears players' jerseys. I try to locate the Shackeltons.

Then: the familiar cry of the Energizer Bunny.

"Woo-hoo! Izzy! We're over here!" Her voice cuts through the din like a blade through butter. She's standing in the middle of the jersey-wearing pack, waving. I raise my hand, signaling that I've seen her (and she can stop now, please), and begin to descend the steps in her direction . . . when I trip and almost land on my face.

Correction: I don't trip. *I am tripped.* Some girl's entire leg shoots out from an aisle just as I'm passing (this is not subtle), catching my foot and sending me flying forward—teeth, nose, and chin first.

Falling is weird. As it happens, you think: Uh-oh. I'm falling. This is stupid. How do I make it stop? I can't make it stop! It all goes through your mind in half a second, and you so badly want to turn back the clock . . .

But here's the thing about luck: Even for those of us who have none? Sometimes it finds you. An extralarge dad has chosen this very instant to get out of his seat and buy nachos for his kids. So instead of shattering my face on the stone stairs, I plow into his solid, wide back. He barely sways. I regain my balance.

"Whoa, are you all right?" he says, his steadying hand on my arm. "Be careful."

"Sorry," I tell him. Then turn.

The girl with the leg at the end of the row looks everywhere but at me. She's pasted a bland look on her face. It's so bland, a test of her brain function would probably reveal zero activity. Everyone in the rest of the row, all girls, stares straight at yours truly, waiting. There's something ravenous about their expressions. Like I'm a bloody steak and they haven't eaten in weeks.

Melissa sits dead center. As our eyes lock, I see her raise her phone. Like a weapon.

With every ounce of will I can muster, I force the fakest, friendliest smile ever. I waggle my fingers in this sickeningly sweet wave. I blow Melissa a kiss.

"Hey, girls!" I call out to them. "Hope y'all are havin' a great time! Go, County!" I pray they shoot video. I suspect one does: the girl sitting right next to Melissa holds her phone up for so long that Melissa grabs her wrist and pulls it down, fury on her face. "What?!" I hear her exclaim, confused.

I climb over people to get to Aubrey and practically fall into the empty seat she's saved for me. I'm shaking with anger.

"Tell me you weren't just talking to Melissa," she says the second I'm seated.

"Oh, I was *absolutely* talking to Melissa!" I assure her.

Aubrey looks like she can't decide whether I'm the coolest or the craziest person she's ever met. Before she says anything, however, her mom, a few seats over, calls to me.

"Izzy! So glad you found us! Here!" She tosses a soft bundle at me. I unfold it: it's a Sam jersey. There's a big blue "7" on the front and back, and "SHACKELTON" emblazoned across the shoulders.

Yes. Another photo op.

I yank the thing over my head: it falls midthigh, like a nightshirt. Aubrey wears an equally big one. I pull her to her feet.

"On my count, 'Go, County!' Okay?" I tell her. A smile stretches across her face. We both turn in the direction of Melissa's crew and raise our fists in a victory pump. I count to three.

"Go, County!" Aubrey and I yell. The hundred or so people around us think we're showing some school spirit, and take up the chant, clapping. Only Melissa and Co. know better.

Aubrey laughs as we fall into our seats.

"I can't believe you!" she says. "You do know we'll be all over her Insta now?"

I shrug. "The best defense is a great offense."

"Funny. Sam said something like that this morning," she replies. "But he was talking about the game."

———

The jerseys never come off. Definitely not during the game, which Aubrey and I spend mostly on our feet, screaming. Most definitely not after the final buzzer, when a couple of County students rush the court—then pretty much everyone does, in a big blue-and-gold frenzy of celebration. I'm right there with them, bouncing up and down like . . . Aubrey.

Who knew? I'm a basketball fan.

We wear our jerseys as we pack the civic center lobby, waiting for the freshly showered-and-changed players to emerge from the locker room and load into the streamer-strewn buses that will transport them back to the high school. With a police escort, lights flashing. With a line of rowdy students following in their own cars, horns blaring.

We wear the jerseys as we fill the Clayton County High gym, set up with drinks and snacks and a microphone for a semi-impromptu celebration rally. We wear them as the team arrives and the scream-cheers begin again, as players take turns at the mike thanking coaches, each other, their parents. We wear them as captains Darius and then Sam step up to speak.

We definitely wear them for the pictures Aubrey asks me to snap. All four Shackeltons line up.

It's the first face-to-face I've had with Sam since the Tracfone death the other night. I will my hands to hold steady as I tell them to say "cheese."

There's so much to say and absolutely no good time or way to say it. So I don't even try.

But then, as I hand Aubrey her phone, Sam deals with the awkwardness.

"You look good in seven," he says, stepping close so only I can hear. He's doing it again: that hands-jammed-in-his-pockets-watching-me, smiling-with-his-mouth-closed-and-head-tilted thing.

Even though the gym is a crazy zoo of noise and people, he manages, in that moment, to be the guy my baby brother bounced off at Four Corners.

I'm beginning to understand why girls become psychopaths when he dumps them.

"You play good in seven," I return. "By the way, I'm keeping it. No way you're getting this jersey back."

"It's all yours," he assures me, smiling in this slightly surprised, totally pleased way. You'd think I'd just handed him a jumbo bag of Swedish Fish. "You're coming back to the house, right?"

"No way she's not." Aubrey moves in. She loops her arm through mine. "Mom wants us to head over there now. She's got serving people to help and needs to let them in."

A couple of parent types approach to enthuse all over Sam, and Aubrey pulls me away.

We continue to wear the jerseys as we unlock the house for the "serving people," who turn out to be caterers (caterers!) bearing trays of tinfoil-wrapped food. Two women and a guy, all dressed in black slacks and white shirts, get to work: popping trays into the Shackeltons' double oven, setting up drinks on the patio, and arranging stacks of heavy-duty paper plates, napkins, and those silver-looking utensils that are actually disposable.

I resist the urge to ask Aubrey how much her mom is paying them. Catering looks way more fun than working the cash register at the Meadowbrook convenience store.

The jerseys also stay on as guests—many of them wearing their own jerseys—trickle in. They stay on as the trickle becomes a stream, becomes a torrent. The team, friends of the team, parents of the team, hangers-on of the team, coaches and staff—they all find their way to the Shackeltons' big backyard, which is alive with laughter and voices. Which smells of cooked meat and smoke and springtime as Mr. Shackelton fires up that behemoth of a grill.

We all wear the jerseys, but the players wear their Virginia Boys Regional Championship T-shirts. They wear them as they snap multiple goofy pictures of themselves, then post them, then laugh hysterically as the rest of the Clayton County High cyberworld comments on them. They wear them as they beckon to me. A group of the guys. Standing near the wall where not long ago I was hunkered down in the mud with Roz. I look around for Sam, but he must be inside.

They wave me over, again. John. Darius. Ned. Three other guys whose names I only know from the game program.

"Izzy, right?" Ned begins when I wander over. "Didn't we meet the night of the semifinal game?"

"Actually, it was the game before that," I say.

Ned contracts his brow, thinking.

I decide to refresh his memory. "You were hauling stuff. Out to the pool house?"

His eyes open wide.

"Ha! Busted!" one of the guys crows.

Ned eyes me with fresh respect. And caution. Like I'm a friendly Doberman he's not sure he should pet.

"Yeah, that's probably not a good topic around this crowd," John says, winking.

"Understood," I tell him, winking back.

"We were wondering," Darius says. "By any chance ... are you the Steamer Girl everyone is talking about?"

I take a long drink of seltzer from the red cup in my hand

and glance around the yard. Melissa was wise enough not to show her face, but two of the other girls from "pool house" night are here. Chances are pretty good they date these guys.

I need to be careful.

"That's probably not a good topic around this crowd," I echo, tilting my head toward the girls. Who are definitely watching us. The guys catch on immediately, and laugh.

"Fair enough," John says. "Hey, can we take a pic?"

I shake my head and begin backing away, toward the house. "Nah, but thanks," I tell him. Before they can argue with me, I cross the flagstone patio and head inside. It's almost time for the food to come out, and in the kitchen the caterers have kicked it up a notch. I wander in to watch. One of the women catches my eye and smiles.

"Can I get something for you, miss?" she asks.

At first I'm not sure who she's speaking to. Then I realize: *me.*

When did I become "miss"?

"Oh, no. Nothing, thanks," I tell her, smiling back.

She hesitates. "Is everything okay? Do they need something outside?" She seems concerned.

"No, it's great. Everything's great," I tell her.

She waits. It occurs to me I'm getting in her way. She has a job to do, and as long as I stand here, she's tasked with serving. Me. The guest. I turn to leave the kitchen, and as I do I knock over a stack of mail at the end of the counter. It flies across the floor: bills, flyers, catalogs. As I hurry to gather them, one piece catches my eye.

It's imprinted with a logo in one corner: little blue people beneath a green roof. With their arms raised up in a familiar "Say Amen!"

The Habitat newsletter.

"There you are!" I hear Aubrey exclaim. She's tracked me down. "Yikes, what happened?"

"Hurricane Izzy," I confess. We quickly gather the mail.

"Dad wants to make a toast before we eat," she says. "Let's go outside."

I follow her. As we cross the living room, I can't help asking: "Aubrey, do your parents belong to Habitat for Humanity? I see you get their newsletter."

Aubrey slides open the big glass doors. "Probably. My parents belong to a lot of groups," she says. Nonchalantly. The same way she'd confirm that her parents also own a lot of socks. No biggie.

We're still wearing our jerseys while Mr. Shackelton makes an emotional toast about the team, the season, the "family" of Clayton County High students, faculty, and staff. Everyone claps—Mr. Shackelton is clearly the Man; Charlie Crawford would have liked him, and not just for his grill—then eats huge portions of awesome food.

We wear our jerseys as the last of the guests head out, the guys urging Sam to join them later at so-and-so's house for another party. Aubrey has fallen asleep with Frank on the big sectional sofa in the basement playroom and doesn't hear Ned and John invite me to come with. I decline—I have to head home, I tell them, but thanks. Mr. and Mrs. Shackelton have turned in for the night and left Sam and me to dry the last of the big serving bowls and put them away in the cupboards. I dry; he puts away because I don't know where they go and besides, I can't reach that high.

I'm still wearing that jersey when I tell him I'm going to leave and he says to hold on. Wait. We haven't really spoken all day.

We're in the big living room. The one with the wall of windows and the huge flat-screen. I'm standing near the sliding door, poised to go. I'm about to return home to the real world, and it's not lost on me, not lost at all, which side of the glass I belong on. It's been an amazing day with amazing people, but . . . really.

Then Sam comes up to me and we're alone, completely alone, for the first time.

"D'you have fun today?" he asks.

"A little," I tell him. "Might have been an okay day."

"Yeah," he agrees. "It was okay." He steps in close and I can smell his warm boy smell, something like cotton and grill smoke and soap. Sweat, because we've been working. "Can I ask you something?"

"Okay."

"Why'd you ghost me the other night?"

"My phone died. I only got it back in service today. I am not kidding."

He looks like he's trying to decide whether to believe me or not. "That's so lame it's gotta be true."

"It's true," I tell him. I have to look up because he's that close and that much taller than me. His eyes seem very big. "Is that what you wanted to talk about?"

"Yes. And no," he says. "Maybe I don't want to talk."

"So what do you want to do, Sam?" I barely say it. I whisper it. Breathe it. Imagine it.

He puts both hands on either side of my face and lowers his lips to mine, and like that I'm kissing Sam Shackelton. This warm, dizzy buzz spreads through me and builds as he slips his hands to my waist and pulls me against him, and threatens to spill over, a too-full cup, overflowing, as he slowly nudges my lips open with his.

That's when a fist-sized rock comes hurtling through one of the Shackeltons' windows and the night is full of shattered glass.

20

For once, Mami doesn't interrupt. She listens, still as a stalking cat, frozen in single-minded focus on my long, unwinding, horrible confession. Like she can't quite believe it but can't make me stop.

Or maybe it's just that I've gone so long telling her so little that she's simply drinking it all in.

At any rate, she's not angry. Even though I walk in the door waaaaay late.

Turns out police take their sweet time questioning witnesses at a crime scene. Which is what Sam and I became, after his frightened parents rushed into the living room to find us dusted with shimmery powder. No blood, no shards protruding from our necks, even though daggerlike triangles lay scattered on the floor inches from our feet. Only a light snowfall of powdered glass in our hair, on our shoulders.

"Don't rub your eyes!" Sam warned me as his mother dialed 9-1-1. He could see the glisten on my lashes, my lips. As his mother dialed and we stood there, stupid with shock, Mr. Shackelton raced outside to see if he could catch a glimpse of the Rock Thrower.

But I knew she was long gone. Of course, I didn't say that. Not to them, anyway.

I do, however, tell Mami. Every single bit. Every awful detail. Like stones I've been carrying for way too long, I unload them on my mother. I realize I'm exhausted, and not only because it's late.

From the spying weeks ago to my new friendship with Aubrey, to Perry's, the basketball games, Melissa, I tell her. Even the kiss. I tell her about the kiss. Because I'm not ashamed of it (wasn't she once a pretty girl kissing some handsome American on a beach in Puerto Rico?) and because it explains the Rock. It explains the Thrower. I get what happened. And why.

You throw a rock and break things because there's nothing else you can do.

And then you have everyone's attention.

"Who is this girl they think did it?" Mami finally asks when I stop for a breath.

"Melissa," I tell her. "She's Sam's old girlfriend. They think she saw us kissing and threw the rock."

"But you don't think that?"

"Melissa has other weapons," I say. "And Roz is always spying on the Shackeltons. Way more than the one time she took me."

"But this Melissa. You say she tripped you at the basketball game? That is very bad, Isabella. Maybe you are wrong. Maybe she did throw the rock."

I shake my head. I'm no Melissa fan, but the truth is screaming at me. "Melissa was part of the tripping but not the actual tripper," I explain. "And yes, those girls are horrible. And yes again, Melissa has the motive. Aubrey was all over that with the cops, telling them how mean Melissa has been to me and showing them the Steamer Girl stuff. But Mami, it was Roz. I know it was Roz."

My mother is quiet for a long time after that. She is thinking; I know the expression. But there's also something there I can't quite place. A mixture of sadness and resolve. Like someone who's decided it's time to put down the old, sick family dog.

"You did not tell them it was Roz," she finally says. It's not a question.

"I can't, Mami. And yeah, partly that's because I don't want to admit to them that I stalked their house, too. But mostly it's because I don't want to get her in trouble."

Mami nods. "But this other girl? Even if she is mean, she should not be blamed for something she did not do."

"She won't. There was another party tonight. A zillion people will say she was there when the rock was thrown. It'll all go down as a big mystery." The Shackeltons will put in motion-sensor lighting. A better alarm system. Maybe even buy a big guard dog. Poor Frank.

Melissa will be fine. The Shackeltons will be fine, especially if they throw enough money at home safety improvements to help them all feel better. I'll be fine. Actually, I'll be more than fine. Because if Sam and I weren't a thing before, we sure are now. Especially since he seems determined to announce it to the world, starting with the police. Telling Mami about the kiss was *nothing* after sitting on the Shackeltons' couch, answering questions from the cops while he held my hand. The whole family (including Frank) seemed distracted by the little ball of intertwined fingers perched on Sam's knee. And the expressions on their faces were priceless when Sam's reply to "Where exactly were you when the rock was thrown?" was: "I was kissing Izzy good night in front of the sliding door."

That could have gone a lot of ways, but while Mr. and Mrs. Shackelton definitely looked a little whiplashed—Melissa's chair in the dining room was practically still warm—they smiled at me. And Aubrey mostly just looked amused. Like her big brother finally got caught with his hand in the cookie jar.

Considering Aubrey might have shrieked I was *her* friend first and thrown another rock at us? That was a pretty good reaction.

Here's who's not fine and who won't be fine: Roz.

And what Mami says next confirms it.

"That Roz. She is not all right, Isabella."

I feel a clench in my gut. I know what's coming. "I know, Mami. But she wasn't thinking straight. All she could see was her best friend with the guy she likes. And I lied to her. I did. Over and over." I try to imagine what that must have been like for Roz. I can picture where she was standing. How long was she out there? How much had she seen before her hand found that rock?

If it had been Melissa and Sam at the glass door, she never would have thrown it. This has nothing to do with the Shackeltons and the assholes at her school and everyone and everything that pisses her off. This is about me. Izzy Crawford. Her best friend. On *that* side of the glass.

There are a lot of things Roz has to put up with. But that's the one that got her.

"You cannot have a friend like that, mija. I know what you are thinking. And I am sorry for her, too. But your life is taking you somewhere else."

"She's not a bad person, Mami. It's just that . . . she did a bad thing. The two are different, you know?"

Mami purses her lips. The way she does when she disagrees. "There are things we cannot control in life, Isabella. Things that are not our fault. But then there are *choices*. And more than anything, our choices are who we are. What we choose to do. Who we choose for our friends. You make good choices. Most of the time." We both laugh a little. "But a person who makes bad choices? You cannot help that person. And they will drag you down."

I can't speak. The knot in my stomach has moved up to my throat.

"Hiding in that boy's backyard was a bad choice, Isabella. Lying to me was a bad choice. You have to cut yourself off from a friend who encourages that."

"I know, Mami. But she's also funny and generous. She loves Jack. She helps me. A lot. Like with rides, and . . . all sorts of stuff. She's really my friend. And I feel bad. I feel bad for her and

I feel bad that I hurt her. But I also feel bad because . . . I'm happy. You know? About all the good things. Like, the new house. And my school friends. And now . . . Sam. He's really nice. Maybe I should feel guilty that he likes me, but I don't. I don't!"

Mami is nodding as I speak, which probably makes what happens next happen. I burst into tears. God, I'm so tired.

"Do you remember, Isabella, when your daddy was alive and we went to the beach in Maryland?" Mami says.

I nod. I remember that vacation very well. It was the same summer as the last Crawford reunion, and we rented a house near the ocean.

"Do you remember the bucket of crabs?"

One afternoon, the three of us were wandering down the beach when we came up to a group of boys who were catching baby crabs and dropping them in a bucket. There must have been hundreds, teensy crabs all scrabbling for a foothold and crawling on top of each other. It was awful and pathetic and fascinating. A little gross, too.

"Your father," Mami continues, "pointed out how the crabs stopped each other from escaping. As soon as one got out of the pile and started climbing from the bucket, the others would grab its leg and pull it back. It was terrible, not only for the one that almost made it but for them all. If they weren't so stupid, they could have made a chain, worked together, and *all* escaped. Instead, they spent their energy preventing the one crab from leaving, and in the end all died."

"I'm sorry, Mami, but is that supposed to make me feel better?" I can't help asking.

"No, not better. Wiser," she tells me. "Isabella, I am working so hard to get us out of the bucket. You are working, too. With your job and your grades and now with the Habitat people. But, Roz? She is the crab pulling on your leg. Daughter, please. If she will not climb with you, shake her off."

We go to bed after that, but I don't sleep. I stare at the ceiling until the first gray streaks of light peek around the window shades and the birds put up a racket. Even though I can tell it's going to be a nice day, I dread getting up. Because I know what I have to do.

21

SHAWN SMELLS LIKE CIGARETTES AND SOUR LAUNDRY. HE STANDS IN the doorframe of the Jenkinses' home in a stained T-shirt and low-riding jeans (the waistband of his underwear on full display). He leers at me when I ask for Roz.

"Come right in, little lady," he says with exaggerated politeness, swinging the door open wide. I step into a room strewn with junk: random shoes, abandoned dirty dishes, brimming ashtrays. The ripe odor of kitchen trash fills the place. There's no sign of Gloria.

"Her majesty is down the hall," Shawn informs me, then bellows, "Roz! You got company!"

I head straight for her bedroom. The less time near Shawn the better.

She opens her door as I'm reaching to knock and our eyes lock. I half expect her to slam it shut, and she hesitates, as if she's considering that very thing. But then her jaw tightens and she tilts her head toward the bed, closing—and latching—the door behind us.

Unlike the chaos in the rest of the place, Roz's room is neat. Crowded, but neat. Her collection of secondhand-store finds is arranged by season and color in her tiny, overstuffed closet, with shoes either in boxes or stacked on wooden racks. In one corner she's set up a folding table for her necklace creations, with plastic boxes filled with beads and loops of string and wire arrayed on hooks. The walls are papered with pages ripped from fashion magazines or Roz's own sketches: eye makeup ideas, dress designs, cool bags.

This is where Roz the Stylist lives. On the other side of the flimsy door held shut by the cheap latch she picked up at Home Depot (the lock on her knob has been busted forever) is her actual life. Pre-Shawn, we used to spend hours in here, both of us lounging on the bed, staring at the magazine pages and spinning out crazy ideas for when she would be Dresser to the Stars. I once asked her if County had any tech classes in fashion design; one of my old schools did.

"Yeah, but they're stupid," she sort of growled. "The teacher's an idiot and the kids are losers. They're not actually into fashion. They just want to get out of taking math."

She plops herself on the bed, her legs outstretched, the pillow a backrest. I stand.

"In case you were wondering," I begin, "I didn't tell the police it was you."

One corner of one eyebrow arches, and her lip curls in a snarl. She looks like she can't decide whether I'm worth laughing at or not.

"Oh, and I suppose I owe you a big fat 'thank you' for that?" she replies. "Don't kid yourself. No one gives a damn what you tell anyone."

Deep down—really way deep down—I had hoped, prayed, I was wrong. That maybe Melissa was as scary awful as Roz has claimed, and she did throw that rock. But Roz doesn't ask what I'm talking about. She doesn't even bother to deny it.

"What the hell were you thinking, Roz? I mean, are you *insane*?"

Her eyes widen. "Are *you*?" she fires back. "What, you think these people are for real? And Sam could actually be into you? Wow. Talk about delusional. If I wasn't so pissed off at your lyin' ass, I'd feel sorry for you. But frankly, you deserve what's coming. Good luck." She folds her arms over her chest and stares at me. "And by the way, *Steamer Girl*, after that little show you put on at the game yesterday, how did you think I'd *not* finally find out?"

"I guess I wasn't thinking," I tell her. "I just wanted to piss off Melissa."

"Well, you sure managed to do *that*," Roz concedes. "It's the first time I've seen someone spontaneously combust on social media. She took off on you so bad that even her friends started commenting she was losing it."

"At least she lost it in the fake world. But what's your excuse? I get you're angry at me. Yes, I hid things from you. The Sam stuff just . . . happened . . . and I didn't know how to tell you and then it was too late. I'm sorry. But that doesn't excuse what you did! Roz, we could've gotten seriously hurt!"

She flashes me her classic give-me-a-break face. "Please. Stop. I made a hole in one of their precious windows. Boo-freakin'-hoo."

"There was shattered glass everywhere!"

"Yeah? So what?" Her voice keeps getting louder. "They'll fix it. But some things, Izzy? They can't be fixed. So when it comes to breaking things? *You* rule."

I don't know how to respond to this. I'm not sure she's wrong.

I'm sorry I lied to her. But I'm not sorry I'm with Sam. And that's the part we can't fix.

"Can I ask you something?" Roz continues. "How the hell did you even *meet* him?"

"His sister goes to St. V's. She sings in my a cappella group."

Recognition unfolds across Roz's face. Like we've been playing a game of hangman, and she finally has enough letters in place to identify the mystery word.

"That's what happened to her!" Roz says. "The little sister. I used to see her around school, then I didn't. What, she transferred?"

"She hated County even more than you do. If that's possible."

"Not possible," Roz says. "I heard she was whacked out. Is she?"

Something in my stomach curdles. Like when you squeeze lemon juice into a glass of milk: not a good mixture. The guilt I feel about lying to Roz becomes something else when she describes Aubrey as "whacked."

"I think the term for it is 'depressed.' She's doing better now."

Roz's eyes narrow. "Poor little rich girl," she fake-sighs. "My heart is broken for her."

"Wow. That sucks." The words come out before I can stop them. "Have you ever noticed, Roz, that the only person you have sympathy for is yourself? Everyone else is a jerk."

She stares at me in amazement. "You actually think you're friends with these people," she says. "That's why you defend them."

"I'm not 'defending' anyone. I just don't hate everybody."

"I have news for you, Izzy. You'll never be one of them. Take a look in the mirror. Guys like Sam Shackelton? They might try you on. But when it comes right down to it, you don't fit. You're just the poor girl from the trailer park. Bet he doesn't know that, does he?"

It's a threat. It's the rock she hasn't thrown yet, and she's letting me know: *I can mess you up.*

Just like I could mess her up by going to the police.

It's amazing how much damage we could do to each other. Like crabs in a bucket.

I carefully unlatch the door. From down the hall, I hear the sounds of the television and Shawn coughing. There's a dish rattle from the kitchen. Gloria's finally up. I realize I won't miss never stepping foot in this place again. I face Roz.

"I'm sorry I lied to you," I tell her. "That was wrong. But from now on, you stay away from me. And my family. Don't come by anymore."

I leave without looking at the expression on her face. Because I know I won't be able to handle that.

22

HERE'S WHAT YOU WANT TO DO AFTER YOU BREAK UP WITH YOUR best friend: curl up in bed and cry.

Here's what you don't want to do: deal with anything important. Like Habitat. But when I swing open our door after the showdown with Roz, there they are in the living room: Mami, Betts, and Mr. Lyle. The place smells like fresh coffee, and they've all got pens in their hands and open notebooks on their laps. Planning is happening. Which is fine as long as it doesn't involve me.

No such luck.

"Here she is!" Mr. Lyle exclaims. So happy to see me. The man has a camera into my soul: he knows what I'm feeling. And thinks it's funny.

"Uh . . . don't let me interrupt you!" I try, edging toward the hallway and my room.

"Just the person we need!" he continues. "Please, join us, Isabella."

As I surrender to a corner of the Scrouch, Mami rises, squeezing my shoulder.

"Café con leche?" she asks, heading into the kitchen. "There is just enough coffee left."

Something's up. Warm milk, heaps of sugar, and a dash of strong coffee is my little-girl comfort drink. It's running neck and neck right now with salted-caramel steamers.

They want something from me. And I'm not going to like it.

"Sure." I turn to Betts. "What are you all plotting?"

"Building schedule," she says. "How do you feel about moving out of this palace before summer's over?"

This is not the answer I expected. "That soon? I thought we wouldn't be in the new house until fall."

"That's what we thought, originally," Mr. Lyle says. "But Betts would like to try something new. A blitz."

"Blitz," I repeat. "I'm sorry, but the only blitz I've ever heard of is from history class. When the Germans bombed London back in World War Two?"

Mr. Lyle laughs. "Exactly, but in reverse. Instead of devastating *de*struction, it's inspirational *con*struction!" God, the guy's peppy. And looks very pleased by his little turn of phrase.

"It's intense," Betts explains. "In the past we've done a few blitz weekends. But I'm proposing a thirty-day blitz, full house, start to finish. I visited a Habitat site in Georgia to see how it's done and it's pretty neat. And volunteers like the idea of working hard for a short period, instead of seeing a project drag on for months."

"There's only one drawback," Mr. Lyle says.

Mami returns, handing me a hot cup.

"It moves our fund-raising schedule up," Betts says.

I'm beginning to see the light at the end of their dark tunnel.

And we all know where it leads, folks.

I take a sip of my café con leche (it's perfect), then place the cup on the end table.

"Let me guess, this is that big dinner thing you were talking about. And you want our whole family there."

"Naturally. You'd be the guests of honor!" Mr. Lyle says. "The donors want to meet you."

I smile at him. Or rather, I force my mouth into a smile shape. "Naturally," I repeat.

"You said you would do this," Mami reminds. A low warning rumble in her voice. Like a truck full of gravel, miles away, that you can hear shift gears as it approaches a steep hill.

"Yes, I did," I tell her. "And you know I don't like being paraded around, but I get why this is important."

Betts clears her throat. "The fund-raising dinner is for large donors," she explains. "But a big chunk of our budget comes from smaller contributions. They add up, those five- and ten-dollar checks. Which is why we also do a letter campaign. For those people who want to give but can't afford a seat at the dinner." As she speaks, Mr. Lyle reaches into an envelope and pulls out an eight-by-ten sheet of white paper. It's printed on both sides, and has the little blue say-amen people logo. He hands it to me, and I can see it's a mock-up: no real sentences, just letters showing where the type will go. And a couple of big empty blocks.

For photos.

"No," I say, handing it back. I hear Mami's exasperated whoosh of breath.

"Izzy," Betts begins.

"What part of N-O don't you people get?" I ask. I say this without anger, looking her straight in the eyes. I don't know how else to convey how serious I am and how little chance they have of changing my mind.

"Sweetheart, no one is asking you to discuss anything painful," Mr. Lyle reassures me. "Just a little something you'd like to share about yourself is all. It's important that we bring the project to life for people! They don't want to write checks for paint and nails—they want to help a family. Let's introduce them to that wonderful family!"

He doesn't understand. Well-to-do, white, educated, well-meaning Mr. Lyle . . . who has never had to remove items from his grocery cart because he doesn't have enough money, has never been stopped by some random kid who fingers the zipper on his jacket and says hey-that's-my-old-one-Mom-dropped-off-at-Goodwill, has never watched his mother give him and his brother everything in the pot and say she's not hungry tonight because she had a big lunch . . . He doesn't understand.

And if you add all the stuff he and Betts and the rest of the Habitat folks don't understand to all the stuff I don't tell them—like that I'm starting to date this amazing guy whose parents are on their mailing list—this whole thing is a nonstarter.

I stand. I have no interest in my café now.

"Count me out of the poverty porn," I tell them.

Mami's eyes widen. "Dios mío, Isabella! What are you saying?"

But Betts doesn't blink. She rests a calming hand on Mami's. "It's a term of art, Rita. Don't worry. But good for you, kid. You're smarter than I thought, and I thought you were pretty smart. That said, you're wrong. No one's exploiting you. And Habitat is not charity. It's opportunity. It's empowerment. You spend a day on-site building your own house and your muscles ache at the end of that day, you'll know what I mean."

"I already know what you mean. And I'm happy to work. So's my mom. But our story is our personal business. It's not entertainment for rich people who want to peer into our sad little lives and feel good about themselves for tossing us their spare change."

"'Sad' is the last word I'd ever use to describe you, Izzy. Or your mother."

"Count me out," I repeat.

"Then you tell me how we're going to raise the money. Because truth is, poverty porn works. Ask UNICEF."

Betts and I are each getting louder and angrier, and Mami's eyes are filling, which is actually pretty bad because usually she gets mad, not weepy.

So Mr. Lyle comes to the rescue. "Will you at least come to the dinner?" he interrupts.

I take a deep breath. "Yes."

"Will you agree to let us interview your mother and include a photo of her and your brother in our fund-raising letter?" he asks.

"I can't control what my mother does," I tell him.

He looks at Betts, satisfied. "I truly doubt people will withhold giving because there are no quotes or photos of the teenage daughter in the letter."

Betts shrugs but says nothing and doesn't make eye contact with me. She's pissed.

"Can I go now?" I ask them. One fight per day is my limit, and this is one too many.

"Yup," Betts says, and begins leafing through her papers.

Mami doesn't look at me, either. I exit.

Here's the thing about bad stuff: it comes in threes. My mother insists that good stuff does as well, but I really can't recall three good things in a row. Ever. But now, as I flop onto my bed and flip open my Chromebook (RubyFish_guest is up!), number three makes its grand entrance. I go to Facebook and see that I've got a message. Which pretty much never happens. I click on it, and . . . there he is. Devil Spawn.

"Hey, Cuz!" the message says. "Long time no see! Thanks for friending me!"

Friend him? In what universe? Then, I remember.

Damn Roz.

23

I STARE AT THE SCREEN. THE BLURRY PROFILE PIC OF THE TAN BOY who seems to be laughing while he's dodging the camera. I wasn't kidding when I told Roz he's like watching a car wreck: awful and irresistible at the same time.

So yeah . . . I reply.

Me: **Hey back**

His message is a few days old, and I don't expect him to answer right away. But within seconds, he responds.

Figures he'd be online the moment I contact him.

Mark: **How the hell are ya?**
Me: **Good. You?**
Mark: **Can't complain. WHERE the hell are ya?**
Me: **Clayton Virginia. Been here about 8 months**

Mark: **Your profile says Gainesville Florida. And your pic looks like you're 10**

Cousin Mark obviously still has no filter. I never figured out whether he was just honest or . . . brutal.

Me: **I don't post much. Gainesville was two moves ago. But hey don't judge my pic! Yours looks like you're running. Maybe from the law?**

Mark: **Mighta been**

Me: **Some things never change**

Mark: **Got that right**

Me: **Speaking of where-the-hell-are-ya: where the hell were ya? You dropped off the Facebook world**

Mark: **I dropped off the real world. Back now**

Interesting. What has MarkyMark been up to? Maybe I shouldn't be joking about incarceration . . .

Me: **??**

Mark: **Long story. Better told in person. Speaking of how come we don't see you people anymore?**

I don't share my cousin's talent for brutal honesty. I also can't throw Mami under the bus. I might be mad at her, but I'm sure not going to tell *him*.

Me: **I don't know. Mami works a lot, we move a lot, it's far**

Mark: **Weakass excuses. Couple tanks of gas and a car is all it takes**

Me: **Well back atcha! Why don't you people come see us?**

Mark: **Maybe I will**

I stare at the screen again. Did I really just invite Devil Spawn to visit?

I can imagine the look on Roz's face right now. Actually, I don't have to imagine: I've seen it. It'd be the face from that day we were wolfing down nacho fries outside the market while I was describing my plans to eat healthier.

Her *WTF?* face.

Roz never has a problem choosing something and sticking with it, whether it's a plan or an opinion. Granted, the plan and opinion she sticks with might suck, but she sticks. It drives her crazy that I waffle. Like, when I call Mark the evil cousin but still want to know what he's up to.

Just like it makes no sense that I'm furious with her *and* wish she was here right now.

I take so long to reply that Mark double-messages.

Mark: **Reunion's in a few weeks. You coming?**

Me: **IDK. Lot going on here**

Mark: **Weakass excuses again. What's more important than fried chicken in the fellowship hall with a bunch of old ladies?**

Me: **Wow make me an offer I can't refuse**

Mark: **You know that's right. But think about it. I gotta go TTYL**

I'm about to close out of Facebook when one last message appears from him. It's a link to the Crawford Family Reunion page. Once upon a time, I'd search for this very thing, but it turns out there are a lot of Crawfords. And they all have reunions. I'd never found the Queen's Mountain page. Until now.

There's not much to it. Mostly just updated info on the next one, plus some photos from reunions past. I scroll through those photos, absorbed in checking out cousins who I haven't seen since Daddy's memorial service, six years ago.

Then one of the photos catches my attention. I recognize it. Not because I've seen it before but because I was there.

It's a photo from Grandma Crawford's sixtieth birthday celebration. I know this because she's wearing the dress I remember from that day, and the corsage Uncle DeWitt had pinned on her. She sits on a chair and she's surrounded by children. All her grandchildren, the Bigs and the Littles. Everyone dressed up and respectable and smiling at the camera. I recognize Amy, Mary, and Ginny. I recognize little Grace and even Jonnie. And Mark. He's standing at the far right end, like he'd just arrived in the nick of time and someone pushed him into the picture.

Here's who's not there: me.

I have no memory of everyone lining up for that photo. It must have been taken post–cake disaster, when my parents took me back to Aunt Carrie and Uncle DeWitt's to change clothes.

That's why Daddy was so angry. Because they took it without me. They wouldn't wait. *She* wouldn't wait, he told Mami. Not five minutes.

I don't know who "she" was. The photographer? One of the aunties? Grandma Crawford? I'll admit I feel bad seeing this. But my father felt beyond bad. He was livid. Mad enough to pack us up and leave and never bring us back.

There were things going on between the grown-ups I didn't know anything about. And it occurs to me that maybe I've been wrong about Mark.

Maybe he's not the worst Crawford.

24

THE SHACKELTONS LOVE TRADITIONS. THEY ALSO LOVE PIZZA. SO IT makes sense my first appearance as Sam's Special Friend (we're not using the B and G words yet) is their Friday-night pizza party.

Which includes adults. It's funny, I never would have guessed that someone like Sam Shackelton spends so much time with parent types. But his friends seem to be the kids of his parents' friends. It's like they're an unofficial club. Of good-looking people with incredibly straight white teeth.

Here's how it works: every Friday the Shackeltons provide dough and sauce, while guests bring toppings and drinks. Anything goes, except anchovies. No. Anchovies. Allowed. You bring an anchovy, even as a joke? Banished from the pizza party forever.

Other than that, once invited, always invited. And there's no need to ask whether it's on or not because it's always on.

You just have to confirm you're coming so they can prepare. Mr. Shackelton comes home from work early on Fridays to fire up the outdoor brick oven, and Mrs. Shackelton starts making dough right after lunch: sourdough, whole wheat, white, beer batter.

Aubrey's favorite is the sourdough white pizza with garlic and fresh basil. Although the whole wheat with sausage is also pretty good. She tells me all this as we haul folding chairs from the basement. They're expecting a big turnout tonight; it's someone's birthday. Mrs. Shackelton ordered a cake.

"What about you?" she asks.

"Huh?" I'm only half paying attention. Aubrey's been talking almost nonstop since Sam picked us both up after school. A complication requiring some seriously creative thinking since he will expect to drive me home after. I *think* I have it handled.

"Favorite pizza?" she says.

"Oh. Pepperoni. No contest," I tell her. I'm distracted, watching Sam, who's helping his dad stoke the fire. I can see them through the glass doors. There seems to be a lot of smoke.

Everything in the house is back to normal already: the glass swept up, the damage repaired. The Shackeltons don't live with duct-taped windows.

"Figures," she says. "It's Sam's favorite, too."

I snap open a chair. "You okay with that?" It's the first time I've asked. Since the Night of the Rock (and the hand holding), there's been a lot not said out loud.

"Sure," Aubrey says. "He's dated worse."

For a second I think she's serious. Then I see her sly smile. I fake-punch her arm.

"Thanks, I love you, too," I tell her. "But seriously. This isn't weird for you?"

"Oh, it's totally weird!" she says. "I don't want to imagine what you two do when I'm not around. Ew. But here's the thing, you were my friend first. So in a way, I introduced you."

Sam chooses this moment to come inside. He smells like smoke. "Bree? Dad needs you."

She skips outside. Really. She skips.

The second the door closes, Sam moves in. His lips brush my ear as he speaks. "Actually, he doesn't. Follow me." He grabs my hand and we race upstairs, both laughing like two kids playing hide-and-seek. It's probably a little mean, but honestly? Bree's been on us like a second coat of paint all afternoon.

I wouldn't mind some Sam-alone time.

We've been texting all week. Mostly dumb stuff, but also updates. Like how after the police questioned Melissa all hell broke loose, not just at school but in their parents' circle. Melissa's folks were pissed the Shackeltons didn't call them first. But after what happened to Aubrey (and after they saw the #SteamerGirl Instagram posts), they decided not to mess around.

As it turns out, Melissa *was* at another party that night. So the identity of the rock thrower remains a mystery.

Sam leads me to his bedroom and closes the door. It's the first time I've ever been alone with a boy in his personal space. Where he sleeps. Dresses. Reads, does homework, texts . . . all the things guys do alone. My mind starts to go places it really shouldn't, especially given that his whole family is downstairs. I look around for something safe to distract me, to keep me from breathing in too deeply the warm-Sam smell of the place, and I fixate on the shelves packed with trophies and plaques. I try to will my heart to slow.

"Wow," I say, pretending to read the brass plates. "Do you ever *not* win?"

He stands beside and slightly behind me, his chest brushing my shoulder. "Sometimes I come in second," he says.

I glance at him. His expression is serious. I burst out laughing. "Oh my god! You mean that!"

Sam looks hurt. "What?"

I don't even know where to begin. He's not being snotty or bragging. He's just . . . unaware of a world in which he doesn't crush it. How can someone be so completely oblivious to his own dominance? That he breathes rare air?

Looking like a sweet, beautiful boy the whole time.

"You're . . . incredible," I tell him. Which is pathetically clichéd but utterly true. So next thing I know, I'm kissing him, my fingers behind his neck and creeping up into that hair I've been dying to touch, and he's kissing me back. Pulling me down onto his bed, his hands on me, at the hem of my shirt and slowly moving up and under, and . . .

"Sam! Mom says come down. John's here." Aubrey accompanies this announcement with a few hard raps on the door. Which is, thankfully, locked.

He groans, burying his face in my neck, which is an unsurprisingly awesome feeling.

"I'm gonna strangle her," he mutters into my ear. But he lifts his head and calls out, "Be there in a minute." We both tense, listening for the sound of her retreating steps. When she's gone, Sam rolls away, props his head on one hand, and stares into my eyes.

"We need some alone time," he says.

"We do," I agree.

"Next week. Friday night. My parents have plans and Bree is going to a birthday party for one of our cousins. We'd have the place to ourselves."

A shiver runs the length of my spine. That's a lot of . . . privacy. With a guy who's had a lot of girlfriends. Izzy Crawford, on the other hand, has had exactly zero boyfriends. And only one makeout session pre-Sam. I don't know if I'd even call it a "session." Or making out. I'd mostly call it . . . forgettable.

Somehow, I suspect an evening alone with Sam would be anything but forgettable.

"What do you have in mind?" I ask. It's an actual question. But when I see the look on Sam's face, I realize it sounded like a come-on. And he answers with a kiss that tells me exactly what he'd like to do.

Someone else pounds on the door. "Dude! Your mom's asking where you are!" John.

Sam sighs, resigned. "We'd better go down."

A decent number of people arrived while we were upstairs. I'm amazed at how comfortable they seem in the Shackeltons' home. As if it's their own. No one bothers to ring: they just walk in, carrying bags of food, helping themselves to drinks, their conversations seeming like a continuation from an earlier party, as if this evening is simply a chance to complete a thought they'd had a few days ago.

They also seem muy interested in me, especially the adults.

As Sam and John disappear downstairs to collect more chairs, I find myself listening in on a conversation:

"Who's the girl with Sam?"

"Donna says she's a school friend of Aubrey's."

"I thought he was with Dan and Faye's daughter!"

"Didn't you hear? They broke up and Melissa hurled a rock through the window!"

"My son says it wasn't her. The kids were all at Paul and Meredith's that night."

"Well, I heard the police are still speaking with her. Faye's very upset."

"This new girl is very striking. Is she Italian?"

"Donna says her name is Isabella."

"She has lovely eyes."

Aubrey interrupts my eavesdropping. "Dad just put two of the white pizzas in the oven. Let's get over there so we can nab a slice before Mr. Taunton eats them both. Look, he's practically standing guard."

I glance over to the brick oven, where I see Mr. Shackelton listening, a pained look on his face as a man with a crew cut and very red face speaks emphatically to him. Crew Cut doesn't seem to be standing guard so much as lecturing.

As Aubrey goes to retrieve a couple of lemonades for us, I wander toward the oven. I stand close enough to hear the two men, but not so close that they notice me and invite me into their conversation.

Which actually sounds less like a conversation and more like a one-sided argument. With Crew Cut Dude doing most of the arguing.

"I'm telling you, Mike," he insists, "it's going to kill property values in East Clayton. And it's wrong. People have worked hard and made sacrifices to create the right sort of community out here."

"What exactly do you mean by 'the right sort,' Phil?" Mr. Shackelton asks.

The question seems to anger Crew Cut. "You know what I'm talking about. Riffraff. People who get in cheap, park their rusty wrecks on the front lawn, and don't maintain the property. Our house values are going to take a hit, you mark my words."

"Riffraff," Mr. Shackelton repeats. "Sure that isn't code for people who don't look like you, Phil?"

Even though the sun has set at this point, I can see Crew Cut turn redder. "You know I'm not a racist," he fires back.

"Well, I know you're not. But I wonder why you aren't upset about the houses down the road from the new development. Half-acre lots, buildings completely neglected. Of course, those owners are white—"

"All I'm saying," Crew Cut interrupts, "is that there are plenty of those Humanity houses in downtown Clayton, and that's where they belong."

Aubrey appears with our lemonades.

"Daddy! Are you burning my favorite pizza?" she demands.

Mr. Shackelton looks startled, as if that's exactly what he's doing. He grabs a long-handled wooden paddle and slides two bubbling pizzas from the oven. He deposits them onto a cutting board, then scoops up two more pizzas and slips them into the oven's fierce mouth. Meanwhile, Aubrey takes this cutter that looks like a miniversion of an old-fashioned tree saw and quick-slices one of the pizzas into four wedges. We each take two, then find seats on the wall.

The wall where Roz and I were hiding a few weeks ago.

"Saved these in the nick of time," Aubrey says, blowing on her slices.

"Does your dad always burn them?" I ask.

She takes a bite. "Not saved from Dad. From Mr. Taunton. Guy's a pain."

I blow on my pizza. I think I agree with her about Crew Cut. "How so?"

"He's always angry about something. His latest thing is some new houses not far from here."

I feel my heart beat a little faster. "The ones about a mile down the road? On the left, where they cut a bunch of trees?"

"I have no idea. Maybe."

"What's his problem with them?" I ask. I stare at the pizza. It smells delicious, but I can't manage a bite. My throat feels tight.

"Somebody have a problem?" we hear Sam ask. He and John Mayhew balance plates stacked with slices in one hand, cans of soda in the other. Sam sits close to me, his thigh pressed against mine.

"Mr. Taunton," Aubrey says, as if that's all the explanation needed.

Sam rolls his eyes.

"What's the dude on about now?" John asks.

"He seems upset about some new houses," I say. I try to sound casual. But all the muscles in my body feel like tightly stretched wires.

Sam shakes his head in disgust. "The guy is such a loser," he says. "Somebody wants to build a couple of houses on old man Jensen's land. It's basically this cow pasture, and Taunton's got his jock strap in a knot about it. He started a group to oppose it and wanted my dad to join, but my parents told him to blow." Sam turns to me. "That's the dinner they're going to next Friday. It's a benefit for that development." He leans into my shoulder and speaks softly into my ear. "And we get the house. All. To. Ourselves."

"Ew. Stop," Aubrey orders. "Can't handle the PDA."

John sort of smirks, then fills his mouth with pizza.

"If he's such a jerk, why do your parents invite him over?" I ask.

Sam ignores his sister. His lips have migrated to my shoulder.

"He lives next door. And doesn't bring anchovies," Aubrey says. As if that explains everything.

It occurs to me these people are very good at a game I've never played. And have no idea what the rules are.

25

Two doors down from the entrance to lovely Meadowbrook Gardens Mobile Home Park is this sweet house where an old lady lives. Alone. At least, I assume she's alone. I've never seen anyone with her when she's out watering her flowers.

I've also never seen her lights on past ten at night, so I'm pretty sure this is a safe bet. Still, as we approach the driveway, a fierce prayer plays like background music in my head.

Please, God. Please. Don't let her come out. Please let this work.

Thankfully, when Sam pulls the Jeep Cherokee up to the garage door, the house remains dark.

"I'd invite you in but they're all asleep," I tell him, unbuckling my belt. I need to make a quick getaway. Before the old lady hears the idling jeep and comes out to investigate.

"I'm pretty quiet," he says, cutting the engine. His smile a hesitant question.

"My mother has ears like an elephant's," I tell him. "And I don't think the first time she meets you should be with both of us sprawled on the couch."

"Sprawled," he repeats. As if it's an option he's considering from the dessert menu. "Interesting thought." He leans in for a kiss, which I'm happy to return.

But then I unlock my door. "Good night, Sam. Thanks for driving me home."

He looks a little surprised. "Uh . . . okay. Want me to wait for you to get in?"

I reach in my pocket and pull out my keys. "No worries," I tell him. "And I'm going around back. Good night," I say again as I get out.

I slip around the side of the house in the pitch dark, hoping I don't crash into something loud, like aluminum garbage cans. Once in back, I peek from behind a bush at the Cherokee's retreating headlights. Not until Sam disappears down the street do I set off for the entrance to Meadowbrook Gardens and the winding walk home.

It's chilly, but the cool air and quick walk help clear my head. Not that clarity helps. Actually, the more I examine my situation, the worse it looks:

1. The Shackeltons are going to the Habitat fund-raising dinner. Next Friday they'll be sitting at one of those round tables covered with a linen cloth, sipping wine with their other rich friends, when Mr. Lyle steps up to the mike to introduce the recipients of all their

generosity . . . and what do you know! It's their son's new/latest girlfriend. From the trailer park.

2. That's if I go. Which would mean I have to back out on Sam's big plans for next Friday. Which, honestly, I'm not at all sure I'm ready for. Gorgeous as he is, he's moving fast. For me, anyway. On the highway of love, Sam Shackelton is a Maserati cruising down the Autobahn, while Izzy Crawford is a tricycle weaving along the sidewalk. Okay, maybe not a tricycle. A two-wheeler. With training wheels. In any case, it's pathetic.

3. But if I don't go to the dinner, I back out of my deal with Mami and the Habitat folks. Epic levels of pissed-off-at-Isabella will occur.

4. Dinner or not, here comes the fund-raising letter. Which the Shackeltons will actually read because they're donors. But their neighbors aren't. This is who Mr. Lyle was talking about: the Buttheads who were holding up the project.

Is that what the "charm offensive" is all about? Convincing people like Crew Cut Taunton that people like us deserve a decent house? I feel a furious knot form in my stomach. Who does he think he is? He knows nothing, *nothing*, about us but already has his mind made up that we shouldn't live near him and his precious family? God, I could just . . . kick something. Scream. Throw something.

Like a rock.

Roz is the only person I know who would completely *get* how calling Mr. Taunton a pain or a loser isn't enough. Only she would understand the *WTF?*-edness of serving that guy pizza in your own house. What was it Aubrey said about Sam being too nice to see how mean some people can be? Maybe he got it from his parents. Too polite to tell the awful neighbor to beat it.

Mami and Jack are sound asleep when I creep in, which is fine, I don't want to talk about my evening. Instead, I climb straight into bed and open my Chromebook, fingers crossed RubyFish_guest is up. I need a distraction.

I'm in luck . . . or not. Because while the internet is up, the first thing I see is a Facebook message from Mark.

Correction: Facebook *messages*. Plural. I check the dates and times: Mark's gone all hypermanic on me, typing up a storm late at night.

"Doesn't this guy have any actual friends?" I wonder aloud as I scroll through. It seems to be a massive catch-up on his life for the past six years, with interesting holes ("I'm doing better these days, and got my GED," he writes, without explaining the parts when he wasn't "doing better"), typical drama ("My girlfriend and I broke up"), and boring complaints ("My boss is a jerk").

Mostly, though, it's about the Crawfords. Not his mom and dad: the extended circle of Crawfords, to which we both belong. Or not. Seems like I'm not the only one who feels like an outsider. He doesn't go into detail, but according to Mark, he's the cousin the Crawfords all love to hate.

Which I get.

"Honestly, Cuz?" he types at the end. "I'm not kidding about you all coming to Reunion. I told Ma you and I were in touch, and she said to tell your momma hey and you all can stay with us. So no more weakass excuses!"

What was it Mami said about choices? They define us. In the big, complicated world of good luck and bad luck and things we can't control, we do control our choices.

So what does it say about me that given all these choices— Habitat dinner or a night alone with Sam? newsletter profile?—I pick None of the Above.

Instead, I move the cursor to the bottom of Mark's long, multipart message and type: "Hey, Cuz. Guess who's coming to Reunion?"

26

Here's what you can count on for breakfast when you're in the hog business: really good ham.

Here's what's an added Aunt Carrie bonus: hot-from-the-oven biscuits, the butter liquefying on contact. Fluffy scrambled eggs. Grits, with something called red-eye gravy poured into a well in the middle. She has this feast ready and waiting for me when I stumble downstairs in the morning. It's the first I've seen of her; Mark picked me up at the bus stop at midnight and everyone was asleep when we got in.

"Oh my lord, there she is!" Aunt Carrie exclaims when I appear. She stands at the stove, where something that smells sausage-y spatters in a cast-iron pan. The sun is bright in her cheery kitchen. She opens her arms wide. "Give me some sugar, girl."

I sink into her warm hug. She's wider . . . and whiter . . . than I remember. Mami's hair is still jet-black, but Aunt Carrie's has morphed mostly silver. She wears jeans and a loose, smock-type shirt. She presses me into her pillowy bosom, then holds me at arm's length.

"Look at you! You're a beauty!" she says. "And so grown up. How did that happen?" We both laugh, and she gestures to a kitchen chair for me to sit. Without asking, she pours me a cup of coffee and begins shoveling food onto a plate.

"It is so good to see you, Aunt Carrie," I say.

"Same here, sweetheart. Goodness." Her eyes begin to fill but then change, as if she's just remembered something. "Your mother called. She's worried sick about you. I telephoned her while you were sleeping this morning to let her know you arrived safe and sound."

A cold tsunami of dread rolls through my stomach at the mention of Mami. The Habitat dinner is over.

And pretty much everyone I care about is pissed at me.

Around the same time my bus pulled out of Clayton yesterday and began its nine-hour winding trip to Queen's Mountain, my phone blew up. Sam had come home from school expecting to hang out that night, and he instead got a text from me saying I couldn't make it. Roz was minding her own business when Mami banged on her door. That's because she'd come home from work expecting me to be dressing for the dinner and instead found a note on the kitchen counter:

Hi Mami.

 To begin with, I am sorry. I am not going to the dinner tonight. And I took the emergency money. All of it. I will pay you back, I promise. I know you are *probably very angry and I don't blame you, but for a lot of reasons I can't explain right now I just can't do this dinner. I'm sorry. Besides being supermad, I'm guessing you are also freaking out and wondering where I am, but I promise: I am safe. Please don't worry. I'm not doing anything bad. I might even be doing something good.*

I will be back in time for school.

P.S. I am NOT with Roz. She doesn't know anything.

For some reason, that postscript prompted Mami to march immediately over to Roz's. (That was after Mami tried calling me maybe twenty times. I didn't answer even once.) I know this because the first texts last night were from Roz.

Roz: **WTF Izzy? Where are you? Your mom just here**
Me: **Sorry I told her you don't know**
Roz: **???**

To which I did not reply. Then:

Mami: **Where are you?**

Didn't reply to that one, either. Then:

Sam: **Hey. Just saw your text. You ok?**
Me: **I'm fine. Sorry to cancel. Rain check?**
Sam: **Sure**

Roz: **?!?!**

Mami: **I am calling the police.**

Mami doesn't make empty threats. So:

Me to Mami: **Please do not do that. I am safe**

Me to Roz: **Long story cant talk now**

Sam: **Should I be worried?**

Me to Sam: **??**

Sam: **You realized I AM an asshole?**

I stared at the screen. Did he honestly think I'd changed my mind about him?

Me to Sam: **LOL. No worries**

Mami: **If you do not tell me where you are I am calling the police.**

I started to type *"Fine."* Then thought better of it. If Mami put out some dragnet for me, who knew how far she'd go? Definitely the VC girls. Aubrey. Which would lead to Sam. So:

Me to Mami: **I'm on a bus headed to Queen's Mountain and staying with Aunt Carrie and Uncle Dewitt. I'm going to the Crawford reunion. Don't call police**

There was a very long pause after that. I could practically feel her thinking. Then:

Mami: **Tell Carrie hello from me. Let me know when you arrive.**

I stared at the screen. Was this a trick? Were the state troopers already on their way? Because Mami doesn't give up this easily.

Me to Mami: **Ok**

Mami: **You should have told me. I am very disappointed in you.**

Which is when I turned my phone off.

"How old is he now?" I hear Aunt Carrie say.

I shake my head, trying to reengage with the conversation. "Who?"

"Your little brother."

"Jack is six. He's great. Hyper, but great."

"Hey: no talking about me behind my back!" we hear. Aunt Carrie and I both look to the doorway.

Devil Spawn has arisen.

"Oh, are you hyper?" I ask him, laying on sarcasm thick so there's no mistaking it.

Aunt Carrie's guffaw is like a bark. "You two!" she exclaims. "Caught right up, I see."

Mark crosses the kitchen and peers into the pan. "I see Cousin Izzy's getting the full Carolina breakfast!"

I look at my brimming plate. "Wait. There's more?" I can't help asking.

Mark lowers himself into the opposite chair. "The pâté de foie gras of the South," he informs me, intentionally mangling the French pronunciation. "Livermush."

I'm really hoping I just misheard him.

"It's a specialty around here. Made from hog liver and

head parts. All ground up with spices, then baked, sliced, and fried."

I feel my stomach buck. Maybe from the "parts" part? Still, I want to be polite. "Sounds delicious," I manage.

A pleased smile unfolds across Mark's face. "Tell you what," he says as Aunt Carrie slides a sizzling rectangle of livermush onto my already-full plate. "This might be my favorite cousin. Right here."

I'm having a hard time wrapping my head around this version of Mark. When I stepped, stiff and sleepy, from the bus late last night, his voice cut right through the cotton that had replaced my brain.

"Cousin Izzy, I'da known you anywhere!" he boomed. Heads turned. It was too late to be that energetic. I faced the direction of the voice. A tall, slim young man with straight brown hair and a ski jump nose was standing on the sidewalk.

"Mark?" I asked. He'd texted that he'd be the one to "collect" me. For some reason, I'd been expecting an enlarged version of the ten-year-old I last saw demolishing Grandma Crawford's birthday cake. Not this guy with the smart jeans and untucked shirt.

He also had "trouble" practically stamped on his forehead. So that hadn't changed.

He shouldered my pack, pointed me toward his pickup, and talked nonstop until we pulled up to the house. He was friendly in a four-pack-of-Red-Bull way. Like he was jet fueled.

"Izzy Crawford!" he crowed as we sped along the dark country roads of Queen's Mountain. "It is good to see you."

"It's good to see you, too," I said, surprising myself. Because I meant it. Go figure.

"Why'd you come alone?" He cut straight to the chase.

"Long story," I replied honestly. "And frankly, I only decided at the last minute." I could see him eyeing me in the dark truck cab.

"Fair enough," he finally said. Like someone who smelled a secret and knew better than to lift the lid off the box.

Now, tucking into heaping plates of Aunt Carrie's good food—the livermush is delicious—he reveals his plans for my day.

"So'm thinking we'll swing by the pens first," he tells his mother. "Daddy and Jim'll want to say hey." He glances at me, mischief in his grin. "Plus you don't want to miss the hogs."

"Absolutely not," I assure him.

"Maybe pack a lunch and take Izzy up to the quarry for a swim?" Aunt Carrie suggests. "It's a nice little hike up there. Get some views. And tonight it'll just be the five of us for dinner. Something quiet before we set the whole clan loose on you Sunday."

"The whole clan," I repeat. "Ready or not."

"Here you come," Mark says. He peers at me across the food-filled table in a curious, expectant way. Smiley, but with a side order of grim. As if I'm a small child standing at the edge of a high diving board, and he's waiting to see whether I'll jump or retreat.

Like he knows something I don't.

Betts is right about one thing: hog stench'll damn near kill you. As happy as I was to see Uncle DeWitt (he looks so much like my daddy I could scarcely keep from crying) and cousin Jim (Mark's one older brother who still lives at home), I struggled to breathe through my mouth and not gag the whole time they were talking. We stood alongside a writhing, stinking passel of piglets, chatting, and they just smiled away, oblivious to the odor.

A dip in the glass-clear quarry is a must post-hogs: fortunately, I had packed a bathing suit. After the initial shock of the cold water it feels amazing, all the sweat from the hike up and clinging bits of dust and airborne dry pig poo whooshing off. Afterward, Mark and I stretch out on the sunbaked boulders, our wet hair streaming.

"You're definitely not a wuss anymore," he says.

"When was I ever a wuss?" I demand.

"Those dresses," he begins. "Talk about lace explosion."

"I hated those dresses. My parents only made me wear them because all the other girl cousins did."

"You were always a little scaredy-cat," he continues. "Practically had to crowbar you off your mother."

"You were a scary bunch. Well, *you* were, anyway," I tell him. "And be fair. You all knew each other. I was the outsider. It's intimidating."

He rolls to his side to get a better look at me. "I wasn't scary. I was . . . rambunctious." I can tell he's trying not to laugh.

"You know what my nickname for you is?" I say.

"Can't imagine."

"Devil Spawn."

Now he laughs. "Oh, I like that! Ha!"

"I wasn't trying to be funny," I tell him.

"I know! That's why it's funny," he replies.

I growl at him under my breath. He's a very frustrating person.

"I like you, Cuz. More'n the rest of the crew." He props his head up on his wrist and looks at me. "So tell me. Why are you here alone?"

His sudden flip from lighthearted to direct is disarming.

"I guess because I am a scaredy-cat. You're right," I tell him, a little surprised at my honesty.

Mark's expression doesn't change. He waits. Like someone who's good at listening.

"I've been keeping secrets from a whole lot of people. And it's about to bite me on the butt in a big way," I say. "Things came to a head and rather than deal with it I . . . ran. Your Facebook message and the reunion happened at just the right time, so I bought a bus ticket and here I am. My mom and this guy I like and my former best friend and the Habitat people are all mad at me, and I don't blame them." I'm running on, like a sentence without punctuation, but Mark holds steady. Until I say "Habitat."

"The what people?" he asks.

"Habitat for Humanity. We're building a house with them."

Mark sits up. "Really?"

I nod.

"Wow. That's cool. I'm impressed."

"You know about Habitat?"

"You could say that. I had to do some court-ordered community service, and I did it volunteering on a build. Best hundred hours of my brief high school career."

I sit up as well. "That's a lot of hours."

"And I deserved every one of them," he says.

I fake-sigh. "Like I said. Devil Spawn."

He laughs, this short punch of sound. Reminds me of Roz. Especially in the way it doesn't sound happy. "Nah. Addiction isn't evil. It's a disease," he says.

A silence falls between us. Finally broken by me.

"You were an addict?"

He doesn't answer right away. When he does, he measures his words. It's a switch from his usual barrel-assing, runaway-truck conversational style.

"I was headed down that road," he says. "Way down that road. Before I turned it around. But I definitely have the tendency. So when you ask *was* I an addict? I'd say no. I *am* an addict. And every day I get up and choose not to drink or use. That's recovery, Cuz. The desire to drink and use never goes away. You just beat it back. One day at a time."

I watch his face, his careful expression. This must be what he meant by dropping out of the "real" world.

"What happened?" I ask.

"Who knows? Starts out innocent enough. Stupid teenage stuff, trying things. Thinking it's cool to be bad. But I never half-do anything, you know? So while my friends might get a little drunk, I'd get a lot drunk. My friends might pop a pill, but I'd lift someone's whole prescription. Luckily, I never got into needles, or any of that. But I was on the verge."

"Wow." Wholly inadequate, but I don't know what else to say. "So what happened?"

"Got caught," he says. "Best thing that ever happened to me was getting caught. Because I was *good* at hiding. I snuck bottles, only got drunk enough or high enough to feel good but still be able to get through the day. Until I couldn't. Until someone found me in their house, rummaging through the medicine cabinet in the middle of the night. Called the cops. Luckily, I wasn't carrying, because they might have shot my ass. Instead, I got mandatory treatment and community service."

"That sounds light, given you broke and entered."

"Well, when it's your grandmother's medicine cabinet and she's the one who calls the cops, things go a little easier."

"Whoa! Grandma Crawford called the cops on you?" This is a stunner. I knew she wasn't the warm-and-fuzzy type, but to turn in her own flesh and blood?

Mark makes this I-know-right? face. "She dialed nine-one-one before she knew it was me," he says. "But when they arrived? She let 'em haul me off."

"Wow," I repeat. I'm actually surprised. For all my jokes about expecting Mark to wind up behind bars, they were just . . . jokes. "Maybe she wanted to even the score."

"I'm sorry?"

"You know, finally get back at you for what you did to her birthday cake?"

I expect Mark to laugh. But he looks serious. "Nah. They still blame you."

I'm not sure I've heard him correctly. "Hold on. *You* apologized. *You* acknowledged you did it. And they still think it was me?"

He puts his hands up in this what-can-I-say? gesture.

"That's insane."

"Welcome to the Crawford family," he says without a trace of humor. "They're not right." Which he still says like "rat."

I sit up a little straighter. I need to make sense of this. "But you confessed," I repeat.

"But you were wearing the cake," he explains. "And people believe what they want to believe."

I don't ask him the obvious—why would they *want* to believe I had done it?—but instead stare stupidly at him. "Was this a mistake?" I finally say. "Coming here?"

He doesn't answer right away, which makes me feel worse. "I don't know what y'all's secrets are, Cuz," he finally says. "But running away from them? That won't help. In fact, it'll make things worse.

"But as far as coming here? Not a mistake. We are all really glad to see you." He places a hand over mine. It's an unexpected gesture of kindness, and I feel my eyes fill.

"That's because now there's a cousin lower on the ladder than you," I say tearfully.

We both laugh.

"Well, you might be right about that," he says.

27

In addition to being the least fashion-forward members of the Christian family, Catholics are musically challenged. Well, maybe not *all* Catholics. I've been to a few churches where it didn't sound like they were tuning cats. Once, when we went to church with friends in Atlanta? The choir there sang from the *Lead Me, Guide Me* hymnal, and their Sunday renditions of "I'll Fly Away" or "Precious Lord" could've won Grammys.

The Queen's Mountain Methodists aren't quite that good, but they're close. When we file in Sunday morning, they're belting out a rousing "How Great Thou Art." It's one of my favorites, which I take as a good omen.

Which I could really use. Word of my arrival spread like spilled mercury through the Crawford clan, and no fewer than two aunts, three cousins, and an uncle had dropped by while Mark and I were at the quarry. Aunt Carrie held them off so we could have a quiet dinner, but now, at the worship service,

I'm on full display. Especially since we're tardy and there are only front-pew seats left. We make the Late Walk of Shame in front of everyone.

"Stare much?" I hear Mark mutter right before the congregation launches into verse two.

I glance back quickly as I lower myself into the pew: every pair of eyes is trained on me.

Holy crap.

"When through the woods, and forest glades I wander,
And hear the birds sing sweetly in the trees . . ."

I recognize a few of the gawkers. Cryin' Jonnie is now a pimply preteen. Ginny looks taller, blonder, and lacier than ever. Mary looks . . . pregnant? An unmistakable bulge pulls the fabric of her cotton dress tight across the front. She stands alongside a guy who looks to be her age. Maybe nineteen?

"When I look down, from lofty mountain grandeur
And hear the brook, and feel the gentle breeze."

Everyone is super dressed up, and I feel every wrinkle in the yanked-from-the-backpack sundress I'm wearing. Along with last summer's worn sandals. My long hair is shower wet and pulled into a damp knot at the back of my neck.

Aunt Carrie and Uncle DeWitt pull out their hymnals, but I know this one by heart. I lean into the chorus:

"Then sings my soul, my Savior God, to Thee,
How great Thou art! How great Thou art!"

Now Mark is staring at me. You'd think I'd just sprouted a unicorn horn.

"You have a beautiful voice, Cuz," he says.

"Thank you," I whisper.

"I never knew you could sing! See, now that's a secret worth sharing. You should—"

"Shh!" Behind us, a middle-aged woman with a line of grumpy-looking children pokes Mark.

"Sorry," he mutters as the next verse begins.

"You are *still* bad in church," I murmur.

"You too, missy," the woman hisses.

Mark rolls his eyes and I try not to giggle.

After the hymn the congregation sits. The minister moves to center front and launches into the opening prayer . . . when I see her. Far left, front, lemony dress.

Grandma Crawford.

She looks straight ahead at the minister, jaw set. Her white hair is molded in helmetlike curls, like she's just had it done and sprayed. She's superthin: all sharp angles and bones. Like dry kindling in a yellow bag.

I've seen so little of either of my grandmothers, but this I know: they are nothing alike. Abuela is all soft curves and hugs, little pats and constant kisses. Her English is worse than my Spanish, so she talks to me with the food she insists I eat and the teary goodbyes after our rare visits. Her church in Puerto Rico is not this blond-wood, well-lighted place: it's candles and plastic statues of saints who have been killed in all sorts of gruesome ways. It's all mystery, blood and gore, with a massive crucified Jesus hanging on the wall behind the altar.

That Jesus scared me when I was a little girl. But it's nothing compared to the nerves I feel now, with all these eyes—like crawly bugs—on me.

I must be staring at Grandma Crawford, because she turns her head. As if my thoughts are lasers boring into her skull. Our eyes meet.

Hers narrow. Not in a mean way. More . . . curious. Like the item she'd ordered from Amazon finally arrived and wasn't quite what she expected when she opened it. Her mouth twists, like she doesn't want anyone to know she's sucking on a hard candy. She turns back to face the minister.

I think I stop breathing. At least, that's how it feels when Mark speaks into my ear, startling me to exhale.

"Real warm and fuzzy, right?" he whispers. He noticed.

I don't answer. I don't know what to think. Or what I expected. Just . . . not that.

The service blows by in a series of songs and prayers, and next thing I know everyone is filing out. Everyone—regular parishioners and Crawfords alike—visits over coffee and donuts in the fellowship hall. Aunt Carrie navigates for me, quietly whispering names when various relatives approach with "Is this Charlie's girl?" or "How *are* you, sweetheart?" I sort of know most of them, especially the older folks. They haven't changed nearly as much as the Littles.

After donuts, the general public leaves and the Crawfords get to work, setting up folding tables and putting out food. For some reason they treat me like a guest, so when I head to the kitchen to help, one of the aunties shoos me away and tells me to go have fun. I'm not sure what that entails, since everyone else is occupied, but then I see a girl arranging a table by herself in the corner.

It's Grace of the "lonely" child question. I do the math in my head and figure she must be thirteen by now.

"Hi. Grace, right?" I begin when I approach her.

She's removing something from a box and turns. Her face lights with recognition. "Cousin Izzy!" she exclaims. "Hey! I heard you were here!" She places the objects she's holding on the table and wraps her arms around my shoulders in a quick squeeze. "Little" Grace is taller than me. "How are you?"

"Bored," I confess. "No one will let me help."

She laughs. "Well, you can help me with these photos. I got dozens. We'll arrange them here and you can catch me up!"

Grace talks nonstop while we work. I hear all about her school and who's at Reunion this year and who isn't and who got engaged and who's got a boyfriend and . . . yeah. Grace'll "talk ya." That's how Daddy always described way-chatty people.

Speaking of: Grace pauses for breath and looks at me meaningfully as she places a picture front and center.

It's my father's formal Marine portrait. And even though I can't stand that photo, suddenly seeing him there, staring at me, threatens to bring on the tears.

"I know you must miss him so bad," Grace says, placing one hand on my arm.

You can't even imagine, I don't say. He should be in this room right now, standing with a brother or two, cold drink in hand, smiling that Big Charlie Crawford smile. I would join them and murmur so only he could hear, "That Grace. She'll talk ya," and see his eyes crinkle with laughter and wink in that our-little-secret way. I would tell him Grandma Crawford looks sour as a lemon in that dress. And Aunt Carrie is so nice. And Mark has grown up to be kind, go figure. And the hogs still stink and the dirt around here's still kinda red and . . .

God, this was a mistake. Charlie Crawford isn't here. He's missing from here more than he's missing everywhere else. The big black hole of Charlie Crawford Is Dead is bigger and blacker in the places where he *should* be. In the places where I remember him. Where I need him.

As hard as it is to feel alone, it's harder to feel alone in a room full of people. And unbearable to feel alone where you're *supposed* to belong. Like, with family. Daddy's what connected us to this clan: he knew all the players and all the rules of their games. Without him, I don't know where I fit or what I'm supposed to do. Definitely not unwrapping foil pans of fried chicken or hauling tables and setting out chairs.

Or even arranging family photos. As if I needed more evidence I don't belong, the next I pull from the box is the one from Grandma Crawford's sixtieth. Where she's surrounded by all the grandchildren. Except me. I set it on the table like it's fire-hot.

"Oh, I remember that day!" Grace begins, but then checks herself. An embarrassed expression creases her face, like she's just walked in on someone using the bathroom.

"Yeah, who could forget Grandma Crawford's birthday," I comment.

Grace smiles politely. "Can I ask . . . why d'you call her that?" she says. "'Grandma Crawford'?"

"My mother," I tell her. "She's strict about how we address

adults, so that's what she taught me to say. You all call her Mawmaw, right?"

"*Meemaw*," Grace corrects. "But she doesn't like it. She thinks it's common." Grace glances around, as if someone might overhear her. "She can be snobby," she confides. "She tried to get us to call her Grand. But Meemaw stuck." She giggles. "Except for Jonnie. His parents warned him to always say 'Yes, ma'am' and 'No, ma'am' when he talked to her? But Jonnie's sort of nervous? So he just called her Ma'am. And *that* stuck."

Something inside me stills. Like Grace hit the "mute" and "pause" buttons simultaneously.

Ma'am says she might as well be black! Jonnie's words about Mami.

I'm so stupid. God, I'm so stupid.

"Could you excuse me?" I say, and walk quickly away before she says another thing. I'm not sure where to go, so I make for the exit doors, in search of a shady tree. Unfortunately, it's hot as hell even in the shade, so I start to walk. I don't know where, just . . . away.

I need to clear my head. Because here's the thing: I'm not sure how bad this is.

And even just a little bad isn't okay.

I've covered maybe two blocks, and my sandal straps are rubbing blisters into my ankles when someone shouts my name. Mark. Of course.

"Where's the fire?" he exclaims, panting, when he catches up.

I decide not to bury the lede. "'Ma'am'?" I demand. "Jonnie calls Grandma Crawford *Ma'am*?"

He hesitates. Like a witness on the stand, worried he might say something to incriminate himself. "Yeah. What, you didn't know that?"

I shake my head violently, my hair whipping itself out of its knot. "No, I did not! You people 'ma'am' everyone! Mami used to tease Daddy about it. Whenever he'd come back to North Carolina he'd lay the Southern accent on thick and start ma'aming every woman in sight."

"Sorry that upsets you. Down here, we call it manners."

I stamp my foot in frustration. "Is it 'manners' that she said Mami might as well be black?" I demand.

Now Mark looks completely confused. "You talked to her? And she said *that*?"

"No! Last Reunion I came to. Remember, Jonnie said she said it?"

Mark rolls his eyes. "You do know Jonnie's stupid, right?"

"It doesn't matter if he's stupid! It matters if she said it!"

Mark scrunches his nose, thinking. It reminds me of Jack. "I do recall something like that," he finally says. "But, Cuz, no one pays any mind to Jonnie. And Meemaw's just mean as a snake. To everyone. I mean, she calls me white trash. To my face."

I stare at him. Does he really think calling him white trash is the same as saying Mami might as well be black? As if painting people who aren't lily-white with a single brushstroke of "other" is just . . . *mean*?

He doesn't get it. Because in spite of everything—ruining the cake, drinking and drugging, breaking and entering—he's still in the picture. And I'm not.

I'm not sure what's going on here, but it's not right. It smells. Like hog stench. Sometimes so strong it hits you clear in the face and you stagger backwards, but most times? It's a hint. A whiff. Something lurking beneath the sweet perfumes and smiles that you can't grab hold of. But it's there.

Mark thinks it's just people being mean or stupid, the way Sam and Aubrey think Crew Cut Taunton is just an asshole. But they don't smell it from where I stand. Downwind.

"I think maybe you're not enough of a hater to see the hate," I tell him.

Now he looks concerned. He takes a step closer to me. "No one hates you, Izzy. Come to think of it, I think my momma likes you more'n she does me."

"I don't mean you guys. Your family's great. You know who I'm talking about."

He takes another step closer. "She's not right. Daddy says she never was, even before his daddy died and left her with four boys. Then she lost a son? Your daddy? I'm not making excuses, but it explains things. She had to be tough to survive, and it sort of left her all shriveled inside. But does it matter? She's part of the past. I mean, you were just in there. It's like an . . . ambulatory care convention."

For some reason, hearing Mark use the word "ambulatory" strikes me as hilarious. Not that I can laugh. But his comment is like cold water dumped on all my hot mad.

"Well, my mother's a widow, too. But I can't think of a single person who'd call her mean as a snake. Except maybe Gloria. And my brother's teacher."

Mark smiles. "You'll have to tell me about that. But for right now, can we head back? It's hot out here and I'm hungry."

I shake my head. I'm done. "You go without me," I tell him. "I'm walking back to your house." It's probably a mile or two, but even if I shred my feet to bloody bits in these sandals, I'm leaving. As I set off down the steamy sidewalk, I feel Mark's eyes burn holes in my back.

"So that's it?" he calls after me. "You're running away? Again? Isn't that why you came here in the first place?"

I wave at him over my head.

"Fine!" he shouts. It sounds like "fahn." "Then you're not who I thought you were!"

This stops me midstep. I turn. I'm a good twenty feet away, but I can see the fierce blaze in his eyes.

"I thought you were Big Uncle Charlie's daughter. And he never ran from anything."

28

THE BUS TRIP BETWEEN CLAYTON AND QUEEN'S MOUNTAIN TAKES an agonizing nine hours because it stops in dozens of little towns along the way. If you drive your own car and obey the speed limit, it's only five hours.

If you're Mark, and speed limits are merely suggestions, you can make the trip in four.

That's the deal we cut after I got in his face and told him to shut-up-and-what-the-hell-do-you-know-about-my-father? He didn't flinch. He said fine, prove you're not a wuss. Come back to the party in the fellowship hall, and I'll give you a lift back to Virginia.

I don't know what was hotter: the sidewalk or my temper. And I still don't know where Mark got off talking about "Big Uncle Charlie," like he really knew him. But here's the thing: my daddy was the bravest. And accusing me of being less than his daughter? Well, those were fighting words. And made me realize, for the first time in a long time, that I wanted to be the girl he would have expected me to be.

No more Isabella "Chicken" Crawford.

Besides, I hate long bus rides.

So I marched right back and got on line for lunch.

All through the fried chicken and biscuits and pie, I prayed. Through the hugs on hugs from people who kept explaining how I was related to them and how happy they were to see me. Through the polite chorus of "How's your mother?" and questions about my brother they'd never met. Through the Littles (now big) and the Bigs (some married) and right up to the moment when I approached the corner table where Grandma Crawford sat.

Everyone paid their respects to her. As the matriarch and sole owner of the family hog business—which, Mark explained, she had saved, even when all the farms around them got bought out by big companies—she was the boss. The so-called iron fist in the velvet glove. She didn't manage the day-to-day operations anymore, but everyone knew: she was the last word.

And they owed her.

I was beginning to see my daddy's decision to join the Marines in a new light.

When I finally had a chance to approach her, Mark came with me. I think it was half for moral support and half out of sick curiosity to see what would happen.

"You remember Izzy, right?" he began. "Uncle Charlie and Aunt Rita's girl? She's come all the way from Clayton, Virginia, for Reunion." The others had bent to kiss her papery cheeks, and I could see her lift her chin slightly, preparing for me to do the same.

I did not.

I stood there and waited for her to speak.

"Clayton, Virginia," she said, her thin lips barely moving. "Is that where you live now?"

"Yes," I said. "We moved there less than a year ago."

"And how do you like Clayton, Virginia?"

I found it odd that she repeated the name. "I like it very much, thank you."

"They're building a house there," Mark added.

One of Grandma Crawford's eyebrows rose ever so slightly. "Building a house?" she asked.

"With Habitat for Humanity," Mark explained.

I shot him a let-me-do-my-own-talking look, but I don't think he noticed. Grandma Crawford seemed amused by his revelation. "I suppose that gives you both something in common," she said. Which should have been nice, but I could tell: it was not a compliment. Although what she said next was probably her version of a compliment.

"You favor your father."

I knew she didn't mean my Crawford eyes. She was talking color. My light skin. I wasn't one of the piglet-pink blondes like Grace, but I could . . . pass. And while I'm not as fair as my daddy, I'm not as dark as Mami. Or Jack.

I'd been hiding for a long time. Behind my school uniforms, behind my complicated car pool plans, my borrowed clothes, all the stories I made up in every new town we called home. But standing there as my grandmother complimented me for favoring my light-skinned parent was the first time I felt shame for all the times I pretended to be something I wasn't. Letting people think I was something I wasn't.

All afternoon I'd prayed for the right words to say to that woman. But not until that very comment were my prayers answered.

"Actually, I don't favor anyone," I told her. "I'm a little Crawford. A little Garcia. And all Isabella." I took a step closer. I wanted to make sure she heard every word. Because it was going to be the last time I'd ever speak to her.

"But if I grow up to be half as cool as my parents, I'll be happy. Especially my mother. D'you know, my daddy loved her so much. He used to say, 'Izzy, your mother is the best thing that ever happened to me.'" I waited for that to sink in. "The best thing," I repeated.

Her old eyes glittered, but other than that, she didn't react.

"I thought you should know that." Then I turned and walked out, Mark following close behind.

He tailed me straight outdoors, the adrenaline coursing through my blood making my feet fast. Once outside, I tried to slow my racing heart with deep breaths.

"Gotta hand it to you, Cuz," he said, "you're something in a fight."

"For that," I told him, struggling not to gasp, "you don't just owe me a ride. You owe me hours."

"Say what?" Mark asked.

"Equity," I told him.

Which is how I find myself two days later, sitting on the Scrouch with Mark, playing with Paco, when Mami and Jack pull up. They weren't expecting us until after dinner, but at Mark-miles-per-hour, we're way early.

"Izzy!" my little brother cries, banging the door open. He jumps into my arms and we twirl. He smells like crayons and playground dust. His little body is warm. I hold on for a long time.

"Jack," I say when I finally put him down, "this is our cousin Mark. Mark, meet Jack."

Mark stands, holding Paco in his left hand while he sticks out his right. He and Jack shake. "Hey, Jack. Good to meet you."

"You're staying in my room tonight," Jack informs him. "I'm sleeping with Mami."

Mark and I exchange glances over my brother's head. We'd been making bets over what the arrangements might be. I just won a dollar.

"Thank you," Mark says. "It's very nice of you to give up your bed."

"That's okay! It's only one night. Then you're going to Ms. Betts's!"

Before either of us can register surprise, Mami appears, a grocery bag in each arm. Mark, wisely, hands me Paco and makes a beeline for her.

"Hey, Aunt Rita, let me help you with those!" he says, grabbing them both. This buys me a second.

"How much trouble am I in?" I mutter.

"Lots," Jack says, his eyes round with concern.

Many phone calls—between me and Mami, Aunt Carrie and Mami, and Uncle DeWitt and Mami—happened. Mark's offer to drive me back, and my idea that he stay for a while, required some negotiating. But now a plan has hatched, and the Clayton Crawfords have a real live relative (who knows his way around a Skilsaw) to help with our build and earn equity hours.

Of course, before any of that occurs, Mami and I have a face-to-face coming.

As Mark heaves the groceries onto the counter, she points him and Jack toward the car to collect the rest of the bags. That should give her about thirty seconds alone with me.

A lot can happen in thirty seconds.

So I make a preemptive strike.

"Mami, before you say anything, I'm so, so sorry I took off without asking first and scared you. I know I probably deserve to be grounded for a decade, but . . ."

Before I get any further, she wraps her arms around me and holds me in a tight squeeze. When she lets go, her eyes are damp.

"I was so worried! Don't ever, ever do that to me again!"

"I won't."

"What were you thinking?"

"I wasn't."

Mami looks as if she can't understand how she gave birth to such an imbécil.

"That Mark. Is this going to be okay?"

I know what she's wondering. Is the wild child we once knew safe to be around now that he's full grown?

"He's tame enough. Jack says he's staying with Betts?"

Mami nods. "She has a little apartment over her workshop. He can stay there in exchange for chores."

Oh, yes. I really like the idea of Betts ordering Mark around.

Outside, Jack squeals with laughter. They are playing, probably while ice cream melts in the car. Hyper, meet Distractible.

Mami settles onto one of the stools. She's switched to her interrogation face. "So. Did you find what you were looking for at that reunion?"

I'm not sure how to answer. I thought I was just avoiding the Habitat dinner.

"I saw Grandma Crawford," I say.

Mami's lips purse. "And how is she?" she asks politely.

"Still mean as a snake," I reply.

Surprise, and suppressed laughter, cross my mother's face. Like she knows she should correct me, but her heart isn't in it. "Isabella . . ." she tries.

"Did you know," I continue, "*she* was the one who said the 'might as well be black' thing years ago? I found that out."

Mami stills. I can't tell whether this is a surprise. She doesn't say anything

"So, how is she?" I continue. "I guess . . . racist?"

Still nothing. I'm used to seeing a little more fire from my mother. Especially when I'm tossing verbal grenades.

"She is not a kind woman," Mami finally says.

"You think?" I can't hold back the sarcasm. "I mean, with family like that, who needs enemies?"

Mami's eyes narrow. And she doesn't say, so much as spit, what comes next.

"No. She is not family."

There's the fire.

My mother takes a deep breath. Like we're settling in for something long. Luckily, the sounds of Mark and Jack and Paco tearing it up continue outside. "My mother has a saying, 'La sangre llama.' 'Blood calls.' I didn't really understand it until I had children of my own. Right after you were born, and they put you in my arms? It was like I recognized you. A brand-new little person, but I *knew* you.

"All of a sudden I understood . . . animals. How mother lions and bears go crazy if you get near their cubs? It's in our bodies, in our blood. You know your own and you will fight to protect them. You will do anything for them. That's what a mother does.

"So your father's mother . . . confused me. Do you know, she wouldn't come to our wedding? How do you do that? Turn your back on your own son?"

"She's racist!" I insist.

But Mami shakes her head, hard. "I don't use that word. It is too simple. Calling people racist makes it easy to lump them together and label them all bad. Prejudice is more complicated than that. So is race. What is race, anyway? Is 'brown' a race? Is 'Latina' a race? I don't know.

"Here is what I do know, your grandmother is very uncomfortable with difference. Color. Religion. Country. State, even. You should hear her go on about Yankees! And I do not mean the baseball team."

We both laugh. Things have gotten noticeably quieter outside. The guys are probably going to reappear at any moment.

"I know she did not like that I'm Puerto Rican. But she

skipped our wedding because we got married in a Catholic church. And Charlie was thinking about converting. That really upset her."

"Was she awful to you, Mami?" I'm trying to imagine what this was like for her. Those once-every-year reunions.

Mami pauses, carefully choosing what she says next. "I am not going to lie to you, Isabella. Her unkindness hurt me deeply. But Charlie's brothers, and the wives, especially Carrie, were very nice. And you were so little, you were fine. But at her birthday, when she didn't wait for you to change clothes and be in the big picture? That was the last straw for your father. And I realized my mother was only partly right. Yes, 'La sangre llama.' But there is another saying. 'La sangre te hace pariente, pero la lealtad te hace familia.'"

"'Blood makes you . . .' I'm sorry, what?" I try.

"Blood makes you related, but loyalty makes you family," Mami translates. "She is blood, Isabella. But being a family is so much more."

I sit on the other stool. I'm more than a little ashamed of all my anger at Mami for not taking us to North Carolina these past years.

"I'm sorry, Mami. For all the times I bugged you about visiting the Crawfords."

"I told myself I didn't want anything from them." She sits up a little straighter when she says this. "I thought we didn't need anything from them. And we don't. From *her*. But Isabella, it felt good to talk to Carrie and DeWitt on the phone. And I am glad Mark will help us."

Jack and Mark choose this precise moment to carry in

the rest of the groceries. My brother's hair is damp with little-boy sweat. Even Paco pants. Mami moves to the counter and begins unloading the bags, giving my arm a quick squeeze as she brushes past. There's more to say but it will have to wait.

"I just met your neighbor," Mark says. "Nose ring? Blue hair?"

"We saw Roz!" Jack confirms. "Can she come for dinner? She hasn't been over in *ages.*"

Mami smiles politely. "Another time," she tells Jack.

Mark sits on the stool Mami just vacated. "So," he says, grinning wickedly, "you've been talking about me." I look at him, confused. "That Roz girl, just now? She walked up to us and said, 'Well, if it isn't the cute cousin.'"

"Oh god," I groan.

"I told her, 'The one and only. And who might you be?' She said she's a friend of yours? We should all go out, Cuz. She's pretty cute herself."

"Isabella is grounded for a decade," Mami informs him from the kitchen.

I aim my see-how-it-is? face at Mark and shrug.

"Izzy skipped the big important dinner," Jack explains. "And it was so good! They had ice cream sundaes!"

"That's awesome," I tell him. I turn to Mami. "So how did that go?" It's the first time either of us has even mentioned the Habitat event.

"Ms. Betts raised all her money. And you would have had a nice time. Everyone was asking for you. There were people who know you. Their daughter goes to your school."

My heart skips a beat. Honestly, there's this clutch in my chest, and for a full second I experience what it must feel like to die.

"Who?" I ask. But I know.

"Mike and Donna Shackelton. Their daughter sings in that group with you? And by the way, they told me you also know their son? Isabella, is that the boy with the rock?"

I'm too miserable at this stage to do more than nod.

But Mami winks at me. "Do not worry," she says. "We did not talk about that. They are very nice. A good family." She's trying to reassure me. Of course, I feel anything but.

Because that was not how I planned to tell Sam.

29

Sam proposes Perry's again. I say no. The last things I need are fresh appearances on social media. The paparazzi will have to wait.

I suggest Pie in the Sky, Betts's epic pizza place in Alder. It's far enough from Clayton that we won't know anyone, plus Mark can drop me off on his way to Betts's.

He can also pick me up if things go badly.

Sam is already there when I arrive, in a prime window seat. He smiles when he sees me cross the room. He wears another electric-blue shirt, like from the steamer nondate. He practically glows in that color.

"This place is cool," I say as I sit. "'Dyou have trouble finding it?" I glance around the wood-dark dining room. It's like an old-fashioned log cabin except with the sort of random junk on the walls you'd find at Applebee's. Plus it smells wonderful. Melted cheese and roasted onions. My stomach rumbles.

"I've actually been here before," Sam says. "The pizza's great." He seems happy to see me but also a little guarded. Like I'm a gift-wrapped box he found on his doorstep, with trigger wires poking out the sides. Making a suspicious ticking sound.

"So, in the interest of full disclosure," he begins, "did I just see you get dropped off by a strange guy in a pickup?"

I make a mental note to share with Mark that Sam pegged him as strange from more than forty feet away. "That was my cousin Mark. And he is *very* strange."

Sam's shoulders relax. "I didn't know you had relatives around here."

"I don't. He's from North Carolina. That's where I went last Friday. To a family reunion. He drove me back."

Sam takes this all in, his eyes never leaving my face, which I find unnerving. I pick up one of the menus on the table.

"So. What's good here?" I ask.

"My parents met your mother on Friday night."

Okay. It's like that. Mark would approve. He told me to be direct.

"Come clean, Cuz," he said. "You can only hide for so long." This, after he'd pried out of me that coming to Reunion was an excuse to avoid the Shackeltons at the Habitat benefit.

"What if he dumps me the minute he finds out?" I asked him.

Mark looked puzzled. "Finds out what?"

"That I'm poor. That we live in a crap place smaller than his garage. That I'm on scholarship at St. V's. I could keep going, but do you get the point?"

"Uh, no one's dumping you. Not to be weird, but you are hot AF."

"Ew. Boundary crossing. First cousins, remember?"

"You are also smart, funny, talented, and kind. If he dusts you because your mom doesn't make much money, then *you* don't want *him*."

Easier said than done, I didn't say.

"Actually, speaking of hot AF," I said. "Sam is . . . so beautiful."

"So you've said."

"And had a zillion girlfriends."

Mark was silent.

"Really popular girlfriends. Pretty. Experienced." We let that last one hang there for a minute. "Like, he doesn't date Catholic school dorks in uniforms, who . . ."

"Yeah, I get where you're going with that," he laughed. "Same thing, Cuz. Use your voice. Say what you want. And what you don't want."

"What if we want different things?"

"Then you shouldn't be together," he said.

"Ouch."

Mark laughed. "Nobody said this was easy," he said. "And hell, I'm no expert. But I do know that secrets don't stay secret for very long. It all comes out, in the end. So rip the damn Band-Aid off and just tell him."

I don't know if Mark Crawford qualifies as any sort of Life Coach, but I decide to go with his advice. I place my menu flat on the table.

"Yes, they did," I say to Sam. "My mom really liked your parents."

"They liked her, too," he says. That's all. He waits. He's set this in motion, and wants to see where I'll go.

I take a deep breath, and leap. "You know that house where you dropped me off the other night?"

He nods.

"I don't live there."

Sam sits back in his chair. His expression has changed from waiting to wary. Like I've taken off the first tiny bit of a disguise, and he's not sure what lies beneath.

"I live the next block over. In Meadowbrook Gardens."

His eyebrows contract, forming this little line between. "The trailer park?"

"Actually, it's a mobile home park. But yes."

"Right. Sorry. So . . ." He pauses. "Why did you have me leave you at that house?"

"Because our place is a dump. And I didn't want you to see it."

He doesn't say anything.

"There's more," I continue. "My mom isn't a nurse. She's a nurse's aide. She doesn't make much money, and since my dad died, we've moved around a lot while she keeps looking for better jobs. We don't get a lot of help because all of her family lives in Puerto Rico. They're broke, too."

Sam waits some more. When he's satisfied I'm done, he speaks.

"Is that it?" he asks.

"I think so."

"Just so I'm clear, was your dad a Marine who died in Iraq? Or did you make that up?"

"That's true."

"And do you go to St. V's with my sister?"

I laugh. A little. "Yes."

"And your family is moving to that new development in East Clayton? The one Habitat for Humanity is building?"

"Yes."

Sam stares at me for what feels like forever but is probably only sixty seconds. He looks . . . hurt?

"You think I'm an asshole," he finally says.

My shock is electric. I feel my whole body startle. "What? No! Oh my god. Not at all!"

"Yes, you do," he insists. "Why else would you not tell me those things? You must think I'm a materialistic asshole who cares how much money your mother makes."

"Sam . . . no."

I feel the beginning of a cry coming on. This is not the reaction I expected.

"I don't think badly of you. I feel bad about me. You've never been poor, so you don't get it. But I was . . . embarrassed. You live in this gorgeous house with these gorgeous parents and you're perfect. You're *perfect*, Sam. And I'm . . . not."

He snorts. Is he laughing at me?

"Right. The perfect family that had no clue one of them was getting bullied into depression. How'd that happen?" He breaks eye contact and stares out the window. His jawline stiffens.

Sam Shackelton is not mocking me. He looks like he's trying not to cry.

"You know what my mom said about yours?" he finally says. "That she was the bravest woman she's ever met. The fact is, my mom blames herself. She blames herself every single day for Aubrey. It doesn't matter how many times we tell her it wasn't her fault. After she met your mom, she said, 'Maybe if Aubrey had had a mother like that she wouldn't have gotten so sad.'" Sam's voice cracks. "It wasn't my parents' fault. It was mine. I was the one who dated that awful girl. And she wrecked my sister. So trust me, Izzy. I'm as far from perfect as they come."

This was a mistake. This pizza place. Because right now the only thing I want to do is wrap Sam Shackelton in my arms and hold him. But our bright-eyed waitress chooses this moment to see if we're ready to order.

"No," I bark. "Give us ten minutes."

The poor woman flees.

"Remind me not to get on your wrong side," Sam says.

"That'll teach her," I say.

We both try to laugh. This is hard.

"Sam," I say, "I'm sorry. I'm sorry I didn't trust you. I think I've been keeping secrets so long I'm on auto-lie."

"I'm sorry if I came across as someone you couldn't trust," he says. "Given my past track record with girls, I can see where you got that idea."

"So. What happens now?" I ask him. I hold my breath. Beneath the table I cross my fingers.

"I could use a do-over," he says. He reaches across the table and holds out his hand, palm up. "I'm Sam Shackelton. Nice to meet you."

I clasp his hand in mine. "Isabella Crawford. It's *very* nice to meet you."

"I'm not perfect. And if you call me that again, I'll get mad."

"Me neither. Perfect, that is. I also despise pineapple on pizza, so if you order anything called a Hawaiian, we're done."

"I was thinking the Meat Me? With hamburger, pepperoni, and sausage."

"Yeah, I'll need a salad with that."

"Also, no more secrets. Not about anything, Izzy. Especially not about the house thing, which, by the way, is very cool."

"Deal," I tell him. "And Sam?"

"What?"

"Since we're not keeping secrets, would you go hunt down the waitress? I'm starving."

Sam treats me to one of his killer crooked smiles and goes off in search of our server.

Meanwhile, I sit back. I cannot remember the last time I felt so light. Maybe it's because my arms are finally empty of stones.

Except for one. But that's not my secret to share.

30

I WAS WRONG ABOUT A BLITZ: IT'S NOT LIKE AN AERIAL BOMBING. It's like ducks paddling on a lake. On the surface, things look smooth. But beneath the water? Those webbed feet are working like mad.

That's what the weeks leading up to the Blitz are like, anyway. It's driven Betts into planning overdrive. She creates this big work calendar, and maps out what needs to happen on every day of the thirty-day build. She's figured out what supplies are needed each day, and who is doing what. From nails to beams to roof shingles to paint, Betts has written it down.

It's a massive job for one person. But she has a "helper."

"She's killin' me," Mark moans one night before dinner. He lies on our living room floor, Paco licking his face. He's too tired to push him away.

"You must taste good," Jack observes. "He never licks anyone like that."

"Salt," Mark explains. "It's from dried sweat."

"Shower's down the hall," I suggest.

"I'm too tired to get up."

From the kitchen, Mami bangs on a pot. She is the noisiest cook.

"First the smoke alarm, now the drums! Too loud, Mami!" I call to her.

"It is not my fault the smoke alarm goes off every time I cook! Just one more month and I will have a real kitchen."

Mark props himself up on one elbow. "That smells amazing. What is it?"

"Arroz con gandules y chorizo," Jack says. "And plátanos."

Mark squints, thinking. He's determined to learn a little Spanish. "Okay, so that last thing you said? Fried bananas. *That* I know."

"Plátanos are not fried bananas!" Jack exclaims. "They just look like bananas."

"So what are they?" Mark asks.

"Plátanos," my brother and I both say at once. Then laugh.

"The rest is rice with pigeon peas and spicy Spanish sausage," I tell him.

"Pigeons lay peas?" he asks Jack. Who giggles and loudly exclaims, "No!" I recognize the beginnings of a hyperfest. Mark, it turns out, is worse than Roz at revving up my brother. Who adores him.

That's because Mark keeps whisking him off to the site to see the latest developments. The delivery of the porta potty. The trucks unloading lumber. And Hair Spray Day, which might possibly go down as the best in Jack's young life. Because he finally got to *do* something.

Once Mami and Betts settled on the actual layout for the house, Betts chalked the outline onto the foundation. She measured everything, marking where every wall and doorway would go. Then, she handed Jack a can of hair spray.

"Go for it, kid," she instructed him. "Wherever you see chalk? Spray. Just don't smudge my marks with your feet *before* you spray. That would defeat the purpose."

"And don't spray your eyes," Mark warned. "I did that once."

"Of course you did," I said. I had skipped the potty delivery but agreed to come along for hair spray. "You were such a train wreck of a kid."

"I didn't do it when I was a kid," he said as we watched Jack get to work.

I burst out laughing.

"Hey, it's an easy mistake to make," he said, defending himself. "And by the way, I still beat your boyfriend in the competence department. Nice guy, Cuz, but he's useless with a hammer."

I smiled. Sam had signed on to help build a toolshed on-site. During the Blitz we'd use it for storage. Afterward, we could use it to keep things like rakes. A mower. Hard to imagine that now we would own stuff like that.

Sam turned out to be a danger to himself and others. He was unfamiliar with the most basic tools, and for all his coordination on a basketball court, he was a klutz on the construction site. More than once he almost nailed his thumb to a wall. He was, however, incredibly enthusiastic. Almost Aubrey-like.

"I think he's more the hire-someone-to-fix-it type. He just doesn't know it," I told Mark, who bit his lip to keep from saying what he thought about that type.

"Let's hope the crew he brings on Paint Day is a little more useful," he said.

That's the other part about a blitz: the crews. On most builds, Betts told us, she had to make do with whatever volunteers showed up on a workday. Sometimes only a few came, so she didn't get much done. But for a blitz, which you finish fast? You don't take potluck. You schedule whole crews that commit to completing, and maybe even supplying the materials for, a single task. For Paint Day, me, Sam, and Aubrey have locked down his basketball team and Veronic Convergence to paint the entire inside of the house. In a single day. Mr. Shackelton's law firm will donate the paint. I requested lavender for my room.

Every other stage and its crew, from roofing to flooring, are also scheduled. Tomorrow, on Blitz Kickoff Day, the walls go up. Mark has been working round-the-clock with Betts to get everything ready.

As he slowly picks himself up from the floor and heads to our shower for a predinner desalting, he groans. "I may not survive to tomorrow's wall raising."

Jack gasps. "But you can't miss tomorrow! It's the most important day of all!"

Mark ruffles Jack's hair. "Just kidding, little man. I'll be there." He winks at me, then trudges down the hall.

Jack looks relieved. He's so literal. "He can't miss Uncle Dickie!" he says. "He must have forgot. Remind him when he comes out."

"I'm sure he didn't forget, bud," I assure my little brother.

How could anyone forget? For our wall raising, Betts called in the Marines.

The day we made window boxes, I had thought Betts seemed unusually interested in Uncle Dickie. But here's what I didn't realize: she'd been plotting a blitz from the beginning. And she knew the key to blitzing was rounding up support. Calling in all your people.

When she heard about Dickie, she knew she'd struck gold. So when she and Mami and Mr. Lyle were brainstorming possible crews for each stage of the Blitz, and Betts mentioned Dickie, they tracked him down. Then he tracked down other guys from Daddy's unit, and eight of them managed to secure leave for the wall raising.

They're at the site when we pull up, and I don't think I've ever seen my mother exit our car so fast. Even though we're early, the place is already hopping. It's like a county fair with power tools. And hard hats. Everyone has to wear these ridiculous plastic hard hats that wouldn't protect you from a falling acorn, but Betts is adamant about safety. Her one rule.

Mami finds Uncle Dickie and drags him over to me and Jack. He and the other guys only just flew in this morning. It's been years, but I'd recognize him anywhere, and not just because he's in that picture I snatched from Daddy's "effects."

"Well. Would you look at these two. Holy cow, Rita, they're huge."

I feel Jack press in behind me, unexpectedly shy.

Not me. Just the sound of his familiar voice is all the encouragement I need. I hurl myself at my father's best friend, who wraps his strong arms around me. It's all I can do not to cry.

"Hey, young lady," I hear him say. "You ready to build a house with your uncle?"

———

It starts with a prayer. Our pastor from St. Bernadette's gives the invocation, blessing all present, and our tools, and this land, and this day, and pretty much the mud and the mosquitoes even, so while he's off on a blessing tear, I look around. It's not just the Marines.

Uncle DeWitt and Aunt Carrie are here: Mark encouraged them to come for the Blitz kickoff, and they plan to help until the walls and roof are up. All four of the Shackeltons are here—"We're going to be neighbors!" Aubrey keeps semiscreeching, she's so excited. The entire Habitat board is here, along with Mrs. Brenda and a bunch of other people from our church.

And of course, Betts. She stands beside me while everyone prays, wearing these badass steel-toe boots and a hard hat that looks like it's seen some years of use. Kind of like her. While everyone murmurs along with Father, I feel her push something into my hand.

A real leather Carhartt tool belt. It's brand new.

And has my name embossed on it.

"Happy Blitz Day," she murmurs to me as everyone chimes in "Amen!" "I figured you earned this." Before I can manage a thank-you she stalks off, calling the building volunteers to gather around so she can give them the rundown.

I'm assigned to a group with Uncle Dickie and a few of the guys from Dad's unit. We're going to frame an exterior wall in my soon-to-be-bedroom, probably the simplest of the walls because it only has one window. As another group sheathes the floor of the house, we gather all the materials we'll need and go over the plans with the master carpenter supervising our crew. It's all a little distracting. Especially because I keep watching Sam.

Mark assigned him to carry stuff. For anyone who asks. In other words, he's the Site Gopher. It's probably the least accident-prone job he could have, unless he whacks someone in the head with a beam. Which is a real possibility. At any rate, whenever I catch sight of him, he's smiling enthusiastically and scurrying off to . . . carry something. So adorable.

"A friend of yours?" Dickie asks. He couldn't help noticing.

"We're dating," I confess. "I'm also friends with his sister."

"Like I was friends with your mom's sister," he says. With one of those faraway smiles adults use whenever they trip down memory lane. Usually I try to change the subject because that smile always means a boring story from their past is next. But I'm starving for any old thing he wants to tell me. "You know, you and Jack wouldn't be walking this earth if it wasn't for your aunt Blanca."

"I thought it was because of you," I say.

"No, ma'am. It was Blanca. I was at a bar in San Juan with some friends, and she came up to me and asked if I knew the handsome guy with the green eyes sitting across the room. Who just happened to be my friend Charlie Crawford. I thought she wanted me to introduce him to her. But no, she thought he would be perfect for her sister. I told her yeah, I knew him, so she scribbled down her address and told me she was having a party the next night and I could come. *If* I brought him. Well, I did. And you know the rest. But none of it would have happened without Blanca."

I've missed this. I've missed these men and their deep laughter and their stories. I miss how I always felt so safe around them. Like everything was right in our little world.

Mami has done her best, but it's been a long time since I've felt that kind of safe.

By midmorning the floor is sheathed and we can lay out all the pieces of our wall, like a giant puzzle, in the room where it belongs. Once the pieces are arranged, we nail them together, basically building the wall while it lies flat. Then everyone lines up, takes hold, slowly lifts, and walks it into place.

Ours is the first wall up, and everyone applauds. Because it's starting to feel like a house. A room. I stand before the gaping hole of a soon-to-be-window, and realize: this is my view. Those blue mountains and pool-table-green hills will greet me every morning. They're not going anywhere, and neither am I.

I have felt my father's absence in every room I enter, in every new town we've called home, for a long time. But this afternoon, in this muddy cow pasture, surrounded by family and friends? I feel Charlie Crawford like I feel the sun on my face and the wind in my hair.

I feel him all around this place.

31

If you google "Habitat for Humanity time lapse," all these cool videos pop up on YouTube. Clouds fly overhead as days pass; trucks whiz in and out delivering stacks of lumber; people race around like ants; and the walls, roof, and shingles magically appear. Usually in under three minutes. Like SimCity on steroids.

In real life? It feels faster. Especially if you blitz.

All Betts's planning pays off, and crew after crew knocks out one stage after another. Before we know it, it's time to paint, and a bunch of guys from Sam's basketball team and pretty much all the VC girls are coming. Those who aren't sixteen yet can't work on-site (despite my pleading, Betts refuses to bend this rule), so Aubrey recruits them to help her set up a post-painting pool party at the Shackeltons'. When I step out that morning, the sun burns bright and it's already steamy. The pool is going to feel good.

Mark is parked in the road, truck idling, waiting for me. For all his complaints about Betts slaying him, he's an Early Bird who seems to run on an endless-charge battery. He's also very chatty, and when I come out he's talking . . . or something? Hard to tell . . . with some girl who's leaning so far into the open driver-side window I can't see her head. When our aluminum door slaps shut, she straightens.

It's Roz.

Our eyes lock, but I'm too surprised to even manage a "Hey." She's too . . . whatever . . . to say "Hey," so before either of us exchanges a single word, she wheels around and rushes back to her place, slamming the front door behind her.

We've been dealing with each other like this for weeks now. Random sightings. Near misses. And no talking. Not even a text.

I knew Mark was intrigued. That whole first night at our house, he'd pumped me for information about the "cute neighbor." As best I could out of Jack's hearing, I'd filled him in, from Gloria and Shawn to the Roz Rules and the Rock. In all fairness, I'd also told him about all the fun we'd had. The clothes she'd lent me. The rides and favors. But always, I'd come back to the Rock. And the impossibility of our friendship continuing now that I was seeing Sam.

Mark was disgusted. He said girls get in fights over the stupidest things. And that was it.

Or so I thought.

I climb into the truck and he pulls out.

"Good morning, Cuz!" he begins. "Already feels like a scorcher! Good thing we're done shingling the roof. Wouldn't want to be up there today."

I don't reply.

"I heard Bojangles' is donating coffee and breakfast biscuits this morning. Love me some Bojangles'!"

Still silence from me.

"Hey, did you know—"

"Tell me I did not see what I just saw," I interrupt.

I wish I could say Mark looks surprised. Instead, he looks anything but. He's like a kid wearing a mustache of chocolate, sitting alongside an empty brownie pan.

"That depends on what you just saw."

"Were you . . . making out . . . with Roz Jenkins?" I demand.

"Might have been," he says. Without an ounce of remorse. Which really pisses me off.

"Are you *kidding* me?"

Now he looks surprised. "Are you?"

"Am I what?"

"Kidding. Because you sound angry and you have no right to be."

God, I hate the way he pronounces "right" like "rat." "I told you about her. And still, in spite of what she's done, you go and get involved with her? Behind my back?" I'm so mad I can barely see straight.

"First off, Cuz? It's a free country. I can hang out with who I want. Second? I didn't do anything behind your back. I did it right in front of your house."

"Can you stop joking, please? I'm serious."

"So'm I." His voice has dropped a notch. "Just because she's not your friend doesn't mean she can't be mine."

"*Friend*?" I can barely keep the sneer out of my voice. "That looked like more than 'friend.'"

"Some friends come with benefits," he adds. And smiles. Still joking.

I try a different tactic. "Mark. This thing with Roz? It's been really hard. Even before the Sam stuff. I needed to make a clean break from her. You getting involved complicates things."

He doesn't answer straightaway. He's quiet, thinking. I can't decide what's worse: when he talks nonstop, or when he gets serious and silent.

"How long has this been going on?" I finally ask.

"A few weeks. I was waiting for y'all to come home one evening when she wandered over. She doesn't much like hanging out with her mom's boyfriend. But you know that."

I try to ignore the obvious dig. And the stab of guilt in my gut. No one knows better than me how Roz feels about Shawn.

"Can I ask you something?"

I don't like the way that sounds.

"Why didn't you ask her to join the painting crew today?"

The idea of including Roz with Sam's crowd is so ludicrous I almost laugh out loud.

"Yeah, and while we're at it I'll invite Oprah and the president of the United States to swing by."

"I hear that Oprah is a big Habitat fan."

"You know what I mean. C'mon. We're not speaking."

"That's stupid talking right now. Give me a real reason."

"We're really not speaking."

"Sure it's not because you're a snob?"

I'm so surprised by that I'm not even mad. At first.

"Since when is the girl from the mobile home park whose brother gets the free lunch at public school a snob?" I demand.

"Since she decided her old friend wasn't good enough to introduce to her new friends," he says.

He has me there. I *didn't* want to introduce Roz to everyone. But that's because she's . . . difficult. Hell, Mami is the least snobby person I know, and she practically forbade me from seeing her.

"Mark," I say, "she threw a rock at me and Sam. We could have been seriously hurt. Backing off from her doesn't mean I'm a snob. It means I have basic survival instincts."

He flashes a give-me-a-break look in my direction. "Sometimes people throw rocks because they don't know how else to get attention. As a former rock thrower myself, I can tell you, doesn't mean they're bad people."

We're pulling into the site now, and I have never been so relieved to see the place. Mark slips out of his truck as soon as he parks, slamming the door and leaving me alone in the cab. I take a few deep breaths. But the tears come anyway.

I miss her. She was my hilarious, badass, knows-my-story-but-loves-me-anyway friend. But what Mark doesn't get is that you could only be *her* friend: everyone else was a dork, or an asshole, or rah-rah, or superficial. He doesn't get that she was the biggest crab dragging me down into the bucket.

And I couldn't pull her up. I could barely hang on myself.

A sharp rap on the truck window startles me back to reality. Sam, flashing one of those eager smiles.

"Hey, no napping! There's work to be done!" he enthuses through the glass. I'm so glad to see him I almost cry harder. Instead, I duck my head and wipe the tear tracks from my cheeks as I pretend to look for something under the seat. When I emerge from the truck, I've got a big smile and hug ready for Sam.

A bunch of the kids are already there, hovering near the snack tent, where Mrs. Shackelton and a couple of other basketball moms are setting out stacks of bright-red-and-yellow Bojangles' boxes. Darius chats with Lindsey and Jamila. Sam introduces himself to VC girls he doesn't know, telling them he's Aubrey's brother. In spite of the heat, everyone's drinking coffee.

I link arms with Min and Ann and smile.

"You guys are the best," I tell them. "Thank you so much for coming today."

All day, it's that easy. It's dusty (we have to vacuum and wipe everything to make sure no grit from the drywall sanding remains) and hot (late May in Virginia can roast) and a ton of work (even with rollers, ceilings are a bear). But as the day progresses and we coat the walls and talk and laugh and visit and tease, it gets easier and easier.

At the lunch break a few of the girls pull me aside to get the scoop on a few of the basketball guys, and Lindsey actually thanks *me* for inviting them to help on the build. It gets easier when Betts does a survey of the rooms and tells everyone they've done a great job. Really easy to slip into the utility closet with Sam when no one is watching and kiss him, my hands in his hair, him pressing me against the (still unpainted, luckily) wall, because despite having no skills whatsoever in the handyman department, he is the best kisser.

And even cleaning up at the end of the day is easy because everyone pitches in. We're all coming back tomorrow for the second coat. But for now, we're hot and sweaty and piling into cars and heading to the Shackeltons', where there is a swimming pool and music and all sorts of amazing delicious things that Aubrey and the other under-sixteens have set up.

The only time it's not quite so easy is when I retrieve my backpack from Mark's truck and ask if he's coming with us to the Shackeltons' and he says no thanks.

"I have other plans," he informs me. Unapologetically. We both know with whom.

"Okay. Well, have fun. See you tomorrow," I tell him. We don't make eye contact. We don't cross that no-man's-land minefield and blow apart this fragile family thing we've only just put together.

But we both damn well know that Roz Jenkins would have loved to be included.

32

AND THEN, IT'S DONE.

There's a toilet that flushes and lights that flick on and off. There are doors that swing without scraping the floor and windows that open to birdsong. The meadow surrounding our yard is alive with these blackbirds that have red streaks on their wings. I could watch them all day. I might. Choose a day to do nothing but look at birds.

Of course, it's not completely complete, but as Betts likes to say, "The perfect should not be the enemy of the done." There's still some final touches, and the yard is mostly dirt, but we can move in. Right after the Dedication.

Mami whips us into packing mode. We've moved a zillion times, but this feels different. Instead of shoving things in boxes without any idea where they'll wind up at the other end, every item I wrap and every choice I make—pitch or keep?—feels hopeful and deliberate, as I choose what to carry into our new house. Our new life. Because that's what it really is. Not just different walls.

We'll U-Haul the big items (like the Scrouch, which is, unfortunately, joining us), but Mark and I make a few runs in his pickup with the fragile stuff. And the special stuff. Two items in particular, which I promised myself would be waiting for me when we move in.

In my lavender room with the white trim, Betts helped me install three shelves. Nothing fancy, just boards resting on brackets. I plan to fill them with books (yet to be purchased), but before that, I've got two things to display there: the plastic hard hat I've worn on-site all month (signed, in Sharpie, by everyone in the Paint Day crew) and my favorite (now framed) picture of my father.

Mark stands in the doorway, watching as I place these on the shelves.

"Finally dragging ol' Charlie out into the light, huh?" He knows about this picture. We talked a lot on that car ride from Queen's Mountain.

"Yup. Showed it to Mami last night."

"How'd that go?"

"Uneventful. I thought she'd get all emotional, seeing a new picture of my dad? But she was, like, 'That's a good one,' and just kind of blew it off when I confessed that I'd taken it." It was not a very Mami-like reaction, which makes me realize my mother is pretty distracted right now.

Mark seems slightly amused. "Guess it was only a big deal in your own mind."

"Okay, can we *not* throw darts at Cousin Izzy right now?" I say. "I'm in a good mood."

I stand back to admire my shelf arrangement.

"Fine! No darts. Not today, anyhow."

I try to scowl at him, but it's hard. My shelves are making me too happy.

"By the way," he continues. "This is for you." He holds out a balled-up white shirt and necklace. "She doesn't want it back."

"Must be covered in cooties," I remark. I'd found Roz's shirt the other night when I was emptying drawers. I'd asked Mark to return it for me.

"Probably," he agrees. "But she says it was a gift."

I try not to reveal how that feels like the stab of an actual dart. Instead, I take them. There's no furniture in here yet, so I shove them on a shelf in my closet.

Mark just looks at me like I'm a piece of gum stuck to his shoe.

I'm so sick of his judgments.

"Go ahead. Say it," I demand. "You think I suck."

He doesn't comment. Which is worse than if he did.

"What do you want me to do? She hates *everyone*. And everything. Except maybe you, go figure. You can't help a person like that. They drag you down."

"I understand. When I got sober, I dropped all my drinking and drugging buddies. I walked away from anyone who threatened my recovery. It didn't leave me with many friends. But I had to do it, so I get what you're saying. Thing is, that's not Roz."

"She threw—"

"Forget the damn rock!" he interrupts. Loudly. "She knows that was a mistake, okay? She's sorry. But it's not like you've even given her a chance to apologize!"

"I was at her place the very next day! And she was not one bit sorry."

"She trusted you and you lied to her. Have you ever apologized for that?"

I don't answer him. I honestly can't remember.

"Izzy, you didn't drop her because she gets in your way. You dropped her because she's an inconvenience. Now c'mon. Aren't you better'n that?"

God, I want to hate him. Devil Spawn. I want to shout at him, *You don't know me! And just because you're hooking up with Roz doesn't mean you know her!*

But here's the thing: he's not wrong. I was embarrassed by her. Afraid she'd blow my cover in front of all the people I was trying to fool.

I have no idea how to fix this. It's probably too late.

"Mark. Can we just . . . get through this move? Get through tomorrow and the Dedication and everything? And then I'll think about Roz? I hear you, okay? I get what you're saying."

Mark walks over to my three wall shelves and picks up the hard hat. I see him reading the names scrawled all over it. All my friends, absent one. When he replaces it, he doesn't look mad anymore.

"Sure, Cuz."

It's dark outside by the time we return to lovely Meadowbrook Gardens. Mami has been busy: our bare-walled living room is filled with cardboard boxes taped tight, and she has emptied the kitchen except for what we need for breakfast in the morning. Since there's no way to cook, she splurged and got us all pizza for dinner. She's also hoping Mark will finish off any leftovers in the fridge—I told her the empanadas had turned, but she insisted they were fine—because she thinks it's bad luck to bring old food into a new home.

As Mark and I stand at the counter with our slices, I clink my soda can with his.

"Here's to the last supper in the ol' homestead," I say.

"Cheers," he replies.

Jack sits on the stool next to us. "Good Lord, good meat, good—" He doesn't finish.

That's because a familiar pounding threatens to collapse our door.

"Mrs. Crawford! Mrs. Crawford, please!"

My little brother aims his terrified eyes at me.

"What the hell?" Mark exclaims.

Mami and I exchange glances.

"Call nine-one-one. And take Jack into the back room," Mami orders as she rushes to open the door.

But before either Mark or I budge, the door crashes open. Figures our last night here the thing would finally break.

There's blood all over Roz's face and the front of her shirt. There's so much blood you can't really tell it's her, except for the hair. She's sob-shrieking and I can't make out what she's saying, but probably that's because Paco is barking and Jack is wailing this high-pitched scream that sounds like a crazy engine revving. Somehow I manage to get my hands on the one dish towel Mami didn't pack and blot the blood out of Roz's eyes. It's difficult, though: she's got a deep cut on her forehead. Like, to the bone. I can see the white. The room spins, and behind the screams I hear buzzing bees.

The telltale signs of a faint coming on. God, I'm such a wuss.

"Izzy. Izzy, close the door. Close the door." Roz is rambling. She blinks rapidly, trying to clear the blood from her eyes.

I fill my lungs with air and will myself to stay upright. I press the towel against her forehead and place her hand over it. "Press. Hard," I order her. I guide her butt to one of the stools. The one where Jack was just sitting. His cries sound far away now. Mark must have hauled him off to the back.

"Close the door, Izzy," Roz repeats. Her voice shaking.

I don't have the heart to tell her that I can't. That she bashed our door in and it's lying flat on the floor.

I feel Mami's shoulder against mine. She leans in close to Roz and speaks directly into her face. "Where else are you hurt?" she says. Her voice sounds strange. She seems strange, amidst all the noise and screaming. Like an iron pole in a windstorm, unmoving, while loose leaves and branches whip past.

"Shawn. Close the door," Roz repeats. But it's too late for that. Shawn Shifflett chooses that very moment to fill the empty space where the cheap door once hung.

He is stumble-drunk. Red-eyed drunk, and bellowing. Mad as salt in a wound, not only at Roz but at us.

"Get yer ass out here, girl!" he shouts at Roz.

She scrambles back, almost upending herself and the stool. She's too frightened to even scream.

"Shawn!" Mami orders him. "Get out of my house."

He laughs. "Soon's you send that little whore home," he snarls. "This is none of your business."

"I told you, you make it my business when you come into my house. Leave now, or else."

"Or else what?" he scoffs.

Which is when Mami whips out the second thing I'm surprised she didn't pack: a kitchen knife. *The* kitchen knife. Our biggest, baddest blade, which we use for everything from peeling garlic to cutting up chicken.

Mami always keeps it razor sharp.

"You can either leave my house with your cojones or without your cojones," she says in her scariest Mami voice. Which is pretty scary. "You decide."

Shawn reaches into the loose front pocket of his hoodie and pulls out a gun. The gun. Roz wasn't joking.

"Get outta the way," he orders Mami. He extends his arm full length and points the gun at her. The barrel can't be more than two feet from her face. Mami doesn't speak. But I see her hand go to her throat. To her Mother Cabrini medal. She doesn't stand aside. Instead, she takes one step, putting herself between Roz and the gun, and I realize: my mother thinks she's about to die.

I'm about to watch my mother die.

Shawn pulls the trigger. The empty chamber clicks.

Roz.

"What the hell!" Shawn roars. He tosses the gun aside and lunges at Roz. But at the same moment, Mark, materializing from the darkness of the hall, tackles him. The impact of those two bodies colliding rattles the walls. It sounds like two sides of beef crashing into each other, meat on meat. Luckily for Mark, the door is down and the momentum is in his favor, so as he and Shawn go flying outside into the dark, he's on top.

And he takes Shawn clean out.

There's a frightened wail. Jack has left his room, his fear of being alone trumping his fear of Shawn. Mami scoops him into her arms and heads back toward the bedrooms. As they disappear, I glance into the kitchen. Roz has pressed herself into a corner, and holds the dish towel to her forehead. Blood has seeped through, and the stain is growing. I go to her.

"I'm sorry, Izzy. I didn't know where to go," she begins.

"Shhh, shhh," I say. I rip a couple of paper towels from a roll and add them atop the dish towel. They fill with blood immediately.

"How bad? How bad is it?" she whispers.

"Mark's got him. I think he knocked him out."

"No, I mean my face."

I don't want to look. I don't want to relieve the pressure and let loose a big gush of blood. But the fear in her eyes is killing me.

I gently lower the makeshift dressing. There's a straight slash at her hairline. At first it looks like a thin red wire, but as blood pools it fattens and spills over. I quickly reapply the towel. She needs stitches.

"It's a clean cut, and it's up high. I think this means you're keeping these dumb bangs." We both burst out laughing. And crying. I put my arms around her and squeeze tight. "It's fine. You'll be fine," I promise her.

"Izzy!" Mark is yelling.

I place Roz's hands back on the towel, remind her to press, then run to the doorway. "Call nine-one-one again," he demands when I appear. "Make sure they're also sending an ambulance."

I take out my phone and try dialing, but my fingers are not my own. They tremble over the keypad, useless. In the half-light pouring through the empty doorframe, Mark has rolled Shawn face-first into the gravel, then pinned him by leaning with his knees into his lower back. Shawn's too drunk and too mashed to do much besides squirm and swear. Luckily for us, we can't make out much of what he's saying. That's partly because he's eating stones and partly because the police are already tearing through lovely Meadowbrook Gardens, blue lights flashing and sirens loud.

33

Ms. Clare insists we can't pull off the Dedication without bread, salt, and wine. And since the person responsible for these crucial items dropped the ball, she sends me and Sam out to Four Corners to save the day.

I'm operating on three hours of sleep and feel like I'm stumbling through fog, even though it's a cloudless, bright day. I'm not sure what part of I-spent-most-of-the-night-in-an-emergency-room Ms. Clare doesn't get, but I'm just about out of bandwidth.

Sam picks up the slack. He's the right amount of upbeat and positive as we climb into the Cherokee.

"I get it," he says about the ridiculous errand. "It's from *It's a Wonderful Life*. I love that movie."

I have no idea what he's talking about. I've been filling his ear about what went down last night, and it occurs to me I'm babbling. Sleep deprivation is a strange thing.

Here's what's stranger: emergency rooms. Where no one seems to get that you've got an emergency. *Hello, people?* I wanted to shriek as this intake person behind the glass started asking Roz if she had health insurance, her date of birth, et cetera, while she was looking like something out of a Freddy Krueger movie.

Mark was pissed. He'd followed the ambulance in his pickup (I got to ride with Roz, blaring sirens and neon lights, the works), and didn't bother to hide his mad when he arrived and found us sitting in the waiting room holding wads of gauze on her forehead.

"She's not fine! She's probably in shock!" we heard him arguing with a nurse in the hallway. "I want someone to see her now!"

"Don't mess with Devil Spawn," I muttered, trying to coax a smile out of Roz. But she wasn't buying it. Her eyes kept darting around the room. Like she expected Shawn to reappear. "Roz, what happened?"

"He just lost it tonight. Came at me with a knife."

I didn't ask what had set him off. There's never a good reason.

"I'm screwed, Izzy," she said, her voice full of tears.

"It's a clean, straight cut near your hairline," I reassured her. "No one will ever notice—"

"They're going to call child services. They have to. There's no hiding this."

"Shhh, don't worry about that. Shawn's cooked. You didn't see. The cops hauled his ass out of there. Dude's gone, Roz, and—"

"My mother was blackout drunk when this went down. They'll never let me live at home now."

A cold knot of dread began to form in my stomach. She wasn't wrong. "Let's just deal with the cut for now, okay?" I tried to calm her. "Don't jump to—"

"Could I stay with you guys? It would probably only be for a little while. Until Mom dries out. Again. You've got room now, right? With the new house? Please, Izzy . . ."

An ask. A bona fide ask. From the girl who never admits she wants or needs anything. Before I could even think of how to reply, Mark returned. Pushing a wheelchair.

"C'mon," he ordered. "I got you into an exam room. Probably still have to wait, but at least you can lie down." On shaky legs, she moved from one chair to the other, keeping a hand on the gauze the whole time. "Anybody asks? You tell them I'm your cousin," he told her. "That way I'm allowed to stay with you." He glanced at me and winked. "Rest of the 'family' is supposed to wait out here. I'll let you know what's going on."

You'd think with all the adrenaline pumping through my body I'd have paced that room like a caged animal, but next thing I remember, Mark was prodding me awake. My neck was stiff and one arm tingled from me lying on it like a pillow.

"I'll take you home," he said. "Doc's working on her now."

I licked my lips. My mouth tasted sour. "What's happening?"

"Stiches," he said. "Finally."

If I felt hollow-eyed, he looked it. With a side order of grim. I couldn't help interrogating him as we climbed into the truck and pulled out of the parking lot. "Is something else wrong?"

"She's just upset," he said. And stopped. I could practically see his mind working.

"About what happens next," I supplied.

"Yup."

"She asked if she could move in with us," I told him.

We let that hang in the stale air of the cab for a long moment.

I thought of my sweet lavender room with the three freshly painted shelves. I tried to imagine a second twin bed in that space. Roz's Crazy Beads worktable crowded into a corner, her fashion photos taped above on the clean, new wall. Her clothes in my closet.

Was it awful of me that my heart sank? I had been so looking forward to decorating, unpacking, lying on my bed, and looking out the window.

But what other option did she have? None. Zero.

And I had so much.

"She's dreamin'," Mark said. Clipped voice. Sort of angry. At me?

"They don't just release you to the neighbors," he explained. "It doesn't work that way."

"How does it work?" I asked.

"I have no idea," he muttered. "But not like that."

I'd been trying to explain all this to Sam, in my sleepwalking state, as everyone was scurrying around and setting up for the Dedication. He'd been doing his best to take it all in without looking too shocked, but what passes for a not-too-unusual night in lovely Meadowbrook Gardens is completely alien to East Clayton.

I'll bet he's never spent a night with his front door duct-taped to the side of his house.

"Sam, I have no idea what you're talking about," I finally tell him.

"You've never seen *It's a Wonderful Life*?" he asks. Like I've just told him I've never brushed my teeth.

"Nope."

"We watch it every Christmas. It's a family tradition."

"Why do I get the sense that if the Shackeltons do it once, it's in the books forever?"

He laughs. "This really is a tradition. When my parents were at the University? It would play nonstop, twenty-four-seven, during exam week. They said it was a great study break."

Sam says "the University" like it's the only one on the planet. But as I'm learning: that's how Virginians feel about UVA. Also known as Mr. Jefferson's University. Also known as Sam's school come September. Which translates to this-is-all-going-to-end-soon. But that's what happens when you date a senior. They graduate.

"C'mon," he prods. "Don't tell me you don't have traditions. Especially at Christmas."

I feel my grouchy meter shifting into overdrive. It doesn't help that I'm so tired. "After all I've said about Roz and Shawn and the hospital and all, are we really going to discuss holiday traditions right now?"

Sam's hands tighten on the steering wheel. "When I'm upset about something," he finally says, "and can't do anything to fix it? I try not to turn it over and over in my mind. That's just worry, and it honestly doesn't help. Instead, I change the channel. Think about something else. Until I can *do* something to fix the problem." He looks at me, concern in his eyes. "I wasn't ignoring you. I was trying to distract you."

I don't even know what to say. As someone who comes from a long line of practically professional worriers, I can't relate to this put-it-in-a-box-and-deal-with-it-later mentality.

But I do get that he was trying to be kind. Not thoughtless.

"Well," I begin, "have you ever heard of parrandas?"

"Never," Sam says.

"It's basically Christmas caroling that starts late at night. We do it at my grandmother's in Puerto Rico. You go from house to house, visiting all your friends. At each home there's food and drinks and singing, and when you finish at one place, the hosts join you for the next. So the group keeps getting bigger and rowdier."

"Sounds like a blast."

"It is," I tell him. "Then on Christmas Day, we usually eat the same things. Roast pork. Arroz con gandules. Pasteles. Those are meat-filled pastries that you wrap in banana leaves and boil. We make them assembly-line style. Everyone crowds into my grandmother's kitchen for hours making piles of pasteles."

One time we went—it was the first Christmas after Daddy died—I remember we couldn't eat them all, so Abuela froze a bunch. She gave us some to take home on the plane, wrapping them carefully in multiple layers of thick plastic. But they didn't clear the gate. Mami cried when the woman in the Customs uniform took them. I remember being so embarrassed by my mother, making a scene over those dumb pasteles.

It occurs to me now that those pasteles were just one good-bye too many on a rough day. An awful year.

"Maybe make them for me when I come home at Christmas break?" Sam says.

I hold my breath. He assumes we'll still be a thing at Christmas.

He is so positive. I want to be like that. Feel like that. Or at least try.

"How about we do them together?" I suggest. "We'll get Mami to show us. Set up our own little pastel-maker space in that new kitchen."

"Deal," he says. He reaches with one hand to grasp mine, even though he's turning into the Four Corners lot. "And I'll bring the movie. You'll love it."

The wine, bread, and salt are waiting for us (Ms. Clare called ahead), and after a quick pickup (she also paid ahead since we aren't old enough to buy wine), Sam books it back. Even though we race, cars are parked down the length of our new road when we arrive. Sam edges the Cherokee onto a patch of grass near the Habitat sign at the entrance to the development, and we walk-run toward the cul-de-sac and our house. Halfway there I notice Mark's pickup. It's parked at a bad angle, and he's sitting in the driver's seat, windows down, talking on the phone. I haven't seen him since he brought me home last night.

"Take these!" I tell Sam, thrusting the grocery bags at him. "I'll catch up."

Sam sprints, waving at Mark as he heads toward the house.

When I approach the cab I hear Mark say, "Izzy's here. Want to talk to her?" He passes his cell phone to me.

"She's a little teary," he says in a half whisper. "But she's doin' good."

I hold the phone to my ear. "Roz?"

"Hey, Izzy." Snuffles. The sounds of someone blowing her nose.

"How're you doing?"

"You can never, ever, say anything bad about that cousin of yours again. Okay?" I glance at Mark. He heard that. Tries not to smile, but he's damn pleased with himself right now.

"I'll try," I tell her, winking at him. "But don't be fooled. Deep down, he's Devil Spawn."

"Promise," she says, a break in her voice. God, she's practically sobbing. What'd they do to her?

"I promise," I say. "Listen, he says you're doing good. Are you?"

"I have forty-five stitches in my head."

"Forty-five!" I can't help it. "For that little thing?"

"It was deep," she says. "So they stitch you in layers. Because it was on my forehead, they brought in a plastic surgeon. He says I'll hardly have a scar."

I remember the white bone of her forehead from last night. Taking a breath, I grasp the side of the truck with my free hand. "That's great, Roz. Otherwise you feel okay?"

"Social services was here this morning," she says. A quaver in her voice. "They want to release me into care. Another foster home, Izzy."

I look at Mark. His jaw has clenched and his mouth is set into this firm line. It's the grim face from last night.

"That's not going to happen," I tell her. Even though I have no idea how this can possibly not happen. "We are here for you. All of us." Despite the fatigue, I hear the resolve in my own voice. I don't know where it's come from, or how I know, but we'll figure it out.

"Okay." Her voice sounds small. Un-Roz-like. "Izzy?"

"Yeah?" From the corner of my eye, I see someone waving at me, just beyond the line of cars and before the crush of people standing in front of our house: Wacky Wavy Inflatable Arm Flailing Tube Man Aubrey. Today's program includes Veronic Convergence singing a hymn.

"I'm sorry!" Roz bursts out. "For throwing that rock and bringing Shawn into your house and all those mean things I said and—"

"Stop! Roz, stop!"

She has nothing to apologize for. Neither of us do. Both of us do.

We're all just doing the best we can. It's time to forgive ourselves. And each other.

"I love you. Okay? I love you."

"I love you, too," I hear.

I hand the phone back to Mark. He holds up a finger, signaling that he'll join me in one minute. As I race-walk toward the house, I hear him say, "Hey. Me again." We'll see if he makes it to the ceremony.

I wend my way through the crowd in front of our house, trying to get to the front porch—where I can see Mami and Jack standing with Mr. Lyle and our pastor—but it's slow going. There must be a hundred people standing out here in the sun.

Every one of them helped build our house.

"Finally!" Jack exclaims when I reach them. A microphone has been set up and it's on, so everyone hears him. Laughter ripples through the crowd.

Mr. Lyle gets things rolling, introducing himself, then our pastor, for the blessing. Then the speakers. A lot of them. Everyone who sponsored or who sent a group to volunteer or who's a big deal with Habitat wants to say something. I get it, this is important. But as the clock ticks, Jack tocks. He's wearing his Church Pants and a stiff shirt—Mami might have used starch when she ironed it—and I can tell this is totally testing his limits.

And he's on a stage. In front of all these nice people.

Finally, it's the part of the program where the new homeowner speaks. Which would be Mami. She has been working on her "remarks" for days now, reading lines out loud and asking me what I think. Asking Mr. Lyle and Mrs. Brenda for advice. She wants to get it just right, and not leave anyone out.

She's printed her speech, and as she steps to the mike I can see the sheets tremble. Her hands shake.

Mami starts to read, but then . . . she stops. She looks up from the paper and out into the crowd and tears slip down her cheeks. She's not going to be able to do it. My brave Mami.

Holding my brother's hand, I join her at the mike.

"I've got this," I tell her.

She nods, her eyes spilling over, and steps back.

I look out. To the left stand the VC girls, who are going to sing the final hymn. The Shackeltons stand with a posse of East Clayton neighbors and basketball parents. There are Mami's coworkers from the hospital, folks from St. Bernadette's, teachers and friends from my school, other Habitat families we've gotten to know. At the very back, sort of off to one side, my amazing cousin, the Devil's own Spawn, stands alongside Betts. She's almost unrecognizable in beige slacks and a white blouse. I think it's the first time I've seen her in something other than denim or flannel.

"For a long time," I begin, "our family has been lost. As most of you know, a few years back my dad died. His name was Charlie Crawford. He was a big man with a big heart, and when he was gone he left a big hole.

"I think we've been wandering, trying to fill that hole and find a place to call home. We've moved a lot. It's been hard. We've been lonely. I don't know how my mom stayed strong, but she never gave up. She never stopped fighting for us, and having faith that things would get better.

"And they did. When we met all of you. I know that Mami would like to thank each and every one of you by name, but that would take too long and it's getting hot and my little brother here is about to melt down." Everyone laughs. They all know Jack. "So I'm just going to say, you have changed our lives. You have become our new family. You have given us a home. Thank you."

When I'm finished and everyone applauds, I make a point not to look at my mother. Because I will absolutely cry, and I know if I start blubbing, I won't be able to stop. Mr. Lyle seems to get this, and he quickly moves to the mike for the final presentations.

He hands the loaf of bread to Jack. "Here is bread, so that this house may never know hunger," he says. He passes me the salt. "Salt, so that life may always have flavor." He hands Mami the wine. "Wine, so that joy and prosperity may reign forever." Then he dangles a set of bright silver keys from a ring. "And keys, so you can open the front door!"

Everyone laughs.

I step down from the porch and join the Veronic Convergence girls. Min gives us the tone, and we begin to sing the closing. It's one I chose: "How Great Thou Art."

As we sing, I look over the sea of heads at Mark. He flashes me a thumbs-up. I'm guessing it's for my impromptu little speech, but maybe not. Maybe it's the music.

Because he's the only person here who would understand how important it is for me to take back this hymn.

34

MOST PEOPLE DON'T DEDICATE AND MOVE INTO THEIR NEW HOUSE on the same day. It's too much. But after what happened, there's no way we're spending another night in Meadowbrook—especially without a functioning front door.

So after most of the Dedication guests leave, Mr. Lyle rolls up in the U-Haul. Paco's riding shotgun with him.

"Not safe. Not safe at all, Mr. Lyle," I chide him when he emerges from the truck. "You're setting a very bad example for Jack."

Paco scampers after him. The little guy starts yapping and running in frenetic circles. It's his first visit to the new house, and he can scarcely believe his luck.

Neither can I. Luck. Who knew?

Mr. Lyle drapes an arm over my shoulder. "I know," he muses. "I'm a terrible influence. You don't know the half of it."

I wrap my arms around him and give him a huge hug. "Thank you," I whisper. "For everything."

When I release him he claps his hands loudly and calls out to the lingerers.

"Hey! Make yourselves useful. Let's help these people move their furniture."

Here's the good thing about being poor and constantly moving: you don't have too much stuff. In a little over an hour, the U-Haul is empty. Thanks to Mami's wife-in-the-military moving skills, each of our boxes is labeled according to content and the room where it belongs, so things like clothing, blankets, and pots are easy to find. And while it's a bummer to see that awful Scrouch planted in our bright new living room, at least . . . it's a bright new living room.

People are slowly, finally, almost gone. We're down to only one Habitat volunteer, who is carting off the last of the Dedication celebration trash; Mr. Lyle, who is leafing through the homeowners' manual they gave to Mami; Sam, who is outside running Jack and Paco into the ground with a ball; and Aubrey, who volunteers to help me set up my room. I'm trying to figure out a nice way to put her off. Because I really, really want to do it alone. To some girls it might seem like work, but this is something I've been looking forward to since . . . forever. I want to savor every little folded sock.

As I'm trying to figure out what to say to Aubrey, there's a knock at the door.

Betts, Mark, and a heavily bandaged Roz walk in. I barely recognize her: there's bruising around her dressing, and her eyes are swollen. Shawn really did a number on her.

"Ay, mija!" Mami exclaims. She rushes over to her and guides her to the pleather armchair.

"Look who we sprang from the hospital!" Betts announces. She looks exceedingly pleased with herself. Like she just pulled something off. Mark looks equally pleased. Like he's her partner in some crime.

Aubrey looks like her eyes might bug out of her head.

"Oh my god. What happened?" she asks. No filter.

"I got a bad cut on my forehead," Roz explains. She manages to look around. "Nice place."

Aubrey plops herself on the Scrouch. "Ouch. Did you need stitches?" she continues.

"A bunch," Roz says.

"I'm sorry, you two haven't met," I jump in. "Roz, this is Aubrey Shackelton. Aubrey, this is my friend Roz Jenkins." I lean in a bit closer and whisper in Aubrey's ear. "My stylist."

Aubrey sits bolt upright. "Oh my god. Oh my god, you're the one who makes those incredible necklaces! I've been begging to meet you. I *love* your stuff!"

Even through the swelling and the bandages, I can see Roz flash me a look. *Is she for real?* it says. I widen my eyes and incline my head ever so slightly at her.

"So, I take it things went well?" Mr. Lyle asks Betts.

She sort of smirks. "Pretty well. Me and my granddaughter here informed them that child protective services would not be needed since she's coming home with me."

I can't help it: I gasp. What the hell?

"It took a bit of doing," Betts concedes, "but when Roz *insisted* I was her grandmother . . . and could tell them all sorts of details about my life, and my dog, Posey, and what the inside of my house looks like . . . Well, who were they to argue?" She glances at Mark, who gives her an up-down high five.

I was right. Partners in crime.

"Wait. You lied?" I'm having a hard time wrapping my head around this.

"Pretty much," Roz says.

"A whopper," Mark adds.

"Dios mío," I hear Mami murmur.

"Aubrey, would you go get Sam?" I ask her. "I'd love for him to meet Roz." Aubrey bounds from her seat and dutifully rushes outside to retrieve her brother. I figure we have sixty seconds.

"What happened?" I demand.

"Izzy, I will not go back to foster care," Roz says. No argument in her voice.

"And she can't return to that awful home," Mr. Lyle chimes in.

"That is true," Mami agrees.

"You were in on this, Mr. Lyle?" I exclaim. I can't believe these people.

"Tangentially," he says. "As an advisor. Of sorts."

I throw myself back onto the Scrouch. "Listen, I get that foster care sucks. And Roz needs a better option. But, it's a law. If she's not with her mom, social services is going to come after her."

Betts snorts. "C'mon, Izzy. You know the only rules I follow are safety rules. And staying with her mother in that dump was not safe. Rita, I could sure use a glass of water."

Betts, Mami, and Mr. Lyle go into the kitchen. I hear them rummaging through boxes in search of glasses. Meanwhile, outside, Paco and the boys are making a ruckus while Aubrey pleads with them to come inside.

"So . . . Roz is going to hide out at Betts's?" I ask.

Mark shakes his head. "I wouldn't call it hiding out. I'd call it finishing high school. Before she takes a little turn in the South."

Now I'm really confused.

"I'm sorry. What?"

"Hog heaven," Roz quips.

He gives her a playful punch. She leans her head against his shoulder.

Wow. Okay. These two are really a thing.

I didn't just miss a chapter. I missed the entire book.

"This is mind-blowing. Give me a minute," I tell them. I take a deep breath. Then another. After some serious oxygenation, I begin to sort it all out.

And it makes sense. Totally. Might not be legal, but in all honesty? Who's going to object? Not Gloria. And a good dose of Betts, followed by all those hogs, might just be what Roz needs. For now, anyway. Maybe forever. Maybe that afternoon she turned her stalking skills on my so-called evil cousin was the day her luck started to change.

Aubrey sticks her head in the door. "I can't make them come in!" she whines.

"We'll come out," Mark tells her. The three of us go to the porch.

Sam and Jack are playing keep-away from Paco, and he's going pure mad. Back and forth, back and forth, they toss his doggie ball, and he races frantically between them, his little tail twirling like a whip. A delighted smile spreads across Mark's face, and he races out to join them.

"Triangle!" he announces, and the three of them toss the ball. Poor Paco.

"Thank you, Izzy," Roz says.

I slip my arm around her waist. "What? I didn't do anything."

She shakes her head. "These are your people helping me," she says. "Your cousin. Your friends. Your family. I don't know what would have happened—"

"You'll like North Carolina," I interrupt her. I can't handle the undeserved thanks. The nagging guilt that I got off easy and still have my new lavender room all to myself. "Hogs? Maybe not as much."

"Betts says the stench can kill you."

"Betts's usually right," I agree. "But, girlfriend, I can't believe you've been spending time with her! She didn't say a thing!"

"She lets us hang out at her place."

I don't ask her to define "us." A picture is finally taking shape.

Sam's phone rings. He calls time-out from the game, holding up his hand as he listens.

"Hey, my parents are bringing dinner!" he announces after he ends the call.

"Oh gosh, Sam, they don't have to do that!" I say. "There's leftover food from the Dedication."

He shrugs. "It's done. Dad made a bunch of pizzas in the brick oven and is bringing them over. They'll be here in ten. Tell Betts and Lyle to stay—he made tons."

As Roz goes inside to deliver the message, Aubrey joins the boys and makes it a keep-away foursome. I watch from the porch. Miles away, beyond the bird-loud meadow and the acres of rolling horse pasture, the Blue Ridge Mountains form a hazy protective circle around us. Sam has promised that this summer he'll take me hiking there, and I'm looking forward to meeting them, up close, for the first time. These mountains I now get to call home. These mountains that will greet me every morning from my window. Like old friends.

I watch my friends and my brother and my cousin play in my yard. My heart is so full. Not in that heavy, weight-of-stones way. In that full-to-bursting, spilling-over, looking-forward way. There is no place I'd rather be, and no one else I want to be.

Dime con quién andas y te diré quién eres.

ACKNOWLEDGMENTS

A SMALL WOODEN SIGN ON THE WINDOW LEDGE OVER MY KITCHEN sink reads: *Home is where your story begins.* It was a gift from my sister, who displays the same sign over *her* kitchen sink. Ours was a story-filled house, and around our table, replete with an unlikely assortment of ethnic foods and accents, laughter, and oft-repeated anecdotes that took on the dimensions of folklore over time, I acquired a passion for the power of story to heal and connect and inspire.

My novels grow from a variety of sources, but *How to Build a Heart* has its strongest roots in those family stories, in particular those my mother, Jenny Padian, tells. I could not have written this book without her inspiration, her wisdom, and most important, her generosity of spirit. Mom is a great cook and an even better storyteller, and while my rice and beans will never approach the perfection of hers, I hope someday to spin a tale as full of heart as she does.

I'm also grateful for the support of my critique partners, Charlotte Agell and Gail Donovan. Their wise observations make me a better writer and their friendship keeps me going in this business. Red Umbrella Gals forever!

Speaking of Red Umbrella Gals: I cannot say enough about the great honorary Umbrella Gal, agent extraordinaire Edite Kroll. Edite has always, *always*, pointed me in the right direction. Her literary instincts are spot-on, and in every one of my books she's helped guide me through the weeds of early drafting. She's also done a spectacular job connecting my work with the right editors, and for that I cannot thank her enough.

Which leads me to the crew at Algonquin Young Readers. I've come to realize that the whole team at AYR plays a part in every book, so let me just say a huge, global thank-you (with a special shout-out to Sarah Alpert, Ashley Mason, Brittani Hilles, Stephanie Mendoza, and Caitlin Rubinstein) for all you do for us writers. At every step along the way I feel supported and know that my work is in great hands. I am lucky to have found a publishing home at AYR, and especially lucky to have the talented and insightful Krestyna Lypen as my editor, working with me through multiple revisions and helping me bring my characters to life.

Thanks to my invaluable readers, Sara Farizan, Tanuja Desai Hidier, and Ann Kelly, as well as copy editor Robin Cruise. Special thanks to artist/designer Connie Gabbert, who imagined Izzy the same way I did and created a gorgeous cover for this book. And a wink and shout-out to Henry Laurence, who first told me about the Pie Rule.

Too many Habitat for Humanity friends, families, and fellow volunteers have inspired and instructed me over time to properly acknowledge here, although I will give a special thanks to Dottie Cattelle, who told me a thing or two that made it into these pages. Dottie embodies the spirit and strength that is Habitat, and I am in awe of the life-changing work they do.

Finally, an endless thank-you to my husband, Conrad Schneider. Your stories have become mine, have become ours, as the years pass and our roots grow and tangle into a single tree. Your support and love has allowed me to live my dream, and has been the greatest gift.